the BADGER kNIGHT

KATHRYN ERSKINE

the BADGER kNIGHT

scholastic press / new york

Library of Congress Cataloging-in-Publication Data Available

ISBN 978-0-545-46442-0

10 9 8 7 6 5 4 3 2 1   14 15 16 17 18

Printed in the U.S.A.   23
First edition, September 2014

The text was set in Adobe Garamond Pro.
Book design by Nina Goffi

TO MY SISTER, JAN,
AND ADVENTURERS EVERYWHERE

There were many times I thought I'd die — by disease, arrow, or even hanging. An early death isn't unusual in England in 1346, especially with my afflictions, but in wartime the risk is even greater. War can make you do strange things, things you never thought you'd do. At some point, you have to decide if you're going to accept the challenges. I challenge you to read my story. You may think what you will of me, but please don't judge me until the end. Then you can decide what you would have done if you were me.

—the BADGER

CONTENTS

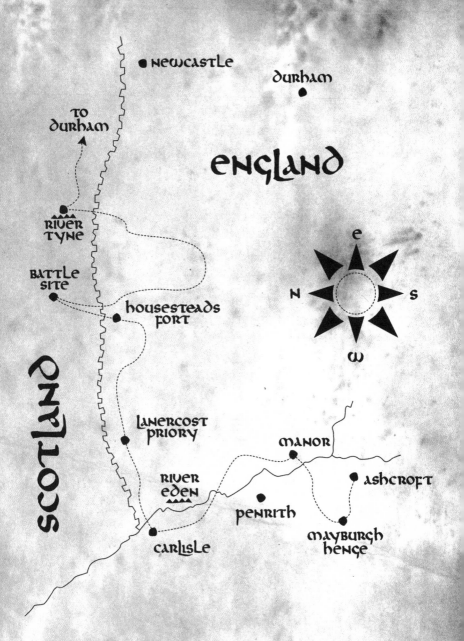

chapter the first

In Which I Sneeze, Wheeze, and Curse Much

IF IT WEREN'T FOR THE ARCHERS, THE PAGAN SCOTS would pour over the border and kill us all. It'd be worse than the plague that took my mother and sister eight years ago. Good Aunt says the plague should've taken me because I'm so useless. Father says I may be different but I have as much right to live as anyone. And, he says, when I find my calling, I'll prove it.

I've already found my calling. I'm an archer. I've been practicing since we lost a third of the village in that plague. Back then, I was a puny, pale, sickly boy, barely five years old. Now I'm almost thirteen . . . and still puny, sickly, and pale as milk. A few people say being tiny and white as an angel is a good omen, but far more say I'm evil, that I was the cause of that plague, and that they see the devil in my eyes. If they do, I didn't put him there. I'm no devil. Nor am I a tiny angel. Underneath my odd-looking outside I'm just me. Adrian. A boy — well, almost a man. They'll see.

I pick up my bow. The ash wood feels firm, yet flexible, in my hand. The weight is perfect. I made it myself, mostly. It's a precision weapon. It's not near as big as a longbow, of course, but I can dart in and out and reload faster than the five or six times per minute a longbow archer can handle.

I draw back my bow and aim. My left eye is weaker so I only use my right and, on a sunny day like today, I spread dirt under my eyes to cut the glare so I don't have to squint as much. I may be called Badger, but I can hit my target every time.

King Edward would be happy to have me fighting alongside him. He won the battle of Crécy last month because of expert archers like me. There hasn't been such a victory since the battle of Sluys in 1340, but I was only six then so I wouldn't have been much use. At Crécy, though, I like to imagine what I could've done. . . . Squinting, I see just where my arrow will hit the French soldier who tries to kill our king. He doesn't see me. Silently, I release my arrow and watch it fly, hitting its mark, piercing it.

I imagine the cheers from the whole army. "Adrian of Ashcroft has saved us!"

But a real voice booms in the distance. "Adrian!"

"Coming, Father!" Quickly, I pull my arrow from its target, which, in truth, is only the birch tree I use for target practice. I hide my bow and arrows in its hollow trunk.

Father still doesn't know I practice archery, but he knows what a fine shot I am. And he knows how much I want to be apprenticed to the bowyer and make bows myself. Everyone in the village says the bowyer is a good, fair, and honest man. That's true, but he's also my father.

Oh, I know it's unusual to be apprenticed to your own father, but since he won't send me away — he's so overprotective! — what better fit is there? And I know he thinks I'm small and weak, in body as well as mind, thanks to Good Aunt, but I'm not wasting any more of my time at that stupid school!

Fleeing the woods, down the hill, I see Father standing outside our shop. I run as fast as I can, tripping on a tree root. Though I keep from falling, my arms flail as wildly as a goose's wings.

Father's shoulders droop. His head drops, too, as I speed up to show him how able I really am, although my chest squeezes and the wheezing starts.

Panting, I stumble in front of him. "Yes — Father." I bend over and clutch my knees as I gasp for air. I sound like a yelping dog. Father looks away. As always, he gives me time for the air to return to my lungs.

I try to slow my breathing as I listen to Peter the journeyman inside the shop sorting through the arrow tips, finding just the right one to attach to a shaft. Father trains Peter to make arrows, although bow making is his prime profession. When I raise my head and squint past Father, I see Peter hold up a pointed tip. The sun streams through the door and glints on the steel, and I want to be where Peter is right now, doing something useful, not like me.

I stand up as tall as possible and look at Father, eagerly, because maybe he'll let me carve an arrow or attach the point, the true harbinger of death. And maybe he'll finally realize I'm ready to be his apprentice. He's a master bowyer, the only one for miles around. It's a kingly calling. I await his word as if he were the king himself.

"Adrian, I need you to collect goose feathers."

I hear Peter snicker and I imagine the entire village snickering.

"But, Father, that's child's work!" I realize how much like a child I sound and try to sound more like a man. "Wouldn't you rather I help you with the bow making?"

"The bow is nothing without the arrows."

"Then the shafts, Father, let me make those!"

His eyes darken at my insolence even though he knows that I can carve a stick into a great weapon — and shoot it as well as any man. Still he doesn't look at me. He dare not, lest he see Mother in my face, and that's too painful. I don't blame him. He clears his throat. "You know what Good Aunt says."

Father is a man of few words, but "Good" Aunt more than makes up for him. She has badgered him near to death with her story that I'm too sick and addlepated to be his apprentice. But I'm only sick and clumsy around her because I want to be elsewhere — anywhere that's away from her. And I have no skill with a plow, but that doesn't mean I have no skill with a bow. Still, she has poisoned Father's brain as badly as she has poisoned Uncle's. Or maybe in Uncle's case it's the ale.

"Adrian!"

I jump. "S-sir?"

"The feathers," he says simply, but his eyes tell me that he has been watching me and is all the more convinced that I'm a sickly simpleton.

"Father, I —"

"Whist, go now. And," he adds quietly, "wipe the dirt from under your eyes."

Peter hears him, though, because he starts chuckling. He thinks my poor eyesight is amusing.

Father whirls on him. "Peter!" His voice is as piercing as an arrow. He cannot stand for people to make fun of my weaknesses. Somehow, his defending me all the time only makes me feel worse, as if he believes me too weak to take care of myself.

When I'm out of earshot, I mutter, "God's bones!" and worse curses as well, anything that won't get me struck down by the good Lord himself. Truly, I'm not angry with Him but with Father and my aunt, the wretched woman who plants such evil thoughts in his head. I only say "Good" Aunt since Father thrashed me for the other name I called her. It was but a shortened form of her full name, Hellewyse. The first syllable describes her well enough.

I walk slowly, ready to live up to the name of ill addlepate if my only role is to be goose-feather collector. I'd rather wander the countryside. Become a juggler or a tumbler. Surely then people would respect me. But I'm more like the baited bear, tethered to a rock while folks laugh and dogs bite at me until there's nothing left. I drag my worn boots toward the north end of the village, where the water attracts the geese and their wretched feathers. I feel useless.

All my life I have heard of Ailwin the Useless, although I never met him. He died the week I was born, which is why most in my village believe that I am to take his place, especially upon seeing my tiny size and odd looks. Ailwin the Useless had a short leg, a hunchback, and one arm that wouldn't work. Also, he was blind. I am nothing like that, but people still say that being useless is my destiny.

If Father won't let me be a bowyer then the only other thing I can do well is shoot an arrow, so I have to be a soldier. Oh, I can read and write better than any of the boys at school, but I think it's a worthless activity. I pretend I'm slow because Bryce wants to be the top scribe, so he thrashes me if I look smarter than he does. And how many scribes does one village need? In truth, who would hire me for any trade? At worst, I am a bad omen. At best, I am useless. So I will end up like Ailwin the Useless, who begged for food and scraped manure off the reeve's boots just so he'd be allowed to stay in the village, although he was little better off than Thomas the leper.

It is not much of a life.

Father says, *Don't worry, Adrian, for I will always take care of you.*

What I want to say to him is this: *You can't always take care of me because, someday, you will be gone, and Good Aunt wants nothing to do with me, so what will become of me then?*

And even more, I want to say this: *I don't want to be taken care of. I want to take care of myself. I want to be a man.*

But instead I simply say, *Thank you, Father,* because I know that's what he wants to hear. It always makes him smile. I suppose he feels that he couldn't save my mother and sister so at least he can protect me.

"Oy, you dolt!" a man yells, and I see it's Uncle, in the field to my right. He's sweating under the effort of making Bessie move. A more stubborn, odiferous ox I have never met, but she's Good Aunt's pride and joy. They're two of a kind. I skulk past, lest Uncle decide I should help him. Sometimes it's useful to be slight and pale. I do cast a curse at Bessie, however. I've been trodden on too many times by that stinking beast.

As I round the path, a man on horseback rides up the hill at a fast trot, looking left to the alehouse and right to some of the village houses. I stop. He's an unusual sight. The man has a full head of brown hair although he's as old as Father. His britches are leather and his jacket is fine and looks soft as moss. And it's scarlet.

He stops his horse and startles a bit when he looks down at me. I realize I still have the dirt under my eyes, but it's too late to get rid of it now. At least my hood is up so he can't see how white my hair is.

He speaks quickly. "Boy, do you know where the bowyer resides?"

I can't help but grin. "Yes, sir! That man is my father!"

"You are right to be proud. Point me in the direction."

I turn and point behind me. "It's half a mile, on the right, sir."

He nods and slaps his reins, but the horse refuses to move. The man sighs and stands in his stirrups, and soon I hear and see why. His horse's piss steams the air. It's not cold out but the horse must be hot from a long ride.

When the horse is done, the man takes his seat and waves to me. "Perhaps when you're a big lad, you can be apprenticed to a bowyer."

I feel the steam come out of me like his horse's piss. I'm already old enough to be apprenticed. Soon, just after Michaelmas, I'll be thirteen. But I still collect goose feathers because Father says it's a skill which only I have, to find the feathers that come from one side of the goose for one side of the arrow and feathers from the other side of that same goose to balance the arrow so it veers not to the right nor to the left but straight so as to meet its mark and kill a man.

That may be true, but collecting goose feathers with boys half my age, and even girls, makes me a laughingstock. I may not be much larger than the little boys, but most in my village have known me since birth and know me to be twelve — maybe ten or eleven if their memory is as short as my size — but not six, like the giggling scalawags who point at me and laugh. I try my best to ignore them, but it's as easy to ignore Thomas the leper with his bell, and the screams and mayhem that accompany him.

I stomp off, directly into a pile of dung, most likely left by Bessie herself. I curse, loudly. It seems, lately, what I do best. I try to cheer myself by jumping over piles of Bessie's dung, pretending to be an archer on the battlefield, leaping over the bodies I have slain. I carry my longbow and all fear me. No arrow can slay me. No man can —

A heavy object hits my head and I fall face-first and slide in ox dung. It stinks badly but at least it's soft and breaks my fall. Beside me lies the piece of oak branch that hit my head.

I hear the laughter of Bryce and William and Warren, like an evil king and his entourage. Before I can rise, I feel a large foot come down on the side of my head. I hear Bryce's laughter up close, the swine. William and Warren, his rotten little piglets, take turns kicking me. "Badger! Badger!" they shout because of the dirt under my eyes.

Bryce grunts at them as if to say I am his kill and what do they think they're doing scavenging his meat. They stop their attack but it's not much relief. Bryce pushes his boot down harder on my head, squishing it sideways like the lid of a coffin coming down on me so all I can see is a fly in the dung. Unlike me, the fly is free, and mocks me by rubbing its legs together, the way Good Aunt rubs her hands together in glee before applying the fire-heated cups to my back to clear my lungs. God's lungs! All I can hope is that a coughing fit doesn't come on.

The tightness in my chest begins, and I curse myself for having thought of wheezing because now I've brought it upon myself and it's my own fault!

Worse, Bryce thinks my cursing is meant for him.

"Dare you call me addlepate? Is that what your puny brain thinks of me?"

Actually, it's exactly what I think of him, but never would I say it out loud.

"You sniveling, red-eyed freak of nature!"

I want to remind him that no one has claimed to see red in my eyes for at least a year. Except Good Aunt, and I think she's lying.

But Bryce only pushes his foot down harder. "What did you call me?"

I answer only with a cough, a wheeze, and a pitiful sound I don't mean to make but can't keep from escaping.

I feel his foot lift from my face and for a brief addlepated moment I think, *God be blessed! He's letting me — ow!*

By Satan's arrow, he steps on my back, squeezing the last breath I have out of me and preventing me from taking another.

I panic, my eyes watering, while images of my village spin in front of me. There's a ringing in my ears and my whole world goes black. This is what it feels like to die.

But, if this is death, it's not nearly as painful as I imagined. In death, the foot of Bryce is mercifully lifted from my back. Maybe I've made it into heaven! Air fills my lungs. I hear an "Ow!" yet feel no pain. I think I'm going to like heaven.

There's a thud and a groan next to me. I open my eyes. St. Jerome's bones! What is Bryce doing in heaven beside me? Who killed him so fast? And why is he up here in this lofty place?

Suddenly, a terrible thought enters my mind. *What if I'm in hell?* I squeeze my eyes tight shut and pray for forgiveness for all the foul things I've said about Good Aunt, because surely that's what's landed me here with the likes of Bryce.

I hear the crunching of twigs near my ear and open my eyes to see Bryce lifted into the air. I squint up into his shadow against the sun and, behind him, a Larger Being. For a fleeting moment I believe I've seen my Maker, who has realized His mistake and is preparing to fling Bryce to hell, where truly he belongs. But then I hear gasps and snickers and I know it's not from angels. In fact, it's from William and Warren. Their laughter grows louder when Bryce is dropped on the earth with a scream, a thud, and a moan. I stare at his grimacing face and look up to see Hugh Stout.

"Hello, Adrian," Hugh says, offering me his hand. His blue eyes and tanned face smile down at me and his blond hair reflects the sun as if he is some kind of saint.

I'm pulled out of the stinking manure with a squelch. Hugh's scrunched-up nose must mirror my own, as I would give anything for two sprigs of lavender to shove up my nostrils right now.

"If you want to get that close to the earth you should be a farmer like me." He winks.

I smile back and steal a glance around me for the whereabouts of the unholy trinity, though I see Bryce running away and I know I'm safe with Hugh. He's practically full-grown, bigger than many of the men in our village, and stronger than Bessie the ox. And he's my only friend.

"You'd better wash before Good Aunt sees you," Hugh says.

My relief at being saved from death wanes as I realize I'm back on earth, which means avoiding Good Aunt like a scared pup and whining to Father like a sick child.

"Someday I'll be a Goliath," I mutter.

"Goliath? Don't you remember the Bible story?" Hugh smiles. "You're the young David. Smaller, but wiser."

"I don't give an ox's ass about smaller and wiser! Give me a bow and a quiver of arrows and I'll show you a man's strength!"

But my shouting starts my coughing again, and my lungs are weak from Bryce's heavy boot. I bend over, wheezing, hating myself for doing so.

Hugh quickly opens his bag, pulling out an onion. Drawing his knife, he cuts several pieces, holding them under my nose until my eyes water and the phlegm runs out.

"Blow!" he commands.

I do as he says, for I know he's right. Soon I'm breathing again as the onion vapors clear my head.

"You're better now, Adam?"

I nod, even though he called me his dead brother's name. He never knows he does it, nor do I ever tell him. Always, when I have a fit of coughing, he's reminded of Adam.

Hugh pulls me to my feet, but the bells of the church peal out so frantically we both stop dead. We sniff the air but there's neither smoke nor fire, nor is it Sunday.

Voices shout and feet hurry past. Quickly, we join villagers who've left their tasks and run for the church to hear whatever the urgent news may be.

chapter the second

In Which We Hear of Battle!

"YOU MUST PREPARE FOR BATTLE!" IT'S THE GENTLEMAN in scarlet I met on the road. "The savage Scots are planning to invade again! Soon they will come across the border into our country!"

Hugh and I stand in the crowd at the church, some of the men around us grumbling about who will take care of their fields and families. I don't know why they complain because all I can think is, *Battle?* A battle I might see with my own eyes? A battle where, someday, I can use my alarmingly good archery skills and take out the enemy? I can finally prove my worth!

The fine gentleman has a commanding voice and uses it well. "We need every able-bodied man to join the battle against the pagans!"

Father will need to provide bows and arrows for the entire village, and all the villages around us. . . . He may need my assistance! This could mean my apprenticeship! I open my mouth to tell Hugh, but our priest speaks and I pay attention out of habit, fearing the punishment of his psalm book thwacking my head even though he's far away.

"My good folk, I must take my leave to give comfort at the manor because our dear lady is distraught that her husband and firstborn son are going to battle. I will stay at the manor to teach the noble children since some of you," he says, turning his pig eyes in my direction, "don't know the greatness of learning that is given to you for a mere pittance." He spits the word *pittance* out of his mouth, so disgusted is he with his low wages, according to Good Aunt, and, it seems, so disgusted is he with me and my wandering mind.

I think he's as useless as a pig stuck in muck. On that — and that alone — I agree with Good Aunt. She calls him "Father Fraud" because he's not even a real priest, but a layman who took the position after our real priest was taken with leprosy and went to the leper's hospital in Cambridge. And although he pretends to be a teacher, I can read and make my letters better than he can.

But now I don't have to worry about school! I'm practically dancing with gladness as Father Fraud dismisses us because I'd rather be piercing a tree with arrows than scratching a tablet with letters any day. I give a sly smile to Hugh, who knows what I'm thinking even though he doesn't have to go to school. He doesn't smile back, however. His skin is drawn tight against his face as he sucks his lips in and squeezes his eyes half shut. "What's wrong?"

"I don't want Father going into battle alone and I don't think he'll let me go with him."

"Why? You're almost grown. And you can shoot a bow as well as any man."

Hugh sighs. "He'll say I'm too young, or that I'm the only one to tend to the fields while he's gone, or that I have to take care of my grandmother —"

I laugh out loud at that last reason. "Grandmother? She's the healer who takes care of everyone else!"

"I know, but Father says she's getting old. And it's true that she's weakening."

I think about that for a moment. Hugh's grandmother is like my own, now that I don't have one anymore. Indeed, she insists I call her Grandmother. I suppose she's old but that's no excuse to keep Hugh out of battle.

"It doesn't matter anyway," Hugh says. "He won't let me go."

"Why would he be so foolish?"

He turns to look at me, his flaxen hair falling about his shoulders like mine, only mine is so much paler. Now his usually placid face is pinched and his brow furrowed like the fields. "He has lost one son already," he says. "He will not lose the other."

I say nothing for a moment because it's what my own father says, having lost a wife and a daughter. We're all that our fathers have left.

"But," says Hugh quietly, "I don't want to lose him, either."

I can tell from the way Hugh's jaw is set that he's determined to change his father's mind, and his feet are already heading him in the direction of his father's field.

"I'll go with you," I say, following Hugh, "and tell him that I used to be a better archer than you but that you're now better than I am."

Hugh looks down at me, and smiles. "In truth, we're about the same."

I bite my tongue. In truth, I'm still better. He has merely had some lucky shots lately. But I don't say that. "I'll tell him that Father will give you the best bow."

"He can't. The yew bows can only go to the men."

"But you look like a man, and you'll be fifteen in a couple of months," I say, my head barely bobbing to his chin as I walk next to him, even if I put a spring in my step.

"Still, better not to use that argument with Father. It'll only sound desperate."

As it turns out, it doesn't matter, because no argument we try convinces Hugh's father. I leave Hugh at his field, working alongside his father. Usually, they are laughing and talking, but now they are silent.

I walk off, listening to the chatter on the road about going to battle. While I feel bad for Hugh, I'm excited about my prospects of apprenticeship. I practically run back to our shop, hoping I can speak to Father alone, without Peter the journeyman around, who will only make fun of me.

chapter the third

In Which I Dislike Good Aunt,
Even More So than Aforementioned

WHEN I ENTER THE WORKSHOP, I SMILE BECAUSE THERE'S no sign of Peter, who most likely took off at the peal of the bells. He's second only to Uncle when it comes to loving ale.

Father looks up from the piece of yew he's honing into a bow, examining me closely, as if he knows that my question is of great import.

"Father, I —"

"Adrian. Where are the goose feathers?"

I forgot all about them! "Uh . . . the bells . . . at the church . . ."

"Aye, but that was some time ago." Father's voice sounds deflated, as if a full bellows has just lost all of its air.

"See what I mean?" Good Aunt's voice crows from behind me.

I gasp so quickly I choke, coughing and even — St. Jerome's bones! — starting to wheeze. Water comes out of my eyes and my nose fills up.

"Time for cupping!" Good Aunt barks, grabbing me by the back of my neck like a kitten and dragging me into our room behind the shop.

"I'm fine," I try to protest, but my voice is weak and raspy.

"Sit!" she commands. "Tunic off!" She turns to the doorway to the shop. "A fire, John! And make it large!"

Father moves slowly, whether in quiet support of me or because he doesn't like the smoke of a big fire inside, I don't know. Either way, he succumbs to Good Aunt as everyone does and, if she wants a roaring fire, that's what she'll get.

Cowering under my aunt's dominance is not the picture I had in mind. I look desperately at Father as he mounds the twigs and pieces of wood and starts a blaze, but he avoids my eyes.

Good Aunt pulls the cloth bundle of glass cups out of her bag and they jiggle against one another as if laughing at me. I shudder because I know what's coming. Gleefully, she puts the glass cups on the edge of the fire, licking her lips even as the flames lick the rims of the small glass bowls. I close my eyes.

Good Aunt tries to cure my phlegmatic condition only because she wants me to be useful in her fields. My cousins are girls and, while they're nearly as strong as her precious ox, Bessie, she wants to keep them soft and pretty to find them husbands and get rid of them, especially Jane, who is fair of face, although that's the only fair thing about her. Inside, she's much the same as Good Aunt, if not worse. The younger one, who's a year older than me, is quieter but looks exactly like Good Aunt, so must be as bad. I avoid them both. Uncle is the best of the lot and he's no prize. She has henpecked him so much that his head is but a nub and he spends most of his time running around like a chicken with his head cut off. Usually with a tankard of ale.

Good Aunt is humming softly now, in her trance. Sometimes I think she remembers my mother, whom she loved, although it's hard imagining Good Aunt caring for anyone, but if I sit very still and quietly, as now, she puts my mother's cloak gently over my shoulders and feels for the spots where she thinks my chest is fullest of phlegm by rubbing my back, softly and kindly, the way my mother did. And for a moment I'm taken back in a trance myself, and I feel my mother's hands, her warmth, and her love.

As soon as the first cough comes out of me, however, it's over, because Good Aunt remembers it's me, not her dear younger sister, and she yanks the cloak off and whacks my back with a force that a wench would reserve for her ox, except that she loves Bessie too much so she takes it out on me. After that, she pulls the searing-hot glass cups out of the fire and presses them to my back.

"Ow!" I yelp and scream, barely able to contain my curses, and struggle to get away from the burning glass, but I can't escape the clawlike grip she has on my arm.

"You are a chicken, nephew!" Good Aunt says over my screams.

It's at times like this that I understand why Uncle runs to the tavern for ale.

When Good Aunt is finally done I'm left alone to lick my wounds. But not for long, because my younger cousin appears with the daily pot of runny pottage and puts it on the fire. I don't even look at her. I'm certain she's laughing at me. She puts a piece of bread near me, as if I'm a leper who can't be approached too closely lest I infect her. To show her who's master, I bat it away. She stands there a moment, saying nothing, then takes her leave.

Good Aunt remains in Father's shop, lecturing him on how best to care for me, which basically amounts to letting me work in her fields so I can "gain strength" and "breathe fresh air." Fresh air? Behind Bessie's big backside?

"He's young and needs to grow a little larger," Father says quietly. "I will not have him malformed before his bones have even grown."

"Well," Good Aunt says in a huff, "he's not so young and, as I've said before, his bones will grow little more. He's small and puny and will be so forever."

I grit my teeth so hard I am sure they'll break.

"Besides, he can at least reap the grain. Surely that's not too much for his precious bones."

"Hasn't he done that for many years?" Father asks.

"He has helped, yes, but not done the task without me."

"Most farmers have more than one person in the field with them. I'm not sure that is a sign of Adrian's weakness. Besides, I wish him to have schooling, too."

"Hmph! What good is it that he can read and scribe? Who would employ such an odd-looking child, weak-eyed and sickly, whom they fear is possessed?"

Father jumps to his feet but she stands her ground, holding a hand up. "I'm only repeating what others say, John.

You know that." She shakes her head. "You must prepare him better for the world. You coddle him. And you spoil him! He speaks whatever is on his mind and gives you no respect!"

Father looks away. He has heard much the same from the priest. I believe I have a permanent dent in my head from where Father Fraud has hit me with the psalm book for every "insolent remark" I make. Still, Good Aunt has no room to talk because what's she doing right now but speaking her mind and giving Father no respect?

"Indeed," she continues, "even my sister would've demanded more of him."

I look through the doorway into the shop as Father flashes her a grim look and maybe even Good Aunt knows she has gone too far.

Her voice turns whiny. "I simply need help, having only two girls and a husband who is . . . often taken with illness."

I think she means *ale-ness*. Besides, while I've never seen my older cousin in the fields, I've seen the younger one there, usually when Uncle has gone to the alehouse, so I know she's capable of working.

"I understand," says Father, "but I need his help, too."

She waves a hand. "Any child can collect goose feathers!"

"Not true," says Father, an edge creeping into his voice that makes me smile, "and since you don't know the arts of bowery or fletchery, I'll not have you lecture me on that."

"I won't try," she says, her voice as stiff as her body, "I'll only point out that cooks are highly valued and I do provide that service for you."

Father glares at her. "And I pay you well, don't I?"

They stare at each other, like two soldiers, waiting for their knight to tell them when next to strike.

St. Jerome's bones! I swear she brings us the food her own family won't eat because it's such pig slop. I think she stretches the bread with sawdust and the broth with Bessie's piss, and likely thinks her blessed ox's piss is a gift too good for either one of us, since she blames us both for the death of her sister. She claims that Father drove Mother too hard, weakening her so that she died from her illness. My role in Mother's death was being weak with fever so Mother kept me wrapped in her own cloak in front of the fire. Also, she fed me broth, which, Good Aunt insists on reminding me, was at the expense of herself and even my baby sister because without milk from Mother's breast, little Abby was in a weakened state and ready to succumb to the fever. I barely remember those days that Good Aunt is so happy to remind me of, and what does she think a sick five-year-old could do?

And yet, I do blame myself. My mother gave her life for me and what have I amounted to? Little more than the small, weak, shivering boy I was then. The thought angers me. My mother didn't die for me to be Good Aunt's serf; I will be Father's apprentice.

I stand up in the doorway between the two rooms and they both turn to me. Good Aunt is in full battle form. I know I'll only raise her ire if I'm too direct. "Is there no one else to help Uncle?"

"Well," she snaps, "Bess, of course."

"Other than an ox, I mean."

Good Aunt bristles. "I was not speaking of Bessie! I was speaking of your cousin, *Bess*." She turns to Father. "See? He doesn't even understand the difference between the two."

I look at Father pleadingly. Surely he doesn't believe her. It's not my fault that she named her younger daughter after her beloved ox.

Father gives me a placating nod, knowing that sometimes Good Aunt goes too far.

She sniffs. "Bess is strong and good with her hands."

Now that she has opened the gate, I may as well walk in. "What about Jane?"

Her face darkens and sours into an overripe plum. "Jane? *Jane?*"

Maybe I shouldn't have walked through the gate, open or not. Father rubs his temples. If his head is not already aching, it will be soon.

Good Aunt's eyes are fiery. "Jane, who is the fairest in the village, most likely in all the king's lands? You would have her work *in the fields*? Have you no judgment?" She bellows on, sounding like a cow suffering a painful birthing.

Jane may be fair of face, but not fair of temper. Still, all the boys in the village, except Hugh, trail after her and were actually drooling when she was crowned May Queen this May Day past and the one before that, and every May Day as far back as I can remember. Yet she delights in tripping or slapping any boy who approaches — after coyly inviting him to approach. It's a stupid game and yet most boys continue to play. Why, I don't know. Myself, I can't even stand calling her my cousin.

I notice Father rubbing his head harder and Good Aunt's hands flying around as wildly as her words.

"I'm sorry, Good Aunt," I say. "Truly, I would no more want to see Jane in the field than I would want to see you." By which, I mean I'd like to see them both slogging away.

Her prune-ish face makes an attempt at a smile, I believe. I think she doesn't hear the insult. From Father's smirk, half hidden behind his fist, I believe he does. When I give him a quick wink, he loses his smile, however.

"Think on it, John," she says as she lifts her excess kirtle. "The fields would be good for him."

I believe Father and I both sigh with relief when she leaves.

"Father, what I wanted to ask —"

"I have found ash, sir, but no more yew." It's Peter at the door with a bundle of wood, and I roll my eyes in frustration, though neither of them sees.

"Very well," says Father, "we must make do with what we have. The point is to complete as many longbows as possible in a week's time."

"And that's where I come in!" I say.

They both turn and look at me like I'm a nightingale who has mysteriously appeared in the middle of winter.

"I can be your apprentice now, Father. The time is here."

Peter lets out a snort but turns away upon seeing Father's frown.

Father stares at me for a good long while. "That knight who spoke at the church, George de Cluny, will be back in one week to pick up all the bows we can make. I don't have time to teach you, nor can you contribute much in seven days."

"I know a lot already, and the demand for bows and arrows will increase throughout the war. You'll need another hand."

"Indeed I will," Father says somberly, and my heart jumps. "De Cluny is sending another journeyman to assist me."

My heart sinks. I look at Peter. He's no longer smirking. In fact, he's already working on the wood he brought in. Bringing competition from elsewhere will likely make him be more serious about his work and forget about the alehouse. As for me, another journeyman means I have no chance at being apprentice.

"I'm sorry, son. For now, I need you to collect as many staves and goose feathers as you can for the arrows."

"That's all?"

"And you may practice your letters —"

"The priest is leaving! Haven't you heard?" The anger comes out in my voice and, while Peter glances warily at Father, I'm not reprimanded.

Father only sighs. "And, eventually, you'll be needed in your uncle's field."

"What!"

"He'd like to pay his way out of battle but I'm afraid that's where he'll end up eventually. Good Aunt is right enough that there'll be no one to work the fields. They're still family. We must help."

"But I could do so much more —"

"You will, someday, I'm sure." But he doesn't sound sure at all as he turns back to his wood.

"When, Father? When? I'm not a child! I may be small but I'm almost a man! Don't you see? Are you as blind as Ailwin the Useless?"

His shoulders stiffen but he neither speaks nor turns around. Peter is frozen, too, though his eyes manage to glare at me as if to say, *You had best take that pagan mouth and be gone!*

I storm out into the dark. It's night now, and I'm grateful for its blackness so that no one can see the angry tears on my face.

chapter the fourth

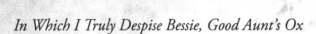

In Which I Truly Despise Bessie, Good Aunt's Ox

WE HAVE PUSHED AND WORKED AND SWEATED AND STILL only gotten Bessie through two rows of Uncle's field. I'm wheezing and Uncle is not much better. He wipes his face with his sleeve and says he must "deliver a message to the alehouse."

"Shall I deliver it for you, Uncle?" I can't resist asking, if only to hear what he says.

"No, no, it's . . ." and he mutters something unintelligible. It doesn't matter. It's a lie, anyway. He only wants to go drink ale, much ale, while he leaves me here in the field. "Start this row, and I expect it and two more like it to be done by the time I return."

What? Has he had too much ale already? How can I plow one row myself, much less three? We've worked together all morning and only done two.

There's a spring in his step as he heads for the alehouse. Maybe it's a mistake for his main field to be so close to it. He can see the alehouse from almost every angle.

The sign swings in the breeze above the door of the ale-house, knocking against the building, but it's quiet compared to the drunken commotion there'll surely be in a few hours, when work is done for the day. That's when Uncle brings his dice along with his thirst. Good Aunt ignores his gambling because he's so good at it. I think she hopes he'll buy his way to yeoman soon. Uncle just wants to buy his way out of battle.

The smell of fires warms me enough that I ignore the breezes. Though it's only September it's a cold day. The smell of baking bread from the mill fills my nostrils but isn't enough by itself to fill my belly. I'm reminded that it's almost suppertime. Lately, I've been famished although I eat as much as usual. I hope I don't have some vile disease. But if I had a vile disease, wouldn't the food be coming out rather than going in?

I ponder such things to pass the time as I move one step forward, sometimes backward, through a solitary row in Uncle's field. My feet are sore and Bessie won't cooperate no matter how hard I push or yell or swat at her.

"St. Jerome's bones, I'll beat you till you bellow!" I cry, but she ignores me. I poke her with the goad — not hard, for she might turn and trample me — but enough for her to know there is someone back here who expects her to work for her supper, same as I have to. I can only hope that Uncle will be too gleeful with ale to remember which row he left me on. Maybe I can make him believe it was me who plowed the two rows we already did.

The next step I take lands me on my back because my foot has slipped out from under me. As I smell the stench

I realize why. It's Bessie's dung! Fresh and odiferous! St. Jerome's nose! It's even in my hair, so the smell will be surrounding me all day!

I catch movement beyond the field's fence and I jump up quickly, lest it be the unholy trinity ready to pummel me while I'm down. But it's my cousin, carrying a large loaf of bread and something else, which is a mystery because it's wrapped in cloth. It's Bess — the cousin, not the thing wrapped in cloth. She puts that on the ground at the edge of the field with the bread on top of it.

Her face is prune-ish, as is her body, just like Good Aunt's. I can't stand the look of her. Why doesn't she just leave the food and go home?

As if in answer, she says, "Father said I must stay because you need help."

I stare at her as if that's the most outlandish thing to say, as if I had not just slid on my ass. "I don't need your help." Even as I say it, I wonder at myself. Don't I want help? Yes, but not hers. She's most likely laughing at me behind her pinched face.

Grabbing the plow, I push with all my might and yell at the stupid ox. Repeatedly. We don't move.

"She won't work like that," my cousin says.

"She won't work at all!" I reply.

"She will for me," Bess says quietly.

I fling my hands off the plow, step back, and cross my arms. "Splendid. I will eat, then. You take the beast."

I strut to the food pile, break off a piece of bread, and stuff it in my mouth. Unwrapping the cloth, I find eel, which

I love, and decide to eat most of it. Uncle won't mind. He's happy with ale.

I settle comfortably in the hollow trunk of an old tree to eat. I watch Bess deal with Bessie, who snorts and farts, whether because of a change of driver or just being herself, who can tell. But what my cousin does next amazes me. Instead of prodding Bessie's back end with the goad, she goes to her snorting front end and proceeds to talk to her and even pet her! I've heard of shepherds singing to sheep to calm them but talking to a belligerent ox? She's as addle-pated as I supposedly am! I laugh out loud but before long I stop.

Bessie stops complaining and stands like a docile pig while my cousin goes behind her to take hold of the plow. Bess makes a clicking sound and — St. Jerome's legs! — that beast begins to walk down the row, not fast, but still she's moving, and it's forward movement, faltering only when meeting the largest stones that take extra effort to move. I stare at my cousin and I think she sees me out of the corner of her eye.

I feel the hot blood rising to my face and my breath comes more rapidly. Fine! So she knows how to handle an ox. I don't even want to know how to handle that beast. I'm only here until — hopefully — Uncle buys his way out of battle.

I'm amazed, though, at how Bessie keeps moving for her. And how my cousin's sweet-talking seems to calm the ox. And how strong my cousin is with the plow, practically lifting it out of the earth when it gets stuck. That piece of iron weighs more than Uncle. I can barely move it. How does she handle it like that, skinny as she is?

I begin to sneeze. When I look down and see the moldy green stuff growing all around the tree I'm sitting in, I groan. And then sneeze some more, my nose and chest feeling fuller by the moment. I think about what Hugh's grandmother has said of certain plant life. *Some sneezing and wheezing is brought on by plants.* Good Aunt says that's nonsense, the idea that nature can hurt us, but if some plants are powerful enough to cure diseases, why can't some start them?

I move away from the offending plants and try to blow out my nose and slow my breathing. When I look at the field, my cousin is already turning Bessie and the plow at the end of the row. I look away quickly because I don't want her to see me watching and think I'm impressed. Or see the water running out of my eyes and think I'm crying.

And it's exactly when I turn my head that the clod of dirt hits. Not me, this time, but my cousin. From the laughter, far to my left, I know the culprits are the same. The unholy trinity.

The next clod hits Bessie and she flinches.

"Leave her alone!" my cousin cries. "Why would you hurt her?"

Now a clod hits my cousin square in the chest.

"Is that better?" Bryce calls, as William and Warren cheer.

"It doesn't matter," William says, or maybe it's Warren, "I can't tell which is the ox!"

"Fool," says Bryce, "the one on four legs is the ox, the other is so ugly it must be a boy!"

They laugh again and proceed to throw more earth, even stones, and I start to feel sorry for my cousin, much as I dislike her. I'm about to come out of hiding so they'll attack me instead, when I realize that Bess is quite skillful at dodging their weapons. And she ignores their jeers and continues to plow. Amazingly, they leave. Are they afraid of Bess? Or Bessie? While I'm happy they're gone, I'm perplexed and not a little vexed that my cousin seems to have more power against the unholy trinity than I do. I feel completely useless.

Shortly after, Hugh appears. He looks at me quizzically. I hope he didn't see what the unholy trinity did, and that I did nothing about it. But he only smirks and says, "You're letting your cousin do all the work?"

I stand up quickly. "I — she —"

He loses his smirk, eyeing my face and seeing the redness and snot. "It doesn't matter," he says quickly. "I'm here to help, anyway. Grandmother needs you to write out herbal recipes for the lady of the manor. She spoke with Good Aunt and exchanged my services in the field for your scribing."

In truth, I'm delighted, because although I don't like school, scribing is much easier than field work. Still, I don't want to look weak, so I shrug and say, "I could do the plowing, except for that wretched ox."

Hugh turns to watch Bessie. "Your cousin seems to handle her just fine."

I grit my teeth. It appears she handles the unholy trinity, the plow, and the stupid ox better than I can.

"Listen," says Hugh, tilting his head and smiling, "how sweetly she speaks to the ox."

"Yes, they seem to understand each other well, Bess and Bessie. Maybe they're related."

Hugh loses his smile, shaking his head. "Adrian, you shouldn't say such mean things about your own family."

"They deserve it."

"What has Bess ever done to you?"

I have to think for a while. Good Aunt has done plenty. And so has Jane. When I was just a small boy, Jane held me upside down over the well, threatening to drop me inside, simply because I splashed mud — by accident! — on her precious kirtle.

"I'm waiting," Hugh says, crossing his arms like Reeve Elliot, the boss of the whole village.

"I'm still thinking. Ah, yes. She tattled on me."

Hugh scrunches his face in thought. "Are you sure that wasn't Jane?"

"Well of course it was Jane! But I bet some of the times it was Bess, too."

Hugh gives me a disappointed look — I wish he weren't so virtuous! — and walks onto the field, toward cousin and ox. Bess looks away shyly and I wonder if she's following her sister's lead and plans to smack Hugh once he reaches her. But she relinquishes the plow to Hugh and walks alongside Bessie, whispering in her ear.

It's like the picture on the page of our church Psalter for growing season, a happy husband and wife plowing the field with their bovine companion. Worse, it's a living picture of bliss because the "husband" and "wife" even speak. I can't hear what they say, but they're obviously enjoying themselves.

I hear Hugh laugh, and when I catch glimpses of Bess's ugly face I see a smile on it. Why? They couldn't possibly like each other. But Hugh's manner is that of a gentleman, even Good Aunt says so, though he's but a lowly farmer, and he could make the sourest plum smile.

Still, as I watch them, I'm not smiling. I don't like this frivolity. Hugh is my best friend and his smiles and jokes should be reserved for me. Why is he sharing them with the likes of my cousin?

chapter the fifth

In Which I Write Recipes While Hugh Handles Bessie
(and Bess)

MY HAND IS GROWING CRAMPED WRITING ALL OF THE
recipes for Grandmother, and the ingredients are swimming
around in my head: two sprigs of rosemary, a pinch of sage,
a handful of wild onion, some yarrow; crush, blend with
butter, boil for two hours. Coriander to prevent fever, cham-
omile to prevent headaches, thyme can be used to fumigate
against infection, and a crushed bullhorn burned in a fire
will keep fleas away.

The scent from the fire is sweet, though, and it's warm
and dry inside and I'm grateful to be here rather than in the
rainy, muddy fields, like Hugh. I'm even feeling guilty that I
have such easy labor while he will have to work in Uncle's
fields, as well as his own, but neither Hugh nor Grandmother
can scribe, so there's no choice.

Still, I'm somewhat peeved with Hugh for spending his
time with Bess. In the field is fine, but he doesn't need to
walk her home afterward. Does he think she's forgotten the

way? And how he looks at her! As if eyeing a savory meat pie or the best yew bow ever made. It sickens you enough to need Grandmother's potions!

"Adrian, are you listening?"

"What? Yes."

"Crushed spiderwort root? Did you write that?"

I squint at the parchment with my right eye. Even my good eye doesn't work well in this dim light. I see nothing about crushed spiderwort root. "Is that for the melancholy?"

"Nay, it's for loosening the bowels."

I snort.

"You may laugh, but it's no laughing matter when a pregnant woman's bowels are blocked."

"I don't even know how to write *bowels*! It's not a word the priest has taught us."

"Do your best. We're almost done. Then you may deliver some remedies around the village. I'll ask Hugh to deliver the recipes to the manor after mass on Sunday."

Maybe Hugh would like a rest. And I would like to get out of going to mass by saying it takes me a long time to walk all the way there and back. I think Father is getting suspicious that I always have wheezing attacks on Sunday mornings and have to stay home. "I can take them." Maybe I'd even see some knights on their way to battle!

"The manor is some many miles from here."

"I've been with Hugh before. It's an easy walk." In truth, the first time I went, Hugh had to carry me piggyback part of the way home because I had a fit of wheezing. But that was when I was even smaller than I am now.

She shakes her head. "I'm not sure your father can spare you."

I roll my eyes. "Oh, yes, my important task of gathering goose feathers."

Grandmother gives a hint of a smile. "Hugh might like the excuse for a walk, perhaps with a lady friend."

I roll my eyes again. "With Bess. I know."

"He's growing fond of her, it seems."

"Really? I hadn't noticed," I say sarcastically.

Grandmother laughs.

"It's annoying," I retort.

She smiles. "It's a part of growing up."

"Yes, but his growing up is affecting *me*."

"Indeed, it does affect others." She looks at Hugh's father's pack and leather armor piled in the corner in readiness for his trip to battle, gazing at it with the smile a mother gives her ailing baby, although Hugh's father is a grown man.

Why, I wonder, doesn't growing up happen to me? Why is everyone else growing and I'm not? When is it my turn?

Grandmother sniffs and turns to me as if she has smelled my thoughts. "It will happen to you, too."

I look down at my small self and sigh. "Good Aunt says I was always tiny and, having barely survived illness, I should be grateful to be alive, albeit forever puny."

"You'll grow. Not to the size of Hugh — not many will — but you will grow."

"Maybe," I say, although I am not convinced. "She says I'm too sickly to grow very much."

"Doesn't she remember your mother, her own sister, who had the wheezing worse than you but, eventually, it faded? Haven't you yourself seen a difference in your malady over these past several years?"

I stop and think about it. Maybe she's right. I used to have the wheezing every day, many times a day. Now I can go for days at a time without suffering. But will it go away altogether? Not according to Good Aunt. "Good Aunt says —"

Grandmother slaps her thigh sharply. "And which one of us — Good Aunt or I — is the better healer and physic, do you think?"

I laugh outright. "On that there's no contest. You, of course." Good Aunt thinks she knows more about everything. She has even tried giving Grandmother advice!

"I'm not dead yet," Grandmother says, "though she would sorely like to take over my position as healer."

"If Good Aunt takes over we'll all be dead."

Grandmother chuckles but stops quickly, slapping her hand to her forehead. "Ah! Your aunt ordered a complexion remedy for your cousin."

"For Bess?" I'm thinking it'll take more than cream to cure that face.

"No, for Jane."

I am aghast. "Jane the Perfect One?"

There's a twinkle in Grandmother's eye. "A blemish has appeared on her chin and she won't step outside, not even to pass water. I suppose I should've made the ointment before now, as it's past noon and the poor girl must need to be going but" — she looks at me, her eyes still twinkling — "I've been busy, have I not?"

I grin back. "Indeed."

"Nevertheless, stop there first lest Jane needs to be put out of her misery."

I mutter that I have other ideas for putting her out of her misery and everyone else's.

Grandmother winks and gives me a sack with the remedies for others in the village, as well as the vial for Jane. "She should apply it to the offending spot twice a day and, more importantly, tell her to wear a shawl."

"What does the shawl do?"

"It covers her face!"

I laugh, but as I step out in the rain I wish I had a shawl myself. My loose hood is soon wet and lets in too much cold. My tunic is soaked through and I can even feel the wetness between my toes as my boots quickly turn sodden. Still, I know it's worse for Hugh out in the muddy field.

I pass the practice field and see some men with their bows — made by Father, of course — as they try to hit the target on the butt, and miss more often than not. Maybe it's the rain in their eyes. Or their fingers are shivering. Whatever it is, though, it's a good thing they're practicing because they'd best improve their shots. It's a shame that Father can't practice with the men, because he could teach them a lot, but he's too busy with bow making. He can't be spared for battle. That's the one bad part of being a bowyer: You miss the battle itself.

I slog on through the mud and gloomy grayness until I see Gerald Alberton entering the blacksmith's, so I pull his leather bottle out of my pouch of remedies and run inside after him. "Gerald!"

Both Gerald and the blacksmith turn to me.

It's warm and dry inside, with the fire blazing, and I wish I could stay all afternoon, but I hand him the bottle from Grandmother. "Here's your medicine for the stomach ailment and gas."

Gerald takes it quickly, looking away, but turning back to give me his coin in payment.

The blacksmith roars his hearty laugh. "Supping too much, Gerald?"

"It's my new wife's cooking," Gerald answers, "but don't tell her I said so."

The blacksmith laughs again and I smile. "She must be following the recipes of Good Aunt," I venture, knowing that the blacksmith, at least, is always ready to jest.

At first, the men look at each other, somewhat aghast that I have spoken insolently. Gerald makes a sour face, still not looking at me. I see the hint of a smile on the blacksmith's face but he doesn't make eye contact, either. To them I am just a boy, and an odd one, at that. And useless.

I return to the rain and head for Good Aunt's. I hear her before I see her and I startle because I think she's screaming at me. "What are you doing here?"

There's a quiet response and the name "Hugh" mentioned, but I can't make out the rest. I'm relieved Good Aunt wasn't yelling at me.

"Then make yourself useful and feed the chickens!"

"Yes, go, Bess!" Jane's pompous voice shrieks. "Don't bring that mess inside!"

A mud-splattered Bess appears through the door and steps beside the house, pelting the ground with bits of grain. The chickens dash up to her like she's a princess.

I dash up to her, too, because I'd like to avoid approaching Good Aunt. "This is for Jane," I mumble, holding out the vial.

Bess makes a sourer face than usual and takes the vial between her thumb and forefinger as if it's some filth from my body. She disappears without a thank-you or other acknowledgment and I turn away, happy to leave before Good Aunt might see me.

I have gone not ten steps before I hear her. "Adrian!"

I cringe, wondering if I can simply bolt, but she calls my name again. I turn around slowly and am relieved to see it's Bess at the doorway, not Good Aunt. St. Jerome's bones! The girl not only looks like her mother, she now sounds like her, too. What a fate!

"Are you to bring the payment to Grandmother?"

I cross my arms and stare at her. Since when is she allowed to call Hugh's grandmother as if she were her own? Is she now his best friend?

She must see my annoyance because she hesitates a moment, her eyes cast downward and her face turning blotchy pink. "I mean, Hu-Hugh's grandmother."

"Yes," I say, "I can take the payment to *Hu-Hugh's* grandmother." I know it's unkind to make fun of her but I'm angry.

Her face turns even pinker and she disappears inside. In a moment, I hear what I know to be Good Aunt's voice because it's so loud. "I will wait to see if the balm is effective first!"

"But, Mother —"

"Don't 'but, Mother' me!"

"Adrian is w-w-waiting."

"Silence! And stop that fool stuttering!"

Then it's that awful Jane's voice. "This had better work! I won't go outside ever again if it doesn't!"

"You will go out lest you burst!" Good Aunt shouts back.

"Nay, I will not! Never, never, never, never!"

Good Aunt's and Jane's bickering voices merge as Bess appears at the door. She doesn't look at me, but at her feet. "I'm s-s-s-sorry. I c-can't pay." She wrings her hands, and now I feel terrible for making fun of her stutter.

"It doesn't matter," I say quickly, even though it matters a lot. It's wrong and unfair to take Grandmother's herbs and hard work and not pay for it, and Good Aunt knows that. Still, I feel bad for my cousin. "It's not your fault, Bess," I tell her.

Bess looks up at me and I realize it's the first time I've used her name, the first time we've had a real conversation.

As I gaze at her I see the sadness in her eyes. In fact, her eyes startle me in how different they are from Good Aunt's. I hadn't noticed before. They remind me of someone, but I don't know whom. She turns and steps inside before I can look long enough to know whose eyes they are.

But after I deliver the rest of the remedies, give the payments to Grandmother, and walk back home in the gray gloominess of a rainy dusk, it hits me as hard as a branch thrown by Bryce, and I stop short. The rain pelts down even harder as I stand there, my shoulders shivering with the cold, my boots sinking into the mud, my mind bringing back the memories. I realize whose eyes Bess's are. They are my mother's.

chapter the sixth

In Which Hugh Is Besotted with "Bessie" —
My Cousin, Not the Ox

AFTER COLLECTING GOOSE FEATHERS AND BIRCH STAVES all morning, Father tells me to go to Uncle's field to see if I can be of use there. I tell him my feet are sore and show him my blisters. He looks at my boots and says they are too small. Imagine! Something is actually too small for me! He says he'll buy me a new pair on market day but, in the meantime, I must hurry along to the field. I remind him that Hugh is already working there, but still he insists I go. So I go slowly, by way of the practice field to watch the men from the village hit the straw bales with their arrows. Or more likely miss.

The men are lined up a hundred feet from the row of target bales, eyeing them like they are the enemy.

The blacksmith encourages them with his booming voice. "Hit the pagan Scots! Come on, men! If it were up to you, we'd all be *deed* by now," he says, imitating how a Scot would say *dead*.

The men laugh, albeit nervously.

"Ready your bows," the blacksmith's deep voice commands. "Nock!"

I watch the men as they place their arrows in the grooves on their bows.

"Mark!" he booms.

The men take aim at the targets.

"Draw!" As he calls out, the blacksmith draws his own large bow. Perhaps because he's the only one almost as tall as the bow, he's able to draw the string back farther than any other man.

"Loose!"

Arrows fly through the air with a *whup-whup-whup-whup* sound, many of them falling short or to the side of the bales. The blacksmith hits the bull's-eye.

He, and he alone, is a sure shot. I can hit my target as well as he can but, in truth, he can let his arrow fly from farther away and still have the strength behind it to stop a man dead. Other than that, I'm as good as he is.

I watch Hugh's father, his hair almost as pale as Hugh's. He's a fair to middling archer. I see Uncle halfheartedly tweaking his string and letting his arrow fall far short of the target. He's only here because Reeve Elliot watches the practices to make sure all men comply with our lord's mandate to practice. Maybe he's hoping to be asked to stay behind because he's a danger to his fellow men.

Uncle looks around, as if looking for an excuse to leave. I shrink away lest he use me as his excuse. If he sees me he may report my lollygagging to Father, or even worse, Good

Aunt. Still, I drag my feet, which is a good plan because when I arrive, Hugh and Bess are already leading the ox off the main field.

"Adrian!" Hugh calls, waving.

"Are you going to his other field?" I ask him.

"Nay. Your uncle says we are done for the day!"

"So we have all afternoon to practice archery!" I conclude triumphantly.

Hugh's face falls and he looks at the ground, then at me. "Bessie and I are going for a walk."

"You mean, you're walking her to pasture and then you're free. Bess can take her."

"No! I mean Bess, here, and I are going for a walk." A shy smile crosses his face. "I call her Bessie."

A smile crosses her lips, too, but mine are simply cross.

Bessie, he calls her now? *Bessie?* "You're wasting a fine afternoon like this to go for a walk?"

"It's not a waste!"

"When was the last time we had the chance to practice with our bows? Do you want to forget how?"

"I won't forget."

"You seem to have forgotten a lot, Hugh!" I say, and storm off, running to the woods. Hugh calls after me, but he doesn't come after me, I notice, now that he's besotted with my stupid cousin.

I reach our secret place in the woods, where we practice, but my lungs are sore and I have to lie down for a while to calm my breathing, careful not to lie near any evil plants that will make my condition worse. Finally, I'm able to pull my bow and my precious arrows out of the hollow tree trunk, and I can't help but admire my beautiful weapons.

Soon I hear the blacksmith's voice in my head: *Nock! Mark! Draw! Loose!* I spread some dirt under my eyes to counteract the bright sun, close my left eye, ready my bow, and take aim at a single leaf fifty feet away. On my second shot I split the leaf in two. As I practice more, I can hit a leaf on my first try, even when it sways in the breeze. I lose all sense of time and feel like I'm in another world.

Until I hear someone approach through the woods, and I grab my arrows, stowing them quickly with my bow inside the tree trunk. For years I haven't been discovered and I don't intend for anyone to find me out now. When the time is right, I will shock them all. So I stand and look up at the branches to divert attention away from the trunk and to show that I'm simply addlepated Adrian looking at birds.

But then I see who it is and I relax. "So, you've finally come to your senses?"

"Good Aunt," Hugh says in a mocking tone, "decided Bess had chores to do. Besides . . ." He frowns and looks at the ground.

"Besides what?"

"Bess says I shouldn't abandon my friendship with you or you'll like her even less than you do now."

I'm surprised that Bess would care about me, or what I think of her. And it pains me just a bit that she feels I like her so little.

"I don't *dis*like her," I protest. In truth, I did, but now I see that she's not like Good Aunt at all. Or like Jane. She's like . . . Bess. And that's a much better thing.

"Maybe you should treat her better, then," Hugh says, an edge to his voice.

"I will," I say, and I mean it.

He deigns to look at me again. "Good." And he smiles. "Come on, let's shoot!"

We challenge each other to hit a leaf, a knot on a tree trunk, even a stone thrown into the air.

"Honestly, Hugh, we're better than almost any man in our village. We should be the ones in battle."

"Don't remind me," Hugh says.

"You've had no luck with your father?"

"None." He sighs. "And you? Does your father see you as an apprentice yet?"

I snort. "Maybe I'll run away to battle because I'll work with a bow much more that way than in my own father's shop."

Hugh shakes his head. "You're too young for that."

From him, the comment angers me. "I'm almost thirteen." And I'm hoping to see some battle, no matter what he thinks. There's always a way around things, I've found.

That's when my brain comes up with a splendid thought. "Hugh! I have an idea for after mass on Sunday."

"There is no mass Sunday. The priest sent word that he's needed at the manor."

"How did you hear?" But I answer my own question as he does, "Good Aunt." Her ears are the size of giant fishing nets and she catches the news before it has a chance to reach anyone else.

"The reeve said that the men must practice all day, even though it's a Sunday," Hugh adds.

"Perfect! Because here is my plan: You show up with your bow and arrow and practice with the men!"

"But Father will protest."

"Maybe, but you can claim, loudly, that you are near the age when it's required to practice, and then quickly shoot a target in the center, and after the reeve sees that, he won't let you leave!"

A smile creeps across Hugh's face and he nods slowly. "That could work."

We shake hands and suddenly his face falls. "I promised Bessie I'd go for a walk with her tomorrow."

I roll my eyes. "You can walk anytime. This is important."

"She's important to me, too," he says quietly.

I hold my tongue so I don't offend him, and try to think of a more artful way to say what I mean. "Why not spend most of the day at the practice, then the late afternoon and evening with her?"

He looks doubtful. "Maybe you could spend some time with her? Until I'm free?"

I stare at him. "Hugh! She's not a newborn lamb who needs to be tended each waking moment."

"But your dear Good Aunt will come up with chore after chore for her if she's anywhere in sight." He fairly spits out "Good Aunt," and I have to laugh.

"It's not funny! It's unfair to Bessie. Jane is treated like a queen and poor Bessie is treated like a — a —"

"An ox," I finish for him.

"Your aunt is most unkind."

"Haven't I been telling you that for years? And all you've said is, *Oh, Adrian, you shouldn't say mean things about your own family.*"

"I have seen the error of my ways."

"Finally!"

"You may say whatever you wish about your aunt. And Jane. Your uncle's not so bad. And Bessie is a peach."

I know he means my cousin, not the ox, and I don't even tease him about it.

"I just don't want to abandon her all day." He says it in such a lovesick way I can't help but grin.

"You can tell her that you'll be longing to see her all day." I put my hand on my heart and make swooning eyes. "Oh, my darling Bessie, I don't know how I can last an entire day with just putrid bows and arrows in my hands instead of your sweet face."

"Stop it!" says Hugh, although he's grinning and red-faced.

"My dear love," I continue, "I pine for you each moment —"

"Adrian!" But he laughs.

"My heart fair breaks at the thought of not seeing you for minutes, nay hours. I gasp my last breath —" And indeed I do because Hugh punches me, not hard, but enough to knock me over, and I start laughing so much it's hard to breathe.

chapter the seventh

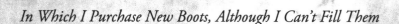

In Which I Purchase New Boots, Although I Can't Fill Them

IT'S MARKET DAY AND TOM THE COBBLER HAS COME ALL the way from Penrith. I head for his stall to buy my new boots because Father says Tom's boots are of the best quality. For the first time, Father is letting me buy them myself, along with tallow he needs for the arrows. Perhaps he realizes I'm almost a man. Or, more likely, it's because he's too busy with the upcoming war. He gave me his whole money pouch, although he says to be frugal. I don't know why. He makes plenty of money and he insists on living well below our means. Where does all that money go?

Reeve Elliot is already at the market. I clutch Father's money pouch and look around quickly, because the reeve is also Bryce's father. I hope the unholy trinity is not nearby. The reeve would do nothing to stop them because he thinks Bryce is God's gift.

Uncle walks by with a tankard of ale that he tries to hide behind his back when he sees the reeve. When Reeve Elliot notices him, Uncle makes a mocking bow.

"I'm pleased to see you have some decorum," Reeve Elliot answers, also mockingly, "lest I should have to report you under the sumptuary laws."

Uncle looks up, both shock and anger on his face. "Me? With my plowman's tunic and muddy boots, which have no sumptuous long and pointed toes, I might add."

"It's your daughter I'm talking about."

The anger drains from Uncle's face as his eyes shift back and forth, as a boy caught with his finger in a plum pie, and looking for escape.

"Her shoes curl up at least an inch beyond her toes . . . possibly two."

If it's two inches, then the reeve is within his rights to charge a fee. I know Bryce's boots have curly toes that are likely two inches too long. Reeve Elliot thinks he and his family are far above everyone in the village.

"That's my wife's doing," Uncle says, "if there's anything amiss."

"Then," Elliot sneers, "perhaps you should have a word with your wife."

Uncle mutters, but this time I hear him. "I'd rather control the ox than that beast."

"A man who cannot control his own wife is —"

"I didn't say I can't!" Uncle says, his chest puffed out and hands on his waist.

"See that you do," the reeve says, and turns to pay for his new shoes. They are a bright, rich brown that's almost red. And they have long, curled-up toes.

"Badger," I hear Bryce hiss behind me, making me jump.

Bryce laughs. His father turns and, upon seeing Bryce, smiles. When he sees me, the smile becomes a grimace, and he raises his eyebrows.

"I — I'm here for new boots," I stammer, although I'm angry for feeling that I have to explain myself.

"I trust your father is wiser than your uncle," the reeve says, as if giving me a warning. "Common boots for common craftsmen." He walks off with a flourish.

Common craftsmen? Father is a bowyer! The king himself is indebted to Father for his knowledge. That's far better than a pompous fool like Bryce's father. All he does is collect money from all of us for the lord of the manor.

Bryce shoves me and laughs coldly. "You'll never amount to anything."

His words sting. He's not merely ridiculing Father's profession, but also my size and strength. St. Jerome's bones! Now I know what kind of shoes I'm getting!

I try to enter the stall but Tom's wife's backside blocks my way and it's too wide to get around. I'm about to ask her to move but she lets out a shriek.

"This is from your side of the family! It's your brother's bad blood in his veins! Our son is a thief and he always has been!"

"Nay," says a man's voice, which I think is Tom's, but I can't see around the aforementioned backside of his wife. "Pippin wasn't always bad. Think on his boyhood. Remember he pulled you out of the stream when you fell in?"

"Aye, because I slipped down the bank trying to get back the penny he stole from my pocket!"

Tom's voice does not boom as much. "He brought us bread when we had nothing to eat."

"Which he stole!" she screams.

Meekly, Tom says, "Maybe he's like Robin Hood."

"Pah! Robin Hood, indeed! He's an evil dolt! I'd ask the devil himself to rip his heart out, it's so black with his vile actions. And now that men are being paid good money for soldiering supplies, he's having a heyday stealing from them. It disgusts me!"

Tom's wife may be coarse but she's also right. I've heard of several people who've been robbed by Pippin. And he was always mean. Just like Bryce.

She whirls around and makes to storm out of the shop, nearly knocking me over. "What do you want, boy?" She doesn't wait for an answer but marches off, muttering.

Tom gives me an apologetic smile and motions outside. "I have children's shoes out front."

"I want those," I say, pointing to a pair on the wall behind him. They are a rich brown leather, almost as red as the reeve's, with long, pointed toes, even curling up slightly.

"They're fine boots, fit for gentry." He eyes my clothes. "They won't last long in a field."

"I don't work in a field!"

He smirks, picking up a shoe he is sewing, and I feel my ire rising.

"I'm Adrian Black of Ashcroft, John the bowyer's son."

He grunts and nods, seeming to accept the importance of Father's position, as well he should. He puts down his sewing and hands me the beautiful pair of shoes.

I put them on and the soft leather feels like feathers on my feet. "How much are they?"

I gulp when I hear the price, but it doesn't stop me. "I'll take them."

"They're too big for you."

"Father said to buy them overly large because my feet grow so fast." Those aren't Father's exact words, but he said something like it.

"Aye, but these are big enough that they violate the sumptuary laws."

I look down at my feet and try to measure in my head if the pointy end of the shoe is more than two inches beyond my toes. It is. But it makes my feet look large. And it feels good to stand out as big, even if it's only my feet. I decide it's worth the risk of being caught by Bryce's father.

"My toes are almost at the end of the boot," I say.

Tom clucks and shakes his head but is willing enough to take my money when I pull it out of my pouch. I walk out of the stall with pride and soon learn how to walk in oversize, pointy shoes without tripping. Much.

I get a good deal on tallow because I carve new pieces of wood to replace the rotten ones on the peddler's cart. And I tell him the tallow is for the war effort. Still, I hope Father doesn't count what's left in his money pouch.

Carving the wood reminds me that I could be making bows, if Father would only realize that I could help the journeyman de Cluny sent. Stephen is nicer than Peter, but not as fast. I know the feel of a bow so well, I could do a better job than either of them.

When I hear the unholy trinity behind me, yelling, "Badger, Badger," I take off at a run, as fast as my shoes will allow. I feel like a badger being hunted by bears. They pelt me with clods of dirt but are too busy laughing hysterically when I trip over my own feet, several times, that they don't come after me, and that's all I wish for.

I wish for a little more when I get home, however. I wish that Peter and Stephen would stop snickering at my feet and Father wouldn't be so angry that I have "wasted good money on ridiculous shoes." Mostly I wish that Good Aunt were not here, telling Father that this is but more proof that I am a useless addlepate.

chapter the eighth

In Which I Learn My Fate

I SNEAK OFF WHILE GOOD AUNT CONTINUES HER TIRADE so that I'm not around when she decides to send me to the fields or subject me to cupping or the Lord only knows what else. I get to the woods, where my bow and quiver are stashed in the birch tree. Although it feels good to practice, it doesn't feel good to keep tripping over my shoes.

I hear Thomas the leper clapping his spoon against his bowl and I retreat farther into the woods. Sometimes I feel guilty for avoiding him, but at least I don't throw stones at him like the unholy trinity. Thomas calls out a thank-you and Hugh calls back, wishing him a good day. It's all right for Hugh to leave food for Thomas but he really shouldn't get so close to him. Even Grandmother says to keep five paces away, and I've seen Hugh get as near as two paces. I shudder to think of the likes of Thomas, but grin when I see Hugh striding toward me.

Taking a step toward him, I trip over my own shoes, again.

Hugh bites his lip, trying not to laugh.

"What?" I say, challenging him, as I struggle to my feet.

He shakes his head briefly. "Nothing. It's just" — he nods at my shoes — "they don't suit you."

"Why not?"

"They look . . . large."

"Maybe it's my feet that are large."

Hugh twists his mouth around. It's painful for him to hear something that even sounds like it might be a lie.

I sigh. "Fine. They're a bit big, but they make my feet look bigger."

"Why must your feet look bigger?"

I look at him askance. Surely he knows why.

"I wish you wouldn't worry so much about your size."

"That's easy for you to say." I snort.

Hugh starts to answer but I cut him off. "The reeve says Father only does common crafts! And Bryce says I'll never amount to anything. They're such swine. Well, I can wear finery, too."

Hugh lets an arrow fly, hitting the center of a knot hole in an oak. "You wear them to show you're as good as Bryce?"

I glare at him. "I wear them to show I'm of his class."

Hugh lowers his bow and looks at me, disappointment in his gaze. "Adrian, you don't need to prove anything to the likes of him."

Although he's my best friend, Hugh sometimes makes me feel like a fool. It's a part of his nature I don't really care for. I change the subject. "I heard what happened at the practice field. Showing your skill worked!"

Hugh smiles. "Aye, it did." His face grows serious again. "But Father says Elliot is weakening and may wait until I'm fifteen to send me. A lot can happen in that time. Father is not the best shot."

I can't argue with that. "So will you go to battle on your own?"

"I think I must."

"I'll go with you."

He shakes his head slowly. "No."

"What do you mean, 'no'? Of course I'm going with you!"

"I won't allow it," Hugh says, his face getting redder. "Absolutely not!"

"You're not my father so you can't tell me what to do!" I shout back. "I'm just as good of an archer as you, even better, and if I want to go —"

"It doesn't matter how good your archery skills are, Adam!"

He calls me his dead brother's name and this time it angers me that he thinks me a young boy. "I am not —"

"You're still twelve years old. You shouldn't see what goes on in battle. Besides, there'll be few enough men left in the village and you'll need to help tend the fields, carry the water —"

"Carry water? Tend the fields? Have Bessie the ox stomping on me while you're off in battle getting all the glory?" I load an arrow, aim, and shoot a squirrel as it jumps from one tree to the next. It falls with a thud. "You can't have all the glory, Hugh!"

I hear a loud crackling in the trees behind us and whirl

around, bow in hand, in time to see William and Warren running away.

Hugh chuckles. "You scared them off."

"They were probably after me but saw that you were here and got scared."

"More likely," Hugh says, "they saw what a sure shot you are with the bow and that sent them scurrying off like scared rabbits."

I have to laugh because they did look exactly like two scared rabbits!

We practice our archery without speaking of going to battle, but I'm hoping that since Hugh has seen my might, he'll change his mind. At least he's happy about the squirrel I killed because now he has a meal to give Thomas. Despite our arguing, I consider the afternoon a success.

Until I return home. Father crosses his arms and frowns at me. Peter and Stephen look at each other, quietly put their tools down, and edge past me, leaving the shop.

"The reeve tells me that you and Hugh were practicing archery in the woods."

How did he — St. Jerome's bones! The twins told Bryce, who squealed on us!

"I can explain, Father."

"Go on."

Why did I say that? What do I explain? I hesitate. "It's just that Hugh needs to be ready for battle — when the time comes."

"And what about you? Why are you practicing?"

"To help Hugh. You want him prepared, don't you?"

"Aye, and that is what the practice field is for. And the other men." He emphasizes the word *men* to make me feel puny.

"Pig slop!" I say.

I hear gasps from Peter and Stephen outside. Father's jaw drops, as do his arms. Maybe this time I really have spoken too much. But I hurry on.

"Father, you know that most of the men in the village are not as sure a shot as I am! I can hit the center of the target! I can hit a leaf at fifty yards! I can hit a squirrel in —"

"Enough!" Father looks down at me, so angry he's quivering.

I stand my ground, even if he decides to hit me. I will not flinch.

Instead, he stands there shaking, breathing fiercely through his nostrils until, finally, he calms down. He turns to the door and calls, "You are both dismissed for the day!"

I hear the scurrying and whispers of Peter and Stephen moving away as Father looks back at me and we're alone. I'm not afraid. His face is sagging and his arms droop, as if he's a bellows emptied of all air.

Sighing, he sits back down and orders me to do the same. I back up to the stool in the corner and sit.

Father holds his palms together as if in prayer for some time before he finally says, "I know you wish to be my apprentice."

I hold my breath. Maybe he'll finally accept me?

"I have refused because of your mother."

"Mother?"

"She's the one who started you on your letters. Do you remember how she told you stories and showed you the words that made them?"

I remember that. She showed me much. And the things she had no chance to show me, I learned at school, where Father made me start going after she died.

"She didn't want you in this" — he sweeps his hand around the shop — "trade."

"Why not?"

He lowers his voice, as if the walls have ears. "She came to believe that war, and all of its weapons, were merely the toys of kings and nobles, a way for them to gain land and money and power."

"Do you believe it?"

He sighs. "With this war against the French and so many battles with the Scots, and even English noble against English noble, I do wonder at the purpose." He shakes his head. "I've seen too many people die. It's easy to say that it's all for God and country and honor. It's harder to believe it."

"Then why do you stay a bowyer?" I challenge him.

His eyes examine the ground. "I am less and less happy in my profession. Yet it has given me much. I don't need to farm at all and that's unusual, also a godsend, given that we're a very small family and I'm growing old."

And I'm not much use in a field, I add to myself. But I don't want to end up like Ailwin the Useless. "Where are you thinking of apprenticing me, then?"

Father looks away. "You know I have always said that I will care for you."

This time I tell him the truth. "I want to care for myself."

He nods but he doesn't look as if he agrees. "It is better for you to stay in our village."

"And do what? The reeve despises me, so he'll sabotage anything I try. The blacksmith is the only one who'll stand up to him, but I'll never be big enough to handle that job."

"I will always take care of you, Adrian," he repeats.

"Then I'll be an archer!"

"No! If people know how good you are, they will want you in battle."

I try not to grin but he must see the happiness on my face.

He shakes his head. "No, Adrian. It is not good. I do not wish to lose you. Reeve Elliot wants to send Hugh into battle with the men, maybe as soon as a fortnight. Hugh's father is arguing with the reeve right now."

"Why?"

Father looks at me, his eyes wide. "Because Hugh is too young for battle."

"He'll be fifteen by the feast of St. Martin."

"Aye," says Father, "less than two months away. That's when the reeve says he must go — if he agrees to let him wait until then."

"Hugh wants to go," I venture.

"Only because he doesn't know any better."

"Hugh is not a fool!"

"Of course not. But he's young and thinks battle is a glorious thing."

"It is," I say to myself.

But Father hears me and speaks sharply. "You wouldn't think so if you saw him wounded — or worse."

"That won't happen to Hugh! He's too skillful!"

Father shakes his head, closes his eyes, and his voice is soft now. "It's not all about skill. There is much that can happen beyond the soldier's control." He sighs and looks at me. "Fortunately, you're so small that there's no chance of your being sent to battle."

I bristle at his remark. I am not useless! I'm a better shot than most of the men. And I'm older than he treats me. Maybe Father is right that I won't be sent to battle. But who's to stop me from going of my own free will?

chapter the ninth

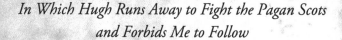

*In Which Hugh Runs Away to Fight the Pagan Scots
and Forbids Me to Follow*

ON MICHAELMAS, THE WHOLE VILLAGE GOES TO CHAPEL
to pray for our good men before they head off for battle. It's
a short service because Father Fraud now stays at the manor
and is eager to get back, probably for a Michaelmas feast,
although no one is celebrating here.

After the service, the men leave the village, walking
north past Penrith to Carlisle. Some have leather helmets.
Some wear chest plates. Some carry pikes. But all have longbows, thanks to Father. I watch Hugh and his father embrace
and see the sadness in his father's eyes. But I know something his father doesn't. Hugh will follow them.

Hugh, Bess, and I meet in Uncle's field near the tavern.

Bess pleads with Hugh not to go. "You don't need to
prove you're brave! I know you're brave already!"

"I must fight beside my father," Hugh says softly. "I don't
want to lose him."

"And I don't want to lose you!" she says, her voice
catching.

Bess cries quietly and Hugh comforts her with one arm, pulling her to his chest. With his other arm, he grabs my shoulder. "Don't follow me, Adrian. Please." Hugh's eyes beseech me and I want to assure him.

"I won't," I say, although what I mean is I won't follow you *now*. Soon, however, I will.

"And take care of Bess —"

"Whist!" says Bess, pushing away from him and wiping her eyes. "How do you think I've survived all these years? How? By my own self!"

Even though she chastises him, Hugh smiles. "I do love that spirit of yours, Bessie."

Bess blushes, smiles, and snuggles up against Hugh's chest again.

I groan and turn away. "Must I leave you two?"

Bess giggles.

I'm about to go, but Hugh stops me. "Adrian, please leave food for Thomas. Now that I'm not here, he'll have no one providing for him."

"Of course," I say, although it turns my stomach to think of Thomas the leper and the scabs on his face and his missing fingers and the stench of him. I know it's not his fault and I know he's suffering his hell on earth so he'll go straight to heaven, but I still can't stand to look at him. But it's the least I can do for Hugh to put food out for him — at least, until it's my turn, too, to leave for battle.

Hugh's voice is quiet and serious. "I must head north . . . toward Scotland."

Bess shivers when he utters the word *Scotland*, as do I.

Only grown, strong men have crossed into the land of the Scots, and many of them have not returned.

After Hugh gives Bess one last, and overly long, embrace, he heads toward the hills. I don't know which one of us is in more pain, Bess or myself, as we watch him walk off on his journey, avoiding the road lest someone try to send him back home. I stare after him and notice that even after walking a fair distance his stature doesn't seem to diminish. He stands out dark and strong against the sun. But then, after raising his arm in a final farewell, he disappears over the hill.

Wiping her eyes, Bess heads for Uncle's far field to weed. It's her plan to be well occupied when people begin to notice that Hugh is gone. Hugh told Grandmother he would be in the farthest fields first so she wouldn't miss him immediately. For my part, I'm collecting staves and goose feathers and pondering what Mother said about learning my letters and how bad it is to be a bowyer. At least, that's what I'll tell Father.

The village seems deserted. There is no celebrating this Michaelmas, no men shouting back and forth to one another, and fewer people on the road. When I pass the alehouse, even the sign that so often bangs above the door is hanging still and quiet. It's almost eerie. As I pass a few women and children on the road or in the field, they only nod or look away. It's as if they're already in mourning. It's just a battle! We'll repel the pagan Scots quickly, our men will be back before St. Crispin's Day, and we'll all rejoice!

I spend the day practicing my archery in earnest since it's my plan to follow Hugh into battle soon. I'll show everyone my might. I'll show them I'm not useless. I'll show them I'm a hero.

Hitting a target is too easy a task, however, and I spend my time splitting leaves, especially moving ones, and even catch myself a rabbit, two squirrels, and one crow, because although a crow hasn't got much meat on it, I don't like those creatures. I move around different wooded areas because I want to avoid the unholy trinity. Also, it's good practice because I can spin around or jump out from behind trees, hitting targets with which I'm not so familiar.

I must admit that the boots Father traded for my pointy shoes are much better for running, jumping, turning, climbing — well, in truth, they're better for just about anything than the pointy shoes. Father says they're better for helping Hugh in the field. Little does he know that it's the *battle*field where I'll be helping Hugh!

As the sun starts to go down, I stop on the road where Thomas the leper passes. Wrapping the crow and squirrels I've shot, I put the bundle in a shallow grave with a cross made of sticks that Hugh always uses as a sign. No one would disturb a grave and Thomas knows it's meant for him. Maybe the squirrels and crow will give him sustenance for a while. The rabbit I save to bring home for dinner. Now that Father knows I practice archery, maybe he'll be happy with what I can provide.

But before I even walk into the shop, I know the news has spread about Hugh. Women huddle on the road whispering and Father is standing outside, a hand over his brow, squinting up the road to the north, as if he'll be able to find Hugh.

When Father sees me, he calls out, "Adrian! Do you know where Hugh is?"

I walk toward him and call back, "No." It's an honest statement. He's on the road somewhere, heading northwest, but I don't know exactly where he is.

"Did he tell you where he was going?"

"To weed the fields." That also is true.

Father cocks his head at me, narrowing his eyes.

I try to appear as innocent as a babe. "Look!" I say, now standing in front of him, holding up the rabbit. "We'll have a fine supper!"

"Aren't you worried about your friend?"

I wonder if I'm playing my role right. "Hugh is well, I am sure."

"Well on his way to battle, is that it?"

I let the rabbit dangle in the dirt and sigh. It's no use pretending. I can only try to make him see reason. "Hugh wants to help his father —"

"Even though his father forbade it? You're his best friend. Couldn't you stop him?"

I shake my head. Indeed, I didn't even try. It was me who put the idea in his head. But he would've gone anyway, I'm sure of it.

Father sighs. "I must try to stop him."

"What? Father, he left many hours ago. You'll never catch up with him."

"Stupid fool!" Good Aunt shrieks from behind me.

I cower, expecting a thrashing for something I've done or not done, I don't know which.

"It's true, then," she sputters. "He had less than two months to wait but he abandons his duty to my fields and prances off to battle like a court jester."

"That's not true!" I cry, losing my fear of her in my anger. "Hugh is brave and noble and has gone to battle to take care of his father! He may even save your own husband's neck since Uncle shoots a bow like a —"

"Adrian!" Father cuts me off.

Good Aunt gives me a sour face but then points her finger at Father. "The only thing more foolish would be for you to go after him. The men will send the stupid boy back home."

"They will not!" I say. "He looks like a man so how will —"

"Adrian." Father doesn't yell at me this time, but his hand squeezes my shoulder. "Your aunt is right. I want to help but it's more likely that he'll happen upon someone from our village or the manor who knows him. Perhaps they'll send him back or at least protect him." He squeezes my shoulder more tightly, as if he'll never let go.

Good Aunt deigns to look down at me again. "Since I've lost my field worker for a time, you'll have to take his place."

I groan.

"First," says Father, "please pay our respect to Hugh's grandmother and give her this." He takes a coin from his pocket and presses it into my hand, although his other hand is still clutching my shoulder.

"Respect?" Good Aunt barks. "Hugh is not dead, for heaven's sake!"

"Still," says Father sternly, "she's now all alone."

Good Aunt rolls her eyes. "I shall take care of this rabbit for supper," she says, grabbing it from my hand so quickly I have no chance to grip it.

I look at Father, who moves his head somewhere between shaking it and a nod, as if to say he gives up and it's not worth fighting her.

I wish now I'd left the rabbit for Thomas.

chapter the tenth

In Which I Pay No Heed to Hugh

I CAN TELL THAT GRANDMOTHER HAS BEEN CRYING. "Is your father going after Hugh?"

She sounds so hopeful I can't tell her the truth. "He was talking about that when I left him."

She twists a sprig of rosemary in her hand. "He must make haste! Hugh is in danger."

"Hugh is very smart and brave, and quick with his bow," I reassure her.

It doesn't work. "You boys do not understand. You don't know the horrors that await him. He'll see things he has never even dreamed of." She looks at me accusingly.

I don't know what she fears he'll run into, other than Scots, but I'm almost feeling guilty now for helping Hugh go. "I'll pray for him," I tell her. "I'll pray that he'll be safe from both pagans and dragons."

"Dragons, indeed! There's enough to be fearful of in this world without men making up horrors." She bangs around her pots, picking some up, slamming them down again. "And the reeve thinks it a good thing that a boy has gone to war! He should be ashamed of himself for putting the idea in the boy's head in the first place!"

I avert my eyes, knowing it wasn't the reeve's fault, but my own.

Grandmother continues. "Will he send his own son? Nay, he says, Bryce is just a boy. Bah! He is large and coarse and belches and farts as loud as any man, but no, his precious Bryce can't be sent to battle." Grandmother shakes her head.

"Silence, woman!"

I jump and turn around to see standing in the doorway none other than Reeve Elliot himself. I swallow hard, holding my breath and hoping that he doesn't punish Grandmother too badly.

"What do you want now?" Grandmother screams at him.

It startles the reeve as much as me. He hands a basket of bread, onions, and some kind of herb through the doorway, and his tone is more submissive than irritated. "From my wife. She bids you well."

Grandmother does not take the basket but stares an evil eye at the reeve, who, upon seeing it and perhaps remembering how some call her a witch, quickly puts the basket down and leaves.

Grandmother looks away, blinking. Eventually, she looks down at the basket. "Comfrey!" she says, reminding me of the name of that herb lying next to the onion. Her body fairly crumples, wrinkling in on itself. "Adrian, I was supposed to send a salve and recipe for our lady of the manor. She needs medicine for her pregnancy pain." Grandmother squeezes her eyes shut and speaks in a whisper, as if she is in pain herself. "I was going to ask Hugh . . ."

"I'll take it," I say hastily.

"Thank you, Adrian." Grandmother sighs and dictates to me while I write on the parchment that I left there. My hand is shaking because I realize what this means. Going to the manor is the perfect cover for the start of my journey. Tomorrow I go to battle!

Grandmother gives me several bags of herbs, telling what they are all for, and I try desperately to remember but my head is elsewhere. "I'll bring this to the manor first thing tomorrow." *And*, I think to myself, *go off to battle*. Despite what Hugh says. Despite what anyone says. It's my turn now.

I go by Uncle's field as the sun is setting and am relieved to find Bess weeding so I can share my plan of going to find Hugh. When I tell her, she stands up and a cry escapes her lips.

"Hush!" I tell her, kneeling down in the dirt, pretending to weed.

She quickly does the same. "How will you be able to find him?"

"He's most likely following the road north and will stop wherever there's a battle to check if it involves the men of our village. The Scots will no doubt try to take Carlisle, as they've tried so many times before and failed. I'll head there first."

Her eyes are wide. "Carlisle? But that's a huge town. How will you find him there?"

Girls know nothing when it comes to matters of war. "I'll look for groups of soldiers, of course."

"But what if they're in hiding? What if they've split into many groups? What if he isn't even with a group but is walking by himself?"

"Bess, I know his walk from half a mile away."

"What if he has crossed Hadrian's Wall and" — she swallows hard — "entered the land of the Scots?"

I can't help but swallow hard myself at the thought of crossing over Hadrian's Wall. Building the wall was how the Romans tried to stop the pagan Scots from entering England, over a thousand years ago. It didn't work for the Romans, either.

I take a deep breath. "Then I will enter Scotland, too." My voice is less firm than I want, but at least my words are strong. Besides, it's unlikely that I'll have to cross the wall. The battles will likely be on English soil. "I'll find him, whatever it takes."

"You're very brave, Adrian."

I've never been called brave before. I shrug as if it's nothing to go off to battle, but I press my lips together to keep the proud grin from appearing.

"I'm so grateful to you for bringing him back, but don't let yourself get hurt."

Bringing him back? What is she thinking? I'm not bringing him back! I'm joining him.

"We'll all feel better once you've both returned."

I nod because that may be true, although it's not happening. Not soon, anyway. But Father will be less angry with me if he thinks I've just gone to bring Hugh home, so I'll let Bess believe that. When Good Aunt and Father question her, she'll have a good story.

"When do you think you'll be back?"

"It . . . may take some time — to find him, and then return. The battle is likely several days' walk, maybe more."

She chews the inside of her cheek and reminds me how much she looks like Good Aunt, though that's not her fault. "I'll make a pouch of food for you — with meat — and leave it behind your house when I bring over your supper."

"Thank you."

She chews her cheek and lip some more. "And from now on, when I deliver food to your father I'll take extra and leave it for Thomas. Hugh would want that."

I nod. In truth, I'd forgotten about Thomas.

"Oh, and will you give this to Hugh?" She unpins the pewter metal of St. Aldegundis from her kirtle.

"Shouldn't you keep it yourself? It's all that protects you." I know the power of St. Aldegundis. Good Aunt says my mother's prayers to her saved me from death, as she's the saint who protects from childhood diseases, as well as wounds and sudden death.

"It's Hugh who needs protecting. And you." Before I can say anything else, she pins it on my tunic, behind the pouch on my belt so no one can see it.

"God be with you, Adrian. I'm proud to call you my cousin."

She gazes at me with the blue-green eyes of my mother. As she leaves, her head down, and arms wrapped around herself, I wonder how I always thought her so hateful.

That night, I wake when it's still dark and Father is snoring. I'm fitful and anxious and can't sleep. Looking outside, I believe I can see a faint light in the east just beginning to turn the black night into dark blue.

Last night I told Father I'd get an early start in the morning for the manor, that it was important to Grandmother since she was already late with the recipes and remedies. He was so distracted that he agreed. He doesn't suspect anything. At least, I don't think he does. Just in case, I decide to leave immediately, lest on awakening he realize the real meaning behind my leaving.

Quietly, I pull on my new boots and Mother's cloak, for there's a fierce chill at this hour. I decide to take my dice — I hear of men playing dice between battles. Mine are a nice set that Father gave me for my birthday last year. I wonder what he was going to give me this year? My birthday is four days from now. Good Aunt says the gifts Father gives me have helped make me the spoiled brat I am. Well, even she will see what a hero I am now.

I dare not even look at Father as I pass him, fearing my guilt might wake him. Outside, I find the pouch of food from Bess and even a small clay bowl I can use for boiling water or cooking food. I bless my cousin for the bread, eel, and large chunk of rabbit for which Good Aunt will surely punish her. I collect my bow and quiver of arrows, which I left behind our house last night.

I am away.

chapter the eleventh

In Which I Am on My Own

THE ROAD IS NOT AS FAMILIAR BY NIGHT AS IT IS BY DAY. And it's *dark*. At first, I'm in good spirits because I'm on a man's journey. I have herbs, a salve from Grandmother, and the recipes that prove I'm going to the manor, lest I be stopped. I have a bag of food from Bess and my bow and arrows, which I can say are for my own protection now that there is a war on. Above all, I have my pride to keep me strong.

The road is also much louder than it is by day. Dead leaves crack under my feet as if I'm breaking branches with every step. The acorns crash from the trees like heavy stones the unholy trinity throw at me. Even the wind blowing against my cheeks seethes and howls as it rushes through the leaves of the trees. I want to yell at it to stop but I must stay silent lest there are spies, robbers, or pagans on this path.

I try to take my mind off the road and contemplate how far the woods go; they seem so immense. Do they stretch all the way north, through Scotland, and beyond? To the end of the earth? Are there dragons there, as some people say? I slink past the gnarled tree branches that look like freakish arms reaching out to clutch me. I wish I really were a badger so I could scuttle out of sight. At the very least, I wish I had a dog or a goose or even that horrible Bessie to bear the brunt of whatever creature might attack, be it man or beast. At least Bessie would bellow and give me warning so I could hide somewhere. Grandmother said that dragons are nonsense and that there's much in nature to fear without other horrors. I agree with Grandmother right now, at least the part about there being enough in nature to fear.

I'm relieved when I come to a clearing. I can see the henge in the distance to my left, the circle of stones from people a long time ago. And I wonder about ghosts or, worse, redcaps with their sharp teeth. Redcaps are said to hurl boulders at people, so why couldn't they pick up one of the standing stones and toss it at me? The only defense is to say Bible passages out loud because that makes their teeth break. I wish I had memorized the psalms better from our Psalter. They're even in English instead of Latin, so it's not that hard. I hope that speaking words, loudly, that are close enough to the psalms will keep any redcaps away.

I walk quickly past the henge and soon am passing the copse of oaks on the hillock, the sun just beginning to peek from behind them. The glint reminds me of the night my mother brought me here when I was very young. It was a Midsummer's Eve, before my sister was even born. Mother had birthed a baby boy who died, and I can still feel her sadness and how strongly she clutched my hand. We sat in the field and watched the flying lights illuminate the trees. They look like bugs but we all know them to be the souls of babies who never had a chance to be baptized before they died. Now they must fly around at night, glowing for all eternity.

I wish I could see my baby brother's soul now, but it's too late in the year for that. And too close to daylight. Instead, I walk on and find myself entering woods again and sinking into darkness.

When I finally see the old Norman tower of the manor I realize I'm even more thirsty than hungry, though I'm hungry enough to eat a bear. I run down the hill and around to the back of the house, jumping over the dried-up moat that used to be there for safety years ago. Now there's no moat or wall, but the house itself is a stone fortress.

The gates are open and horses are in the stable yard as I cross through. I pass squires, or perhaps young knights, talking in low voices. They must be speaking of battle. Near them, several boys, younger than me, practice fighting with wooden swords. How I wish I were to the manor born so I could fight with a sword!

I knock on the wooden door of the kitchen next to the manor house, although it's half open. It smells rich and muttony. The cook works over the roaring fire and doesn't hear me, so I step inside and call out, "Good day!"

She jumps. "You! Boy! What a fright you gave me! What do you want?"

"I've come from Ashcroft to —"

"You came all the way from Ashcroft? In the dark?"

She looks so angry I don't think it wise to point out that it's light now.

"With ghouls and ghosts and thieves on the road? Foolish child!"

She steps toward me and it's only because I'm so nimble that I avoid her hand that tries to smack my head. I smile sheepishly at her from the other side of the table and pull the parchment out of my bag. "I wanted to get the recipe and this salve to my lady's physic as quickly as possible."

"Well," she grumbles, "that is a good cause." She looks past me. "Thomas!"

I whirl around and am relieved to see it's not Thomas the leper, but a boy, younger than me, carrying a headless goose by the neck.

"What?" the boy says, backing up a step. "You said goose, didn't you?"

"Aye, give it here!"

Thomas the boy runs to give it to Cook.

"Now you must go see Roger."

The boy steps back, shaking his head vigorously. "I'm not sick!" He eyes me, crunching up his nose, then points at me. "*That* boy is sick! Look how pale he is!"

Cook rolls her eyes. "Take those recipes and salve to Roger."

Thomas leans away from me even as he snatches the parchment and pot of salve from my hand. Throwing me a final grimace, he runs off.

"Never mind Thomas," Cook says, turning her attention to me. Her voice is kinder now, as if making up for Thomas, but I've been treated far worse. "I suppose you want some food, boy?"

"Yes, madam, I would be very much obliged."

She pours me a large bowl of stew, some of the best I've ever tasted, and gives me not just a hunk of bread but also some cheese! She puts a tankard of watered-down ale in front of me and I gulp it down. I eat fast, too, so I can be on my way.

Cook smacks my shoulder. "Slow down, boy, or you'll make yourself sick!"

After eating and giving my thanks, I start to leave, but Cook catches me at the door. She gives me bread, cheese, and a lecture about all the evil travelers on the road, especially Pippin, the cobbler's son, whose thieving is at full tilt now that there's a war on, and who can sniff out fools like me from miles away.

Again I start to leave but am stopped at the door, this time by the lady of the manor herself. She has dark hair, soft skin, and rosy cheeks. I've never seen her up close before, but now that I do I think she's more beautiful than Jane. Or maybe it's because she smiles. I bow my head but can't stop from staring at her overly large stomach.

Cook smacks the back of my head. "Stop your gawking!"

My lady's voice is gentle. "Who are you, young man?"

"Adrian Black of Ashcroft," I say, standing up straight, "John the bowyer's son. I'm delivering recipes for Grandmother, the woman at Ashcroft who is well-known for her remedies. Well, she's not my real grandmother, because I don't have one, but rather my friend Hugh's. He —"

Cook shakes my arm. "Whist! She didn't ask your life story!"

But my lady is smiling widely now, though she tries not to show it. "It's fine, Cook. Go on, Adrian of Ashcroft."

"I — I was only saying that Hugh will be a healer himself, a physic, I imagine."

"And you, Adrian, what will you be?" She smooths her rich green kirtle around her growing belly, as if caressing the baby inside.

"A bowyer," I say proudly. "And until then, an archer."

"Indeed," the lady says, losing her smile and looking out the door into the distance. "For every bowyer we need a healer."

"Hugh is a great one."

She turns back to me. "He is your age?"

"He's almost fifteen, my lady, a grown man." And then I add, "Much like me."

Cook snorts, but my lady smiles. "He resembles you?"

In truth, Hugh has a handsome, chiseled face, while mine is only memorable for its pale, wan, sickly look. Everyone likes Hugh Stout. People would rather avoid me. Father Fraud only teaches seven boys, and he knows all their names, except mine. He just points to me and asks the other boys, *What is* that?

"Well," I say, "Hugh is stockier and stronger and a head taller — but we're both masters with the bow."

"Aye, and modest, too," says Cook, rolling her eyes.

"This Hugh — is he studying to be a physic?" the lady asks.

"He has studied his whole life, my lady, and learned everything Grandmother has taught him."

The lady sighs. "We could use a good physic here. Still, we must be happy with our lot, even if it's not exactly what we want. Isn't that right, Adrian?"

"Yes, my lady," I say, although I don't mean it in the least. I don't want to be puny, weak, or useless, and I intend to change all of those things, not be happy with them.

The lady reaches into the purse tied to her belt and pulls out some silver coins. "Let me pay for the scribe your grandmother hired to write the recipes."

At that moment, I realize that I have no money. What a fool! How will I buy food or supplies for Hugh or myself? But I shake my head. "There was no scribe, my lady. It was just me."

"You know how to write?" She raises her eyebrows as if she doesn't believe me.

"I was taught by Father Frau — I mean, our priest. Only because my mother felt that scribing was better than bow making."

The lady smiles. "I believe I would like your mother, Adrian."

"She died in the last plague, eight years ago."

"That's very sad," she says, looking down at her belly. "Then I will pay you both for delivering the recipes and scribing them." She drops three groats into my hand.

That's a whole shilling! I stare at the coins until Cook clobbers me on the head, again, to remind me to say thank you.

"You are wrong about one thing," my lady says. "A scribe *did* write those recipes, Adrian. You are the scribe." She even makes it sound like a good thing, not something I should hide as I'm so used to doing around Bryce. "Godspeed. I pray you get home safely."

chapter the twelfth

In Which I Break New Ground . . . or It Breaks Me

WHEN I LEAVE THE MANOR, I AM ON A PART OF THE ROAD, the woods, the world that I have never seen before. Going to the manor on my own was a first, because I'd only been with Hugh before. But now, I am truly on my own. Every step brings me closer to Scotland, and battle.

I stop after losing sight of the manor and stare ahead. Not because I'm scared. It's wise to get your bearings and know what you're doing. It is then that I hear the sounds of metal on metal, and it's moving this way. A fight! The battle? Already?

I hear a brave English soldier's voice. "Cowards! Heathens! Scum!" There is more clashing of swords, yelling and jeering, and it's getting closer.

I jump behind the bushes on the side of the road. There are too many of them for me to take them on single-handedly.

"Next time," the Englishman says, "I'll have other soldiers with me and will take back my money and more!"

It's not a battle taking place but a robbery. The pagan Scots are robbing a soldier! I wish he'd run them through with his sword!

But the Scots only laugh at the soldier, who must've run in the other direction because the heathens are coming toward me! I crouch lower in the bushes, my heart pounding. My first pagans!

They're laughing and cheering and jeering, three men, dressed much like I am, but their hoods cover their faces and they have swords as well as bows. When they pull their hoods off I'm stunned.

I recognize the tall man from the market fair, although he's not from our village. "These are good times," he says. "Men are getting paid for their soldiering services in advance so they can buy their equipment."

"Aye," says a shorter man, whom I don't recognize, but his accent is also English. "The land is rich!"

It sickens me that it's our own Englishmen who would attack someone as brave as a soldier. Have they no honor? All for money?

After that, I pay heed to Cook's lecture about the dangers of the road. I seem to walk as many miles sideways as I do forward because I keep running away from the road, deep into the woods, to hide from pilgrims and traders and anyone else who might be evil. I keep my bow in hand, lest there be someone in the woods who tries to take me unawares.

Soldiers, in particular, I avoid as if they're all Thomas the leper, because if they're pagan Scots they might eat me alive and if they're English they may threaten to do so for coming into battle when they'll think I'm about nine years old. Or for being a white-haired evil omen. Even if someone dragged me back to my village alive, I don't even want to think of what punishment Good Aunt would boil up for me.

At one point, the road and the land around it are wide open with only sheep fields. I don't want to waste time hiding in the woods, so instead I pretend to be a shepherd boy. I make sure my bow and arrows are well concealed under my cloak and my white hair is hidden under my hood so as not to draw attention to myself. When no one is on the road, I hurry, but when I see someone, I look at the sheep as if I'm tending them.

It works until several knights on horseback see me. One of them calls to me from the road and I look the other way. Maybe he'll think I'm deaf. He calls again and, though my heart is pounding, I walk toward one of the sheep. I talk to it soothingly, like Bess does to Bessie, hoping it will stay calm. Kneeling beside it, I lift its hoof and examine it, as if I know what I'm doing.

The man calls a third time and rides over to me. I can't ignore him anymore when he nears and demands, "Didn't you hear me calling, boy?"

I look around me. "Oh. Were you speaking to me?"

He lets his horse's reins drop and thrusts his arms in the air. "Who else is in this field but sheep?"

"Um . . . no one?"

He glares at me. "I want to know if any knights have passed through this field today."

"None that I've seen," I tell him, although I don't mention that I've just arrived at this field myself.

He grunts, as if reading my mind. "How long have you been here today?"

"Oh, all day. Since early morning, sir."

"Funny," he says, rubbing his chin, "I passed by here early this morning and did not see you."

I feel myself shrink, wishing I could hide behind a tree and not be seen. Happily, that gives me an idea. "I — I may have been sleeping, sir, over there," I tell him, pointing to a copse of trees I notice nearby. "Please don't tell my aunt," I add hastily, hoping he'll believe my story. "She will beat me for sure!"

His grimace is almost a smile. Turning, he calls to his men, "No luck here," and leaves me without another word.

I breathe a sigh of relief and stay with the sheep at least an hour in case he comes back to check on me.

Finally, although it's only late afternoon, I stop by a small stream to sleep, finding a soft mossy patch under a tree. I know I should walk farther, while it's still light, but I'm too tired, having started before dawn. I finally get a fire started with my flint. Making fires is not my strong suit. I ate only a bite of bread at midday so I allow myself a piece of the eel and more of the loaf. I'm doing my best to make the food last as long as possible.

I see some mushrooms at arm's length, and that's where they must stay. I would love to pick and eat them, because they can be quite delicious, but just as I can't tell one herb from another, I can't tell one mushroom for another, and the wrong one can poison you as quick as a pagan Scot can cut off your head.

I fall asleep quickly, but while it's still light I wake up and my heart is pounding. I can't get my breath. I realize that I'm lying right on top of some mushrooms, which, while they make a nice, soft place for my head, must have started my wheezing. Quickly, I back away from the mushrooms. I plunge my head into the stream, cold though it is, to wash all trace of the offending mushrooms off me.

Thankfully, there are still glowing embers from my fire, so I add more tinder and twigs to start a good flame, and pull out the elfwort from the pouch of herbs. Using the clay bowl from Bess, I soon have hot water that I put the elfwort in, and I breathe in the steam. I force myself to drink the bitter tea, even though it's without the honey that Grandmother usually adds. Whether it's the vapors or the elfwort, I don't know, nor do I care, because now I'm breathing easier.

Just before dawn, the rain begins. As it falls harder, I get up and move lest I get too cold. Soon, it's pouring like bucket after bucket of water dousing the fire at the tithe barn two years ago. Why didn't God send rain like this then? I don't need it now.

The rain makes my leggings and tunic stick to my skin like large, clammy, cold hands that refuse to let go. I trudge through the muddy woods, trying not to slip, rejoicing every time I avoid a fall. As the water rises, every floating stick I see I'm scared is a snake, and I jump out of its way. That's when I slip and fall. Each time. I'm tripping so much it feels as if I'm wearing those long-toed shoes again. I can only imagine how much slower my progress would be if I were.

The footpath becomes like a creek, deep enough in places to reach almost up to my calves. I hug the edge of the path, but that makes my back scrape against the bushes and trees, which deposit their cold rain down my back.

When I reach the River Eden, it's so swollen that it's like a wild animal roiling. The wind that I thought was bellowing yesterday morning is nothing compared to the deathly roar of this water. I walk along the bank, hoping I'm going in the right direction to find a bridge, hoping that there actually is a bridge or some narrow place I can cross, preferably with a log or stones that are up high out of the water.

After what feels like hours, I finally find a log across a narrower part of the water. It's down a muddy embankment about four feet, but the log looks solid and long enough to safely bridge the width of water. Even so, I'm not happy about having to walk along a slippery, wet log across a rushing river, but I say a prayer before heading down the bank.

Maybe I picked the wrong prayer because no sooner do I descend the muddy bank than my feet fly out from under me and I'm in the water with a crash, flailing to keep myself from drowning, clutching for anything. For several terrifying moments there's nothing to hold on to. When I grab at a bunch of branches my face is scratched and my arms are yanked near off, but I hold fast, pull hard, and I'm soon on the other bank, panting and relieved. Until I turn back to the water that I have conquered and see a sight that makes my heart stop.

I watch my sack of food swirl down the river, and I'm helpless to stop it. I can't swim. If I go after it I may lose my life as well as the food.

I'm so cold from being wet, yet it's now dark and still raining and I can't see the path. I don't know which is worse: Stop for the night and freeze, or keep going so that my body stays warm but I risk falling in the river and drowning.

In the end, I find a place under several trees, one of which is rotten and has fallen against the live ones, making a partial shelter. I'm still rained on. I'm still cold. I can't make a fire because every branch and leaf is as soaked as I am. I hug my knees, shivering, hoping I find the battle soon because no matter how bad Father says battles are, I'd rather dodge swords and axes, and send arrows flying, than huddle in cold, wet misery.

chapter the thirteenth

In Which I Am Known as a Master Archer

WHEN I AWAKE, I'M STIFF AND COLD BUT, PRAISE GOD, the rain has stopped and the sun has even come out! I'm much happier, except for my belly, which reminds me, over and over, that I need food. "Shut up, Belly!" I tell it, but, as usual, it doesn't listen.

The sun is already high in the sky, so I get moving, stiff and soggy though I am. My cloak is starting to dry although it stinks of wet sheep, which is not my favorite smell. I walk along the edge of the muddy road because it's not as bad as squelching through the woods. I can't believe that with all yesterday's rain I'm thirsty. I keep looking and listening for signs of water.

Before long I hear a stream — hoorah! I head left into the woods, following the gurgling sound. It quenches my ears just like it will soon quench my thirst.

I stop short when I hear voices, and pull out my bow and two arrows. I creep closer, softly, so I can hear, crouching down behind a line of ash trees. Two men are sitting down together, facing the stream. Even looking at their backs I can see that one is large and wears green, and the other, much thinner, is in brown and looks like a twig compared to Big Green. Big Green is eating, but I can't tell what. He has a large money pouch on him and I wonder if he's a merchant or a thief. The Twig Man is filling a flask with water. He has a loaf of bread next to him and my belly starts grumbling so loudly I fear they'll hear, so I put both arms across my stomach. I so want to ask them for food, but I don't know if they can be trusted.

I see that they're speaking now but I can't quite hear what they say, despite Big Green's booming voice. The Twig's sounds whiny and sour. I can hear the tone of their voices but can't make out the words. While I thought the gurgling sound of the water was beautiful music before, now I wish it would shut up so I could know what the men say.

Eventually, I hear "boy run off" and "his father" and "near Penrith" and I can't help but crawl closer, bow in one hand, arrows in the other. I lie in some low witch hazel bushes, flat on my stomach, barely ten feet away but unseen.

The Twig shrugs. "It's not the first time a boy has run off to battle, nor the last."

"But this one is tiny and sickly, his father says. He looks odd and appears to be aged eight or nine, though he be almost thirteen."

I grit my teeth.

"He'll turn and run for home before long," the Twig says. "What can a small boy do out here?"

I grip my arrows so tight I fear I might snap them.

"By all accounts he's a master with the bow," Big Green says.

My ears perk up at this. Master? Me? Who calls me that?

The Twig grunts. "A child? A master archer? Ha!"

"So his father says."

Father? Father said that? I feel the pride swelling up my chest so large I wouldn't be surprised if my huge chest sticks out from the bushes and gives me away!

"Pah! That's merely a father's love."

"It's said that the boy can shoot a squirrel as it jumps between tree branches or a crow circling overhead, even if it's foggy."

The Twig shakes his head as if not believing. I want to jump out and proclaim, "It's true! I can!"

"And," Big Green says, his voice rising, "that he can shoot a leaf off a tree at fifty feet even in a stiff breeze."

The other man shrugs. "It's no great skill to aim at a tree and hit some leaf. Many an archer can do that."

"Aye," Big Green says, his eyebrows rising, "but can they name which leaf?"

It takes a moment for what Big Green says to sink in. I know because the Twig's head jerks and he turns to stare at the other man. "Nay," he says, his whiny voice half disbelieving, half questioning.

It's Big Green's turn to shrug. "That's what they say."

"I'd like to see such a boy."

It's all I can do not to jump out from behind the trees and say, "It is I! Adrian of Ashcroft, near Penrith . . . *master* archer!"

"Well, if what they say is true, then no doubt the boy can take care of himself."

Big Green turns to face the other man and I see the smile fade from his lips. "His father fears that he'll be put to use. A small child in a tree shooting a bow could do some damage before . . ."

The Twig stops what he's doing and looks hard at the man. "Before a pagan Scot shoots and kills him."

"Aye. That is his father's dread."

I swallow hard but tell myself that I'm not scared. I don't think anyone could shoot me out of a tree. Besides, they'll be too busy shooting one another.

Big Green stands up with a grunt. "I pulled my cart into the woods and my horse will surely warn me if anyone approaches. Still, I must be away if I want to make Carlisle by nightfall. Safe travels, pilgrim!" He whistles that tune about summer coming, which I think is odd because it's already fall and it's winter that comes next.

The Twig crosses the stream as the large peddler ambles off to my right. He must be a peddler if he has a cart and a large pouch of money. I keep as still as Bessie when she's particularly stubborn, and I remain unseen.

After hearing the men talk about me, I know that I must be even more careful about hiding. It also makes me realize that Father is very worried about me, and for that I do feel bad. I'm happy that he thinks I'm a master with the bow, however. It proves that he was watching all those times I tested his bows. And that he knows what I can do. A *master*, I am.

Even without food, I have high spirits as I walk uphill and down, taking shortcuts through the woods rather than following the winding road. I can also hide better this way. When I trip over an apple on the ground, I look up at several apples hanging from the branches above my head and realize I've found food. Good Aunt says it's only wise to eat apples cooked, so I hesitate for a moment. Then I consider the source of that wisdom and eat six apples raw. They're crisp and juicy and sweet. If I don't puke, I am always going to eat apples this way!

After a while, I allow myself some easy walking on the road, as my feet are tired from stepping on rocks and jumping over logs in the woods. Before long, though, I hear a cart coming and I duck into the woods again. I stop when a sound catches my ear. It's the loud whistle of that peddler. At least, I think it must be him, because he's whistling the same wrong-season song about summer coming. I hide behind trees at the edge of the road. It takes a few minutes for the cart to reach me, and while it does, I get an idea. Wouldn't it be nice to sit in the back of a cart and ride along instead of walk? The peddler said he was heading to Carlisle. Well, so am I. By the time the wagon passes at its slow rate, I've decided to hitch a ride.

It's risky, because the peddler knows my story and might guess me to be the boy — the master archer — who has run off from the village near Penrith. Still, he has a business and wants to make Carlisle by nightfall, so I don't think he'd turn around and drive me all the way to Ashcroft. The worst he'd do is throw me out of his cart once he discovers me and

I'd have to walk, which is no worse than where I am now. In fact, it's better, because I'll be well rested while having made progress north.

The cart moves so slowly that I just need to follow it until I see my chance to hop on. Luckily, there must be a lot of pottery inside, because it makes a jingling racket. That'll cover any noise I make. Still, I must be careful. I know that Bessie is sensitive to any pulling on the plow or cart behind her and a horse is surely smarter than Bessie, so I'll have to choose my time wisely.

When I see the road ahead has some stones and debris from the recent storm, I have my chance. The horse picks its way, slowly, jerkily, over the piles, and I grab on to the side of the cart and gently slide onto the back. The horse whinnies and I cringe, but the peddler talks soothingly for a moment and then goes back to singing.

I crawl slowly under some cowhides, which, though they stink, cover me completely. There are clay pots and bolts of cloth and balls of cheese. The cloth is soft, and just smelling the cheese makes my belly rumble, so I can't stop from eating almost half of the ball. I try to squish it back into a ball as best I can and hope that the damage isn't too noticeable. With a full belly, the singing of the peddler, the rocking of the cart, and the bliss in not having to walk but rather lie on soft cloth, I am soon asleep.

chapter the fourteenth

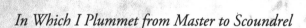

In Which I Plummet from Master to Scoundrel

I WAKE UP AND WONDER FOR A MOMENT WHERE I AM IN the darkness, especially when I see through a crack that the earth is moving beneath my feet! Then I remember I've hitched a ride with the peddler. Next, I notice the noise. There must be a hundred people on the road with all the shouting and laughing and horses and church bells and — wait . . . church bells?

The wagon lurches to a halt, and my head bangs against a clay pot. With all the noise, no one hears my yelp.

"You've arrived just in time," a gruff voice says. "The gates are about to close."

Gates? We must have reached Carlisle!

"Toll, peddler!" the gruff voice continues.

I hear the shaking of coins and the peddler mutter, loudly, "Highway robbery."

The cart lurches forward again and the sounds of horses, people shouting, and bells continue. Soon we come to a halt, and I feel the cart shake from side to side as the peddler steps down with a groan.

"Here, boy!" the peddler's voice booms.

I freeze because for a moment I think he is talking to me, but a boy's voice answers. "Sir?"

"Watch my cart. Here's a penny and there'll be another two pennies in it for you when I come out."

"Yes, sir!"

After a few moments, when I'm sure the peddler has gone, I put my hood up and slide off the back of the cart as quietly as possible.

"Oy! You!" the boy's voice calls out.

I take off running, slamming into the crowd, bouncing off people like a stone skipping in the water. There are so many people! Everyone is yelling at me, even those I don't hit, and I scramble like a rat to get away, helter-skelter. I finally realize that the boy will not likely follow me any farther because he'll want to get his money from the peddler. So I stop and breathe, bending over with my hands on my knees.

Now it's my turn to be run into by the crowds until I'm knocked against a building and end up on my ass, my feet splayed out, at risk of being trampled. I scramble to my feet and flatten myself against the wall of the building, trying to slow my breathing.

As my breath returns I start to focus on everything around me. My eyes and ears and head hurt with the frenzy. There are people everywhere of all different shapes, sizes, and manners of dress, even monks — gray friars and white friars and a black friar yelling to people to repent their sins. His voice is drowned out by the street vendors, calling out, "Fresh fish!" "Last chance for eggs!" "Fine shoes!" "Rushes fair and green!" Other people call out to one another, too, over the vendors' voices and the squeals of pigs and barking of dogs and the clanging of a blacksmith's hammer so that everything blends together like a loud and tuneless song.

And the smell! Trash and horse dung and sweat mixed with baking bread and "Ribs of beef and many a pie!" Meat carcasses and fish stare at me as I pass by the stalls. The scent of leather and spices is around the next corner.

I'm jostled along with horses and carts and I finally realize that we're all on a road. The city is so narrow and close, the buildings even hang over the street, the upper floors jutting out over the first floors so that it looks like they'll topple any second. Signs hang from many of the buildings: a boot for the cobbler, a pig for the butcher, a loaf of bread for the baker. People move quickly and nimbly as if in a fast dance, and everyone seems to know where to go except me.

I walk aimlessly as night falls and the crowds thin, searching for Hugh. One street looks much like another and every place is full of twists and turns. As darkness clamps down on me, I realize that Bess is wiser than I thought. She's right that it'll be hard to find someone here, almost impossible. The town is so large, yet also so closed in with the maze of streets, overhanging buildings, animals, and people. I can hardly see three oxcarts in front of me. What did I think? That it would be sprawled out with open fields like my village, only larger, and I could simply scan the horizon and find Hugh? I am an addlepate.

I round another corner and smell fish and sweat and manure, but above all of it I smell meat pies, and my belly rumbles. St. Jerome's belly! I'm hungry again! I look in the door of a building with a sign that has a plow on it. It's definitely not a place that makes plows, but rather a tavern with long wooden tables with tankards and bowls and hunks of bread. I can smell the ale and meat pies. Sitting on the benches are men, all eating, and I feel faint with hunger.

I start to go inside, thinking to ask the men if they're soldiers and might know where Hugh is, or at least the battle. I might also buy some food. But I'm roughly grabbed by the neck, lifted, and turned to face a large man with a lantern and stick.

The bailiff. Just like Elliot, our reeve, only more important.

"What are you up to, scoundrel?"

"Nothing, sir!"

"It had better be nothing. It's almost curfew and if I find you in a few minutes' time, it's the almshouse for you!" He lets me go, but walks off muttering, "Nothing but a scoundrel."

I don't want to risk getting locked in an almshouse, so I slink away, staying in the shadows, frightened of being caught, but not knowing where to go. When the church bells ring again, loudly now, for the church must be near, I decide to take asylum there.

In the darkness, I can just make out a tower, high above the other buildings, and I slowly find my way there. When I reach it I'm breathless, not from running or fear but from the sheer size of the massive cathedral.

I crouch by the bushes in the dark and watch as a small group of townspeople, maybe even a family, brings baskets to the front door of the cathedral. A monk in black robes greets them at the door and bows to them. I can't hear what they say, but the people leave and the monk uses one basket to prop the door open as he carries in another.

Quietly, I approach, hovering around the corner from the front door, but peeking out to watch, hoping my shroud of darkness will conceal me. Before the monk returns, I see that it's all food! The basket propping open the door is full of apples. Another basket holds meat pies, another bread, and a smaller one has eggs. My mouth is watering.

The monk appears, picks up the basket of eggs, and disappears again. He might give me food if I ask, but then he'd want to know who I am and where I'm from and likely send me to the almshouse. How would I find Hugh then?

Instead, I dart forward, grab a meat pie, then hesitate and take a second one, and race back to hiding. When I'm safely around the corner again, I take a big whiff of the pies. I believe they're mincemeat, that delicious combination of sweet and savory. Hoorah!

The monk returns, picking up the basket of meat

pies, pausing for a moment as he looks at them. Surely he doesn't realize that two are missing? Thankfully, he turns and brings the basket inside. This time, I count how long the monk is gone while I run to grab a small loaf of bread.

I've counted to twenty-nine by the time the monk comes back. He picks up the basket of bread and does a double take, tilting his head at it. St. Jerome's eyes, does he know there's one missing? He looks up, and around, even at my hiding place — where my head is still peeking out from the corner of the building! I dare not move, though, because that would draw even more attention, so I freeze. After a few moments, which feel like an entire school day, he shakes his head as if convincing himself it's his imagination, and he turns with the basket and heads inside. I finally let my shoulders down and take a breath.

Still staring at where the monk was, I see there's only one more basket, the one that props open the door. When that's gone, the door will be shut and I may have no place to stay. Quickly, I dash to the door, hesitating when I see two apples on the stoop. Did they fall out of the basket? Or did the monk leave them for me? I don't hesitate long, knowing he'll be back soon, so I grab them. Once inside, I head for the nave and dive under a pew without stopping to look at anything.

The door shuts and I hear the shuffling of the monk's feet as he carries the last basket away. I quietly munch my supper, although it does stick in my throat somewhat as I realize that today I've stolen a ride from a peddler as well as his cheese. I've stolen food from the monks, which is either their supper or maybe alms for the poor, and am now eating stolen food — except perhaps the two apples left on the stoop — inside of a house of God, which I snuck into. Like the bailiff said, I'm nothing but a scoundrel.

chapter the fifteenth

In Which I Search for Hugh

WHEN I AWAKEN I THINK I'VE DIED AND GONE TO HEAVEN. Angels are singing and a sweet smell is in the air. When I open my eyes, I see shafts of colored light — red, blue, yellow, green! Could it be heaven? Quickly, my addled brain remembers that I'm a scoundrel, so this could never be heaven.

I sit up fast and bang my head on the underside of the pew. Although I see stars, I'm sure it's not heaven. And it hurts. Carefully, I crawl out from under the pew and peek down the aisle toward the singing. What I see makes me catch my breath. I barely notice the singing because my eyes are stuck on the hugest painting I've ever seen. At least, I think it's a painting at first, because it's too bright for my eyes and I can't focus on it. Eventually, I see that there are many scenes of people and animals; some of them I recognize from Bible stories. When I'm able to focus my eyes better, I realize it's a window made out of brightly colored glass. With the sun shining through, the pictures are so bright they light up the very floor of the cathedral. I've never seen so much color in my life, not even at a fair. I feel like I'm in a whole different world.

I've never been in such a massive building. In the darkness last night I had no idea of its size. Our entire parish church could fit inside of it many times over. Our church could fit inside the colored-glass window! I know because below the window are the singers, half a dozen boys and four men, and they're tiny compared to the window. If all six boys were stacked on top of one another, the window would be taller, and if the four men were laid end to end, the window would be wider.

My belly rumbles and I think about food, and also the food I stole yesterday. If I had a penny or two, I would leave those as a donation, but a whole groat? I'll need that to buy food or supplies for Hugh and me. Now I must find more food, and find Hugh. Although I hate to leave the singing, the sound will cover my dash to the front door and outside before anyone notices.

The air is cold, and outside the world of the cathedral the streets are bustling — carts squeaking, pigs squealing, men shouting. I pull my hood tight around my head. My nose breathes in the delicious smell of meat pies and my feet take me to the source. A tavern called the Black Bear. I don't want a bailiff collaring me again, so I walk around to the back. That's where the baking smells are coming from, anyway.

I look in the open door and see a round, bald man sweating as he takes meat pies out of the oven. A woman, her hair gray and face lined, pats out dough and tosses meat onto it. "Can't you go any faster?" she says, nodding her head at the floor. "There's another paddleful waiting to go in."

"I know that, woman!" the man answers. "I can't do two things at once!"

She mutters something, looking up from her work to roll her eyes, and catches me. I suck in my cheeks to make my face as thin as possible, and open my eyes wide and plaintively. The woman's face is stern at first, but her eyes start to twinkle and she even gives me a half smile. St. Jerome's lips! Maybe she'll give me a pie!

I wish I hadn't grinned, because the large man turns around and sees me, his red face squishing into ugliness. "Get away, you filthy rascal!"

I'm surprised enough that I don't move at first, until he takes the paddle the meat pies were on and shakes it at me. I back away, but can't help pleading, though meekly, for charity. "Are there any broken ones you can't sell? I'll eat anything."

"Be off!" the man shouts, turning back to the oven.

The woman grabs some scraps from the table and hands them out to me, just in time, before the man grabs her arm. "Stop, you fool! He'll keep coming back now!"

"Go," she whispers, and as I run off I hear her yelling at the man, "Your fat belly could use a pie or two less today so stop your whining!" She reminds me of Cook at the manor, rough of voice but soft of heart.

When I find a place I can stand without getting trampled, I look at my breakfast. It's two pies with mostly burnt crusts and little meat, but they're a feast for my eyes and belly.

I wander the city all day, looking for soldiers, any soldiers. I follow some, but they seem in no hurry to get anywhere. Perhaps the battles haven't begun. They go to buy supplies, sometimes meet women in the street and go off with them, and almost always end up at a tavern. So many taverns! I could spend days visiting them all looking for Hugh.

I ask a baker when the battle will start, but he simply looks annoyed, telling me to stop being a pest and do something useful.

"I'll be useful as soon as I find the battle," I tell him. "Then I'll fight!" I'm hoping he'll respect my bravery and duty and give me some bread.

Instead, he throws me out of his shop.

After that I look for friendlier faces. An old man on the street smiles at me, so I ask him, "Where's the battle?"

He waves his arms in wide circles. "It's everywhere," he says, in a breathy, spooky voice, "all around us, all the time."

I back away.

When I see groups of soldiers going into the Rising Sun tavern, laughing and joking, I ask the beautiful woman at the tavern door, "Why aren't the soldiers fighting? Why are they all coming here?"

She tweaks my nose and grins. "You, my lad, are too young to know!"

It seems that people speak in riddles here. I'll have to approach the soldiers directly and risk being identified as John the bowyer's son.

I work up my nerve and ask a knight on horseback where the battle is. He asks me why I want to know. When I tell him that I'm going to join the fight, he throws his head back and laughs so hard spittle comes out of his mouth. He rides off still laughing, never answering.

I wait outside of the Stag's Horn tavern until two soldiers come out, their voices slurred from mead. I ask them where I can find the battle.

The big, burly one belches and focuses on me, or tries to. His eyes look so bleary, like Uncle's on a feast day, that they appear to be crossed. I imagine he sees two or four of me. I think I'm right because he demands to know if "we" are spies and who "we" are planning to tell once "we" get such information out of him. He even makes to smack me, but his friend grabs his hands and leads him down the street, laughing.

I'm worn out and hungry. I'm tempted to spend a groat on food, even though I want to save all my money for Hugh. Toward evening, I approach the Dog and Badger tavern, which must be a good sign for me — the badger! And it smells like Cook's wonderful stew. I'm debating whether to go inside to eat, hoping to find a kindly soldier who might tell me where the battle is without laughing at me.

Suddenly, I hear a loud voice in my ear. "Get in line, freak, we were here first!"

I turn to look at a tall boy with mean eyes who grabs my arm and flings me into the street. Other boys laugh.

"Gardyloo!" I hear from the buildings above me. Again, someone grabs my arm and shoves me, this time back against the building instead of into the street. St. Jerome's bones! Is this some city sport?

I pull away from the boy who holds me firm. I am about to fight when I realize that a bucketful of slop lands exactly where I'd been standing.

"Didn't you hear the 'gardyloo'?" The boy lets go of my arm. He's not the tall, mean-eyed one. This boy looks to be about eleven, taller than me but with a young face.

"What does that mean?" But I'm already figuring it out by the smell. It's the water people have passed, and worse. I wrinkle my nose. "Why do they throw it in the street?"

"I wager they don't want to keep it themselves," the boy says.

"But it could fall on people's heads."

"That's why they warn you! 'Gardyloo!'"

"Oh." I pinch my nose because although nothing landed on me, it still smells.

"It's worse on the other side of town," the boy says. "Those with much money eat rich food, which truly stinks."

I think about how smelly Father Fraud is on a good day, but when he eats at the manor his farts are so stinky I can barely sit upright while he yells at me to pay attention. Like I do when Father Fraud's back is turned, I put my fist to my mouth and make a fart sound.

The boy laughs and so do I. He holds his hand out to me to shake. His thin arms and legs stick out from his tunic and leggings. "I'm Henry."

I clasp his hand. "I'm Adrian."

"Where are you from?"

"Ashcroft. It's south of Penrith."

"Penrith," he says, pushing his long brown hair behind his ears. "I've heard of that. What are you doing here?"

"Preparing to fight the Scots."

He looks puzzled.

It feels so good to have someone who is the least bit friendly that I pull the bow out from under my cloak.

His eyes grow wide. "Do you know how to use that?"

"Of course. I'm joining the soldiers to defend Carlisle."

Again he looks puzzled, shaking his head. "There'll be no battle here."

"Why not?"

"The city has paid protection money so the Scots will leave us alone."

I groan. "Then I won't find him here."

"Who?"

"My friend. I'm looking for him, to join him in battle. Do you know where the battle will be?"

Henry shrugs and points at the tavern, and the boy who threw me into the street. "Often there are soldiers here. Maybe one of them can tell you."

I walk toward the tavern and notice that Henry walks with me. I'm grateful because I feel like a fish out of water in this city.

A large gentleman in a red cloak heads inside and I'm right behind him, until that tall, mean-eyed boy hones in and deftly takes the money pouch from the gentleman's wide belt. The man whirls around, but not before the boy drops it. The boy looks at me, smirks, and is gone in little more than a moment. He reminds me of Bryce, the thief! I pick up the purse for the gentleman, and at the same moment someone has my arm in a vise grip. It's the gentleman, who is not at all happy.

"Here," I say, trying to give him his purse, but I can't extend my arm to him because he's gripping it so hard.

"Yes, thief, now that I catch you, you're willing to return it," he says, his face dark.

"I'm not —" He twists my arm so hard I can't help but cry out. "You're hurting me, sir!"

He pulls the purse out of my hand but will not loosen his grip on my arm. "Bailiff!" he shouts. "Arrest this boy! Throw him in the stocks! I've had enough of these hooligans!"

"But it wasn't me! It was —" I look around for the tall boy, but he's gone. So, I realize, is Henry.

"Bailiff!" the gentleman cries again, and I struggle to get away but it's no use.

Men spill out of the tavern, and the men and women on the street gather around, some of them adding to the hue and cry, shouting, "Bailiff!"

Even if I were able to break free of the gentleman's grip, the crowd encircles me, leaving me no way out.

chapter the sixteenth

In Which I Join a Gang

THROUGH THE THICK OF THE CROWD, HENRY AND several other boys appear. A tiny boy tugs at the gentleman's red cloak, saying, "Father, Father!"

"What?" the man cries.

Henry stomps hard on the gentleman's foot, and two other boys grab an arm each.

"Ow!" the man bellows.

"Father!" the little boy whines again.

"Who are you?" The gentleman loosens his grip and Henry pulls me away, yelling, "Boys!" as he runs behind the gentleman, squirreling his way through the crowd so swiftly that while some shout at us, no one is quick enough to grab us. Once past the crowd, he breaks into a sprint. I can barely keep up.

As we run through streets, I notice the other boys are flanking us.

"Where's Otto?" Henry asks one of them.

"Back there," a redheaded boy says, out of breath.

Henry pushes me toward the boy. "Take him to our nook!"

Henry disappears like a shadow.

It's hard to keep up with the other three, but eventually they collapse in a dark corner of the city wall where there's a small patch of dirt between the wall and a large tree. We sit, panting, leaning against the wall, partially hidden by the great oak.

"What's your name?" one of the dark-haired boys asks.

I can't speak yet, fearing the wheezing will start if I don't give myself time to catch my breath. So I simply stare at my boots, trying to calm myself, and thinking, once again, how good it is that I don't have the stupid long-toed shoes anymore. It seems so long ago that I bought them.

A boy taps my foot and I look up. It's one of the dark-haired boys. "I'm David," he says, "and this is my brother, Daniel." He nods toward the slightly smaller dark-haired boy. Now that I have a chance to look at them, I see that their faces are similar in their roundness and thick eyebrows.

"That," David says, pointing at the redheaded boy, "is Nervous Ned." He and Daniel laugh.

The skinny redhaired boy scowls at them, then at me. "What's wrong with you?"

"What do you mean?" I reach up and realize my hood has fallen off in my mad dash.

"Are you some kind of evil omen?"

"I just have pale skin, that's all."

"And white hair," he adds.

"So?" David says with a snort. "Yours is red."

"Oy, there they are!" Daniel cries.

Henry and the small boy who called the gentleman "Father" sit down heavily, leaning against the wall next to us. I stare at the little freckle-faced boy for a moment and then realize that this must be Otto. He's not the gentleman's son. He was a part of the ruse to free me from the gentleman.

"Thank you," I tell Henry. "And you," I say, smiling at the little boy, who grins back.

Henry has already caught his breath and, grinning, pulls several large meat pies out of his tunic.

David's eyes grow wide. "Where'd you get those?"

"I grabbed them off the back of a peddler's cart."

Since there are six of us, we split the three pies in two. David and Daniel share one, the boy they call Nervous Ned shares with me, and Henry shares with Otto, although he gives Otto most of the pie, eating only a small portion himself.

The pie smells heavenly, and I close my eyes to savor each bite. I believe it's pig meat. It's delicious and the fat fills up the holes in my belly like the clay that fills the gaps in our wattle-and-daub house. I cringe when I think of home and Father. What would he say if he saw me with this street gang? Any other time, if a boy gave me half of a stolen meat pie, I would gag. But I myself have stolen food — from a cathedral, no less! I suspect these boys are only doing what they must to survive.

Nervous Ned crouches on his heels. "The night watch-man will be out soon and grab us if we don't get under cover."

Henry sighs and stands up. "Come on, then. We've got to go to the warehouse."

Otto and I are the only ones who don't rise. Henry holds his hand down for Otto to grab and, although the little boy looks unhappy, he clutches on to Henry and pulls himself up.

Henry looks at me. "Where are you staying?"

I shrug, and before I can give more of an answer, Henry answers his own question. "With us."

Ned's eyes open wide and he looks at David and Daniel, who raise their eyebrows.

"Follow me," Henry says, still holding Otto's hand.

Ned follows but also looks back at me. "Simon won't like this." He gets closer to Henry and whispers, although I can hear him. "What are you going to say?"

"I'll think of something."

"But —"

"I'm tired of trying to please Simon!" Henry snaps.

Ned's face tells me he's not satisfied with the answer, but David and Daniel nod, as if understanding Henry.

"Who is Simon?" I ask.

"A nasty weasel!" Otto says so suddenly and loudly that we all laugh, except Ned, who looks around as if this Simon might hear.

We wander down dark streets to the edge of town, to what looks like an abandoned building. A large rat scurries over my foot and I bite my lip to keep from crying out. The boys head for the large wooden door and I hesitate.

"It's a warehouse," Henry explains. "It's a good place to sleep and, as long as we're out before the church bells ring prime, no one will catch us."

I take a deep breath and follow them. Inside, there are voices and laughter, but when we enter the sound stops abruptly. Otto clutches Henry's hand with both his little fists, and I can feel that our whole group is uneasy, not just Otto and me.

When my eyes adjust to the darkness, my heart fairly bursts from its pounding. Standing in the middle of a semi-circle of older boys is the tall, mean-eyed one who tried to steal the gentleman's purse!

"What is this thing?" he demands, looking at me and then spitting at the floor.

I curse myself for automatically taking my hood off. It's second nature when I walk inside, but Simon is shooting arrows at me out of his eyes.

"He's Adrian," Henry says, his voice far weaker than it was outside. "He's from a village near Penrith, and — and he needs a place to stay . . . Simon."

Simon takes his eyes off me long enough to mock Henry, making his voice high and whiny. "And — and he needs a place to stay."

I see Henry clench his jaw and watch his eyes narrow and I realize, with some gladness, that Simon has only strengthened Henry's resolve.

Simon grins at me, an ugly leer of brown, stained teeth. "We are the Hoods, named after Robin Hood. We steal from the rich and give to the poor" — his leer widens — "the poor being us."

The boys around him chuckle. Henry's shoulders slump and he stares at the ground.

Simon's voice grows serious. "We don't give alms to farm boys — or freaks." He glares at me and then at Henry. "What does he bring to the Hoods?"

Henry looks at me, hopeful.

"I — I'm a master archer," I stammer.

"A master archer?" Simon bursts out laughing, and as soon as he does, the other boys do, too, except for Henry and his friends. "There's not much call for archery in the city, even if you are a *mas-ter*," he says mockingly.

I try to think of some other skill I have and come up empty. The name of Ailwin flashes in my head.

Simon circles me, his arms folded, like he is viewing a pig and deciding whether the runt will be allowed in his pen or not.

"Do you have money, farm-boy freak?" Simon asks.

"No," I lie, hoping he can't tell.

Henry speaks up. "Today at the Dog and Badger . . . it's because of him that you were able to run away. He saved you."

Simon stops, his eyes narrow, and he turns slowly to face Henry. There's an urgent whispering that dies down to silence as everyone watches, frozen.

"I mean," says Henry, lifting his chin either in defiance or to be able to look Simon in the eye, "I think it's fair to let him stay the night since he acted as decoy."

Simon's eyes flit almost imperceptibly around the warehouse to gauge the boys' reactions. There's the handful of stoic boys I know who stand by Henry. There's a much larger group of older boys who flank Simon. Some of them look defiant and tough, like their leader, but several of them look at the ground. I think I see in Simon's eyes a momentary flash of fear or anger, I don't know which, before an ugly smile grows on his face. "So there's something farm-boy freak can do. . . . He can be a decoy."

A couple of the older boys chuckle and Henry's shoulders relax.

"Fine," says Simon. "You may stay the night."

The two groups, younger and older, naturally divide. I follow Henry to the draftier side of the warehouse, where boards are missing.

"Thanks," I whisper to him.

He shrugs and gives me an old sack, like the other boys have. He wedges himself in the corner and I sit down next to him. The cold air pushes through the slats and the place smells mostly of dung. Although Father and I live below our means, I have never spent a night in such an abode. I start to feel sad when I think of Father, so I make myself focus on what's happening now.

"I don't think Simon likes me," I whisper to Henry.

"You'd best stay on his good side," Henry says, "if you can."

"I won't be around for long, anyway. I have to find Hugh."

Henry nods. "I think I have an idea how to find Hugh. Tomorrow, I'll take you to —"

"Tomorrow," Simon's voice says from above us — and we both startle, "you and farm-boy freak have a job to do, so there'll be no time for anything else."

Henry nods once, though he doesn't look at Simon.

"You'll bring back six — no, eight — pounds of herring, to show your worth."

I hear several gasps.

"Eight pounds?" a little voice cries.

"Is there an echo in here?" Simon sneers, turning on his heels and striding toward Otto.

Henry jumps to his feet. "Simon! If you want eight pounds, then eight pounds you'll get."

Simon stops and pivots, a horrible leer stretching across his face. "Good boy," he says to Henry, as if Henry is a dog. Simon's eyes dart to me and linger, as he sneers.

I believe Simon has snake eyes, although I don't actually know what snake eyes look like because whenever I see a snake I run the other way. Still, I imagine his are just what a snake's eyes are like. I want so much to stick my foot out and trip him as he walks past me, but I know that will only make things worse for all of us.

Simon returns to his side of the warehouse and murmurs to his compatriots while they all chuckle. On our side, we're silent.

Otto appears at my feet, clutching his sack and staring at me with his large, dark eyes.

Henry nudges me with his elbow. "Can you move over? This is Otto's spot."

I scoot over so Otto is between us, although he snuggles up against Henry.

His wee voice is but a whisper. "Can you tell me a story, Henry?"

I must admit that Henry's soft voice and sweet story, about a little boy who is lost while his mother and father search the world for him, is so soothing that I fall asleep before I even hear the end, although I'd wager eight pounds of herring that the lost boy is found.

chapter the seventeenth

In Which I Help the Gang

THE NEXT MORNING, HENRY, OTTO, THE OTHER YOUNGER boys, and I are out early on our mission to find eight pounds of fish.

"We'll never get that much!" Ned whines. Although he's a head taller than the rest of us, he seems the weakest. Maybe he's young and was just born tall and lanky.

Henry waves his hand dismissively. "We'll find something to make Simon happy."

Ned looks at Daniel, who simply shrugs.

"But first," says Henry, "we're helping Adrian find his friend, a soldier."

"A soldier?" Otto's eyes are wide.

I describe Hugh, and Henry dispatches the others, telling them where to meet us at noon. "And keep your eye out for anything tasty or valuable," he calls after them. "Come on," he says to me, "let's go."

Henry takes me to the hill that Carlisle Castle sits upon, so I can get a better view of the city. We walk almost to the guard gate, across the moat, behind an oxcart delivering goods to the soldiers. Henry instructs me to look at people from there. I strain my right eye to see.

"They're so small from up here, and there are so many," I say.

"Keep looking. Just one group at a time."

It seems impossible, but I do as he says and eventually I realize he's right. It's too much to take in all at once, but broken into little groups, it's manageable. I can't make out people's features but I'd know Hugh's stance and walk from any distance.

Finally, I shake my head. "He's not there."

Next, Henry takes me to a tavern, the Carlisle Arms, and we go inside. Henry asks the tavern owner where the battle is.

"It'll be east of here," the man says, filling a tankard with ale from an oaken cask.

"Where, exactly?" I ask.

He laughs, sloshing some mead out of the tankard. "The Scots haven't given me their battle plan, you knave! They'll be headed for Durham eventually, though. They always are."

"Your friend Hugh must be headed east," Henry says as we leave the Carlisle Arms.

I'm making plans in my head of leaving, but when we meet the other boys at the nook at midday they're looking glum, save Otto, who has two small loaves of bread.

"I'm sorry we didn't find your friend," David says. "We asked a couple of young men who matched your description, but they weren't Hugh."

"Simon's not going to be happy," Ned says.

Even David and Daniel shuffle their feet, looking nervous.

I can't let them get in trouble with Simon. I have to use my money to buy herring. "Where's the fishmonger?"

Otto shakes his head. "It's no use. We tried to filch some and I even begged, but all the fishmonger's wife gave me was this." He holds up one small loaf.

"Then how did you get two?" Henry asks.

"I told her my brother was starving as well, and his name was Henry." Otto's face breaks into a grin. "That's her boy's name, too, so she gave me a second loaf!"

Henry smiles but Ned groans. "Simon will kill us." He looks at Henry's belt. "You could sell your knife."

Henry clutches his side. "Never! Not for Simon!"

"It's not for Simon," Ned whines, "it's for us. Besides, we were all there when the knight gave you his knife. We all helped."

"We did not," David says with disdain, "least of all you, Ned. You were cowering behind an oxcart when Henry grabbed the knife from the knight's saddle and ran it over to him as he lay defenseless on the road."

"Henry could've been run through with that robber's sword," Daniel adds, "but he stepped right in front of the robber to give the knight his weapon."

"Yes," Otto says, glaring at Ned, "that's why Sir Knight gave the knife to *Henry*."

I stare at Henry, who still clutches his belt. I always knew he was a fine person, even if he does have to live on the street and thieve.

"I'll buy some fish," I say. They all stare at me. "I have money. I just didn't want to tell Simon."

Henry claps me on the back and I feel like a savior until we get to the fishmonger and see how expensive eight pounds of herring is. It takes two of my three groats to buy six pounds and I can't bear to spend the last one. How can I buy any food for Hugh?

Henry is grateful. "Simon never expected us to get eight pounds, anyway. He may be pleased enough with this. Especially if . . ." He runs into the fishmonger again and returns a few moments later. "He's going to cook it for us. That'll please Simon."

The boys cheer and Henry runs inside again before I can ask how he managed it, because it says right on the sign at the front of the shop that cooking costs two pence. I'm distracted when I hear a choirboy singing because we are nowhere near the cathedral. I can see its spire far off. I follow the others as they sidle up to the door of the shop. At first, all I can see is the fishmonger, cutting his fish, but he's smiling now, his whole body swaying to the sweet music.

And then I see Henry. He's in a dark corner, singing. It's his sweet voice we hear. He sings for much of the time the fish is cooking, only stopping for one break. When his voice starts getting scratchy and croaky, the fishmonger tells him to drink some water.

"Can I give some to my friends?" Henry asks.

When the man looks out and sees all of our faces, he refuses. In turn, Henry refuses to drink any water himself. His voice gets worse. Quite rapidly. I think it may be on purpose. Finally, the fishmonger invites us all in to drink with Henry, which cures Henry's voice instantly.

"Where did you learn to sing like that?" I ask Henry when the fish is done and the fishmonger wraps it in cloth.

"My mother sang those songs to me. I sing them so I'll remember her. And" — he grins — "sometimes people even pay me to sing."

"You sound like one of those boys in the cathedral."

"Do I?"

I nod vigorously. "Maybe even better. You should see if they pay there!"

He laughs.

"No, really," I say, as an idea takes shape in my mind. "There are choir schools in lots of cathedrals, maybe the one right here."

"I can't go there."

"Why not?"

"Look!" says Otto. "A kitty!"

A tiny black-and-white kitten peeks shyly from behind the wheel of a cart and Otto creeps over to it.

"You can play with him for a little while," Henry calls to Otto before turning to me. "I don't have any money for school and . . ." He looks down at his clothes.

I see what he means. His clothes are old and torn and dirty. I hadn't focused on it before, but he is dirty, too. His face is gray, his hair unkempt, and he even smells a little. Still, I tell him what Father Fraud said about a boy he knew who went to a cathedral school with little or no money, simply based on his angelic voice.

There is hope in Henry's eyes for a moment, then he smiles shyly and shakes his head. "That boy may not have had much money, but he probably didn't come from the streets. His parents likely brought him to the cathedral."

He is probably right, and I think, again, about Father.

"Besides," Henry says, looking over at Otto, who sits with the kitten in his lap, stroking it, "I can't leave him."

It is getting late, so we coax Otto away from the kitten and head back with our fish.

"I hope Simon will be happy," Ned says in his whiny voice.

"Shut up, Ned," David answers halfheartedly. I get the feeling he is just as worried, but what is the use of talking about it?

Otto grabs Henry's hand as we enter the warehouse.

They are right to be nervous. While some of Simon's boys are grateful for the fragrantly cooked fish, Simon is not.

"You're useless!" Simon yells, and I grit my teeth.

With a flick of Simon's hand, two older boys flank Henry, each grabbing hold of an arm.

"No!" Otto shouts, as another of Simon's gang picks up the little boy and walks several steps away.

"Leave him alone!" Henry says, but Simon laughs as Henry struggles to free himself, and I feel sick to my stomach because it reminds me too much of Bryce and William and Warren. And me.

Before I think about what I'm doing, I step forward. "Stop!"

Henry stops struggling and everyone freezes.

"I know I'm useless. And I'll leave. I'll head east as soon as the city gates open." The boys are still holding on to Henry. "So let him go."

Simon narrows his eyes at me. "He still has to pay." He walks and pulls the knife from Henry's belt. A cry comes out of Henry and I know it's not pain or fear, but anger and frustration, because that knife is his prized possession.

Simon's boys are gathered around me, so I can't whip out my weapon or they'll be on top of me before I have a chance to draw back my bow.

Simon turns the knife over in his hand, examining it with his evil smile. "This will do nicely as payment."

"Give him back his knife!" I don't know why I say it, because I have no way to make Simon give it back. And the two henchmen still have hold of Henry. The older boys only laugh at me.

Simon is still chuckling. "I told you, farm-boy freak, this is my payment."

I see the look in Henry's eye. That knife is a symbol that he's a hero, not a scoundrel, even though he must live on the street.

I don't hesitate for a moment. Grabbing the coin in my pocket, I hold out the groat. "If it's payment you want, then here it is."

Simon's eyes flick from delight to doubt to anger. "You said you had nothing."

"It's all I have in the world." This time I'm not lying. "If you give him back his knife, this silver coin is yours."

His eyes widen again, closer to delight, as he eyes the coin. I see the henchmen loosen their grip on Henry in their delight as well.

"Give him the knife," I repeat.

Simon drops the knife but puts his foot on top of it. "Give me the money."

He has unwittingly given me an idea, so I toss the coin behind him and he turns, lifting his foot from the knife, and the two henchmen scramble after the coin as well.

Henry loses no time grabbing his knife and running with his small gang, but not before he grabs my arm and pulls me with them, and we run out of the building at full speed.

After a while, we stop to catch our breath, hiding under a cart in the street.

Simon's voice is close, too close. "Of course he has more! He wouldn't toss a silver coin on the floor if it were his only one! Check every alley."

The crowd of boys takes off in different directions.

"Where can we hide?" Otto whispers.

"They know all the places," Ned points out, "even our nook."

And then I realize there's one place they don't know. "This way!" I hiss.

chapter the eighteenth

In Which I Find Sanctuary

THE CATHEDRAL IS QUIET BUT FOR THE NOISE OF OUR panting. The only person I see is a monk far to the front of the church who likely can't hear us from there. Still, I make us all duck down and scoot to an alcove under some pews, near where I hid before.

No sooner have we settled than Ned squeaks, "They're here!"

He's right. They must've seen us come in. There are ten of them, at least, outnumbering our six. And they're bigger than we are.

Although they call out "Henry" and "Farm Boy" much softer than they would on the street, it's still loud in the sanctuary of the cathedral.

A whimper comes out of Otto. Henry puts one hand on his shoulder, and with his other hand puts a finger to his lips, his eyes widening meaningfully at the other boys.

I can hear the mutterings of the older Hoods and the echoing of their footsteps drawing nearer.

"Look under the pews!" I hear one of them hiss, and my heart sinks. We are found!

"Boys!" It's a man's voice ringing out from the front of the church. "What is going on?"

It's silent. No one moves. Finally, Simon gives a chuckle. "Ah, yes, Father. My little brother is missing and my mother has sent me to look for him."

"I see," the monk says, sounding unconvinced. "Would that be 'Henry' or 'Farm Boy'?"

"Henry," Simon says quickly, "and — and the other is our cousin."

"Indeed. Well, I shall keep a lookout for Henry and Cousin Farm Boy, and tell them to run along, just as I'm telling you to run along now."

The other Hoods are already backing toward the front door.

"But I think they're all in here!" Simon protests, standing his ground, not giving any deference to the monk's station.

"What do you mean, 'all'? These farm cousins reproduce like rabbits, apparently." The monk's tone turns cold. "Your story is thin, boy, and so is my patience. Out! Now!"

His "Now!" echoes in the cathedral such that most of the boys run out of the door and even Simon walks quickly, the door slamming behind him.

The monk drums his fingers on a nearby pew as he stares at the door. Even though it was dark the other night, from his stance I'm sure it's the same monk who carried basket after basket into the church.

"For shame," the monk says to himself, but powerfully loud. "I should have told them that if they wanted food, I'd leave some by the side door of the sanctuary." He clucks his tongue a few times and strides off toward the front of the church.

Henry looks at me, quizzical. "Is that for us?" he whispers.

I nod my head, grinning. Just like he left me those apples.

The monk leaves the sanctuary, a door closing behind him.

Ned looks around nervously. "What are we supposed to do now? Where will we go? We can never go back to the Hoods."

"You could have your own gang," I say, and I imagine my face looks as surprised as all of theirs, because the words tumbled out of my mouth without my even thinking them.

"But how?" says Ned. "Simon will run us off before we have a chance to get at the food."

"Then you have to be faster," I say.

"He knows where all the good shops and taverns are already."

"Then you have to be smarter."

"He knows everyone who might give us anything."

"Then," says Henry, smiling at me, "we'll need to make new friends, won't we?"

I think about Cook at the manor and Grandmother. "There are people around who will be good to you. In my village, there's —"

"But this isn't a village," Ned says, "it's a city. That's different."

"Perhaps, but there are still good people. The fishmonger's wife gave Otto two loaves of bread, and the fishmonger cooked our herring for Henry's singing." I try to remember the name of the tavern where the woman gave me meat pies. "At the Black Bear, I think it was, the cook tossed me two pies."

"No," says Ned, "that fat man tries to paddle us!"

"But the woman who works there is kind." I answer Ned's doubting look. "Truly. She may be loud but she has a soft heart."

David nods slowly. "It could work."

"I think it's time," Daniel says.

"I think it's dangerous —" Ned starts before he's interrupted with "Shut up" and "Nervous Ned" from David and Daniel.

For my part, I can't help but laugh. "You live on the street, Ned. It's already dangerous!"

The others laugh, too, and even Ned shows a hint of a smile.

"What should our name be?" David asks.

"They already have the best name, the Hoods, after Robin Hood," Daniel says.

"We could be the Robins!" Otto says.

David snorts. "Named after songbirds? No thank you!"

"Henry," I say.

"What?"

"Henry is a king's name. Why not be . . . the Kings?"

Henry raises both arms in victory as the others cheer.

"Whist," I say, although I'm smiling. "It's a cathedral."

Henry nods. "I've never been in here before."

The other boys murmur their agreement.

"Really? But it's a house of God, meant for everybody," I tell them.

"But we're nobodies," Otto explains.

"That's not true," I tell him, "you're the Kings!"

We hear Daniel's belly rumble and we all laugh. Henry and I each go to a side door to find the food the monk promised. There's nothing at my door but Henry returns laden with two loaves of bread, a pitcher of milk, and a pot of honey. We sit at the feet of a statue of Mary and feast, no one talking because we're too busy eating.

Eating honey reminds me of something, and I count the days. "It's my birthday today!"

David and Daniel shrug.

"So?" says Ned.

"So, usually my father gets me honey cakes and buys me a gift."

They stop eating and stare at me as if I've said today is spring when really it's fall. "Truly," I say.

"Is it a feast day?" Henry asks.

"No. It's just something my father does for me." When I look at all five of them, their mouths hanging open, I wish I'd kept mine shut. They don't have a father. They don't have anyone who would do anything special for them. They've probably never received a birthday gift in their lives.

"What kind of gift?" Otto asks.

I remember my dice and I pull them out of my pouch. Their eyes are so wide and impressed that I decide Father won't mind if I'm generous. "You can keep them," I say.

Daniel grins. "Really?"

I nod. "I'll show you how to play after we eat."

"We know how," David says, "we've just never had any of our very own. It must be nice to be rich."

I'm about to say I'm not rich but, compared to them, I suppose I am.

Otto is the last to finish and is in such bliss by the end of the meal that he even closes his eyes. "Thank you for the food, Henry."

"It's not I, but the monk we should thank," Henry says.

Otto licks the honey from his fingers and puts his hands together. "Thank you, Father Monk," he whispers, and scampers off to join the other boys, who are exploring the cathedral.

I chuckle. "He was praying to a monk?"

"He's only seven," Henry explains, and then, as if to himself, "the same age I was when I took to the streets." He looks longingly toward the front of the church. "I'd like to thank that monk, too."

"You're not much of a thief! You didn't even steal the food. It was given to you. And you want to say thank you."

Henry smiles at me wryly and shrugs, but looks toward the altar again.

I can tell he still wants to give his thanks. I sigh. "All right. I'll scribe a note." It's the least I can do, given how generous the monk has been.

Henry sits up straight. "You can scribe?"

"It's not that hard." What's hard is focusing my eyes in this dim light, especially at the end of a long day.

I take a piece of parchment and my goose feather from my bag, and use soot from the altar candles mixed with my spit as ink. I write my thanks in both Latin and English, and I scribe large letters so I can see them better: *Gratias, Thanks.* Henry is much impressed and calls the other boys over. They gather around me, watching.

"How do you do that?" David asks.

"Can you show me?" says Daniel.

"What use is it?" Ned asks, and everyone looks at him. "I mean, it's not as if we'll ever be scribes."

"Still," Henry says, "everyone should know how to write his own name, Ned." He looks at me. "Will you show us?"

They're all looking at me now, even Ned. And so, underneath the *Thanks*, I sign all of our names, except mine. I decide to use a disguise, because what if Father discovers I came to Carlisle and sends for word through the clergy? This is what I write, and I read each boy's name out loud, except mine:

hENRY
OTTO
ĐAVIĐ
ĐANIEl
NEĐ
ThE BAĐǤER

"Oy," says Ned, "why is my name so short and yours gets two parts?"

"Because he's twice as important as you," David says with a laugh.

"And he's traveling in secret," Henry adds.

I stare at him. How does he know? I never actually said that. He smiles back at me, I think with respect.

"Which is me, again?" Otto asks anxiously, leaning over the parchment, as if he fears he will forget within moments.

I point to his name and explain it so he can remember. "It's a circle, two crosses, and a circle. If you fold it in the middle, it's exactly the same on both sides."

He grins. "I'll remember it now."

Henry grabs my arm. "Adrian, could you scribe *Kings* for us?"

"Why?" Ned asks.

"We could leave each other messages, like where is a safe place to sleep or a good place to ask for food."

Ned looks pained. "But I'll never remember another whole word!"

"How about just the *K*?" I draw it for them, even a simple version of a *K*. "See? It's a tree with an arrow's tip stuck into it."

They all agree that they can remember that.

David takes the note and he and the other boys practice writing their names with their fingers — on the floor, the walls, the pews — everywhere, as if they're claiming it all for themselves.

"Don't forget to deliver the note," I tell them. We decided it should go with the milk pitcher and empty pot of honey by the side door where the food was.

"Are you really leaving tomorrow?" Henry asks.

"I must. I have to find Hugh and help in the battle." It makes me feel important, saying it out loud.

"You always have a place in Carlisle," Henry says somberly.

"The far-right alcove pew?"

He punches me playfully and we both laugh.

Suddenly, I have a thought. "Henry! Give me your knife!"

His face falls but he pulls it out slowly, takes a long look at it, and hands it over to me. "It's yours."

"No, it's yours, and I'm going to make sure it stays that way."

With my own knife. I carve the letters into the wooden handle of his: H-E-N-R-Y. He watches me silently the entire time, while the other boys talk and even begin to play dice. I look up from my work long enough to remind them that this is a house of God and not a place for dice. After that, they settle, talking awhile until, one by one, their voices hush into the whispers of the cathedral and they are asleep.

When I finish carving, I hand Henry his knife.

"Thank you. I don't know what I'd do without it."

I want to tell him that I know. He's quick and gallant and clever. He's a leader, though he's so young. Even I can see that. He reminds me of the knight who came to our village looking for the bowyer with his fine clothes and fine manners. Henry may not have the fine clothes and fine manners, but he carries himself like a knight. Maybe leaders are born that way, and there are leaders in every class, not just among nobles and knights. I think Henry would be brave and true even without a knife.

But I'm suddenly tired, too tired to say all that, so I simply bid him good night and have dreams of being chased by Simon and the Hoods while I defend the younger boys with my bow, except that the arrows are knives and all of them have carved on them: A-D-R-I-A-N.

The next morning, I wake before anyone else. Streams of painted light splash the stone like colored water. It's as magical as the first time I saw it. I gawk at the colors on the floor and at the even brighter colors in the window.

When Otto talks in his sleep, I look at him and the boys around him. It'll be sad to leave. This is the first time I've had a whole group of friends, not just Hugh. And friends who look up to me, I think. I'll miss them, especially Henry, who I wager would be just as brave on the road as he is in the city.

I have an idea and go back to add a message to our note. However, when I get to the side door, the note is gone. In its place is a huge loaf of bread, a large hunk of cheese, and — God be praised — a whole bowl of sweet apples!

I hear footsteps approach from behind me and I freeze.

"I thought you'd gone." It's Henry.

I turn and smile. "Not without saying good-bye. Look" — I show him — "more food."

He grins. "We'll eat like kings!"

He takes the bread and cheese, heading back to the others, and I pick up the bowl of apples. Underneath it, I see a blank piece of parchment and three pennies. I give the money to Henry and tell the boys to go to the Black Bear for food.

After eating, I scribe a message, glad that the other boys can't read, telling them I'm giving thanks, which is true.

Thank you. May God bless you and these boys — they are good. Please help them. Use a K to mark safe places for them to rest or find food. With sincere thanks.

—the BADGER

chapter the nineteenth

In Which I Smell a Rat

I'M FEELING LONELY AS I HEAD EAST FROM CARLISLE. I'M looking for my oldest and best friend, but I've left all my new friends behind. It was so tempting to stay with them, especially when Otto clung on to me, crying, "Don't go!" I promised him I'd return.

I try not to think about that, and think about battles instead, practicing archery in the woods, which lifts my spirits, although I find no food. It's hard to keep one's spirits up on an empty stomach, and by sundown I'm feeling wretched. For the hundredth time I look in the bag of herbs Grandmother gave me, wondering if any of them are fit to eat. I'm almost ready to eat the remedy for colic because I'm feeling as colicky as a baby.

It's when I'm praying to God for salvation, at least for my stomach, that I breach the rise of a hill and see something through the trees, outlined against the setting sun, as if surrounded by a heavenly light. A priory! A place of God and monks — and food! I fairly run down the hill, thanking God all the while for sending me this salvation.

But I stop short when I see an apparition moving in the trees. It's a gray ghost or ghoul! And it's headless! I jump behind an oak and freeze. No wonder there were no animals about all day! Now I'm petrified. Stuck. I can't run away!

"What is *that*?" the ghost says.

Maybe because it's the way Father Fraud always refers to me I think that the gray shape may be a priest, not a ghoul. I peek from behind the tree.

Still, when the figure pulls off its hood, I breathe in sharply, squeezing my eyes so I can barely see, fearing that he may reveal a skull or the jagged teeth of a redcap.

"Don't be afraid," the voice says. "I'm Nigel."

Nigel? That's hardly a name for a redcap. I open my eyes all the way and see it's a man, now that he's standing up. He's thin and stooped over but not much older than Hugh. He squints at me, his eyes like a turtle's. And he has a tonsure. He's a monk!

"Do you need help?"

I nod.

"A place to rest?" Nigel asks.

I nod again.

"Come. Follow me." He turns and heads toward the priory.

I see now that he carries a basket of mushrooms. He must've been stooped over collecting them. That's why he looked like a headless ghoul.

"What is this place?" I ask, walking after him.

"Lanercost. Have you not heard of it?"

I shake my head.

"Where are you from? What's your name?"

"People call me the Badger," I say, but I don't tell him where I'm from.

His eyebrows rise. "The Badger? Ah. You need say no more. I ran away myself, desperate to become a priest. Is that what you desire?"

I shake my head, maybe a little too forcefully because he begins to laugh. "Never mind. You look like you could use some food."

I nod my head just as vigorously and he laughs again. "Let's go to the kitchen!"

I quickly decide that I like Brother Nigel. He's not mean, like Father Fraud, nor does he smell as much. As we walk toward the priory, I ask him what he has heard about the battle.

"The Scots are heading to Liddesdale. We are due south, right in their path. They could be here in a day or two. It's not safe for you to stay here long. They may attack the priory."

"Pagan Scots!" I cry, as we walk through the stone arch of the gatehouse. "Even a priory?"

As if in agreement, I hear a man shouting from the courtyard and horses whinnying. "Those pagans! They have stolen the entire cartload!"

A man dressed in white with gold chains around his neck shakes his fist at two knights on horseback.

"Who is he?" I ask.

"That," Nigel sighs, "is our prior."

"The head of the priory?"

He nods, bowing his head and crossing himself in front of the large stone cross that sits to the left of the church. I follow suit but am distracted by the prior hurling random curses at King David and all the Scots and wonder how such a man ever became a monk to begin with. I'm also struck by the carving of a female saint high above the door.

"That's Mary Magdalene," Nigel says reverently, bowing his head at the same time the prior hurls curses worse than I've ever heard. Nigel explains in a whisper. "Since the Scots might attack, the prior had his knights escort another cartload of valuables to a safe place. Apparently, it's now stolen."

The knights trot off, leaving the prior moaning about all the stolen riches.

"My lord," Nigel says, bowing as he approaches the prior, "I have found a young shepherd boy, lost, and I ask your leave for him to stay until we can find his family."

The fat prior looks down his hooked nose at me, and after muttering something about a devil child, he asks, "How does a shepherd boy manage to get himself lost?"

In truth, I didn't even know I was a shepherd boy until Nigel said so. "I — I —"

"I don't care," the prior says, waving his hand. "He's your responsibility. I have other things to worry about. Brother Nigel, did you record all the items in the cartload that has now been stolen?"

Nigel's face turns pale. "But, my lord prior, you told me that Brother Bernard was taking inventory, so —"

"I said no such thing!" the prior shouts. "This is why you will never make a good scribe, Brother Nigel! You can't be relied upon for even the simplest of tasks. It's not the first time you've forgotten to record provisions — not to mention destroying provisions, like breaking pitchers of wine! You're worse than useless!"

Nigel keeps his head bowed but I see his jaw clench, just as mine does.

The prior continues to rail, and I feel so bad for Nigel I want to tell the prior to shut up. He waves his arms around wildly, like the players at the market fair last summer who put on a dramatic production. He's dressed like the players, too, with his fine cloth, gold chains, and rings on his hands. Gold rings with gemstones! On every finger!

Finally, Nigel is dismissed, and I follow him in silence. I don't know what to say, and I feel especially bad for him now because the prior has sentenced him to many onerous tasks and three days' fasting for his supposed transgression. For some reason, I feel like the prior is lying.

Nigel leads me through a cloister and to a large basin to wash my hands. I follow him to the kitchen, which is dark but smells warm and delicious. There's a veritable bounty of herbs hanging from the rafters that would stun and delight both Grandmother and Hugh. I look around at the shelves laden with loaves of bread, jugs of ale, pots of honey, and items wrapped in cloth, probably cheese and meat. So much food it's enough to make one want to join the priory!

"This is Brother Cuthbert," Nigel says, leading me over to an elderly, stooped-over monk.

The wizened monk smiles at us and pats Nigel's arm. "It's mutton stew today, Nigel, your favorite."

Nigel's head drops. "I'm sentenced to fast for three days."

"Oh, dear," says Brother Cuthbert, losing his smile. "Our esteemed prior has found some fault with you. Again."

"I think he's lying," I say, and both brothers look at me, their eyes wide.

"Whist!" Nigel says. "Don't say such things lest you want a punishment worse than mine!"

But Brother Cuthbert smiles at me with a twinkle in his eye.

"I must clean the privies now," Nigel says. "I'll be back to take you to the dormitory soon." He leaves by a small door at the back of the kitchen.

Brother Cuthbert opens his mouth to say something but several monks walk in, and once he glances at them, he quickly turns to the fire and stirs his pot. Instinctively, I pull my hood up to cover my white hair. The other monks talk among themselves, practically pushing Brother Cuthbert out of the way as they fill their bowls with stew and sit at the far end of the table, ignoring me.

Brother Cuthbert gives me a large bowl of stew and a huge hunk of bread. When he turns back to the fire and I see that the other monks aren't watching, I put the hunk of bread in my tunic to give to Nigel later. Brother Cuthbert turns back to me and sees the empty spot on the table where the bread was. He looks over at the small door Nigel went through, smiles, and puts another large piece of bread by my bowl.

When the small door finally opens again, I start to get up because I'm finished eating and expect to see Nigel. Instead, it's a little boy who steps tentatively inside.

"What is it, boy?" one of the seated monks calls out.

"Please, Brother, may I have some food for my family?"

"Maybe if you villagers gave tithes we would have enough to —"

"But we have! We always —"

"Don't interrupt your superiors!" another monk chastises.

The boy stops, but his face is set and stern.

"Run along, boy," the first monk says. "Our prior says we have none to spare."

I cringe at the lie because surely the boy can see all the food in this kitchen, and I wonder how a monk can send a starving child away.

The boy shuts the door behind him overly loud and I slump on the bench.

Brother Cuthbert must feel as I do, for he shakes his head as he stirs the pot.

When Nigel appears and takes me to the dormitory in the darkness, he's rubbing his eyes. He seems so tired I don't want to pester him with questions, but I want to know more about this prior. We climb the stone steps of a large building into a long hallway with many doors. They're all individual cells, Nigel tells me, one for each monk. When he opens the door to his, I pull out the hunk of bread.

He squints at it. I think his eyes are not very good because it takes him a moment to realize what it is, and then he looks almost frightened, quickly closing the door behind us. "We're not supposed to have food in our cells," he whispers. "It brings the rats."

"Then you'd better eat it fast," I say, "lest a large white rat come." I'm thinking, of course, of the prior.

Nigel raises his eyebrows at me but can't help smiling. He makes the sign of the cross, says a quick blessing, and eats so ravenously that I resolve to save more of my food for him tomorrow.

Nigel insists on giving me his pallet while he sleeps on the stone floor. He claims he has done it before and it doesn't bother him. Other than his pallet, there is not much in the room. I see a cross on the wall, a small stool and table, and on the table a board with lots of carved figures on it.

"What's that?"

"Chess," he says, stretching out on the cold floor. "My father carved it for me. Do you know how to play?"

"No. I just know it's a game of strategy."

His eyes are already closed. "That's true," he says, yawning. "Tomorrow, I'll teach you about strategy — and deceit."

chapter the twentieth

*In Which I Learn of Chess, Maps, Mr. Ockham,
and Good and Evil*

I'M NOT VERY GOOD AT CHESS. ALL I LEARN IS THAT PAWNS
are like me. They're small, have little power, and are practically worthless. The queen is the most powerful of all, yet it's
the king who must be caught by checkmate. Knights, bishops, and rooks are strong, although the knights have an
awkward way of moving about the board, jerking one way
and then the other. I tell Nigel that's why the Scots were able
to steal the prior's cart of treasures from his clumsy knights.

Nigel laughs and tells me stories of his own. He has many
from all the books he has read. Even about battles, like this:
Armies have actually catapulted diseased corpses into castles
to spread plague and kill the inhabitants! St. Jerome's bones!
Maybe all that reading Nigel does is worth it.

He has also traveled — along Hadrian's Wall, and into
Scotland! He says Hadrian's Wall is but half a mile from
here! There are even Roman stones that were dragged from the
wall and used to build this very dormitory.

Nigel claims the Scots are much like us and are certainly not all pagans. I think he may just be saying that to allay my fears. I'm not scared, although I suspect the Scots are precisely the type to catapult diseased corpses into castles.

"The forts along Hadrian's Wall are most interesting," Nigel says. "You can even see where the Romans relieved themselves."

"What?"

"It's true. I've seen the latrine at Housesteads Fort. It looks like the foundation of a chapel, perhaps twelve feet by thirty feet. All along the edges there used to be wooden benches for men to sit, also like a chapel, except that they sat there to relieve themselves."

"No!" My voice is so loud it echoes.

"Whist!" Nigel says to hush me, although he smiles. "It's true," he whispers. "There were slats in the wooden benches for the waste to fall into the giant pit underneath, a pit that was deeper than a man's height."

"A huge pit of waste? That piled up in the middle of the fort? What a stench!"

"Nay, that's the beauty of it: The Romans channeled water from the River Tyne all the way to the fort so that the waste was flushed out!"

"St. Jerome's bones!"

Nigel's jaw drops.

"Sorry!" I say quickly. I must remember not to curse inside the priory, although it doesn't seem to stop the prior. "They had a lot of money, those Romans," I say, "if they were able to build elaborate relief . . . chapels." I start laughing but cover my mouth to stop the noise.

Nigel grins. "I know! They were powerful in mind, body, and spirit."

And yet, I think to myself, *they weren't able to conquer the Scots.*

The bells in the church tower ring — again — calling the brothers to their singing. I had wanted to ask Nigel about the prior.

"I'll return soon," Nigel says, "and I'll give you a tour of the priory."

"Can't you skip this time?" He has already been to the chapel once, while I was at breakfast.

Nigel laughs.

"Really," I say, "you can tell the prior you were chasing me around. He said it was your responsibility to watch me, after all."

Nigel hovers at the door, stooped over, a slow smile creeping across his face, as we listen to the feet scurrying past on their way to prayers. He doesn't join them.

I jump up from the stool. "Good! Now we can start the tour!"

Nigel puts a finger to his lips and looks out the tiny window in his door. Finally, he opens it and we slip into the hallway.

When we're outside, I ask him, "Why does the prior wear a ring on every finger?"

He lowers his head close to my ear so he can speak softly. "The prior has a love of jewels. He's like a magpie grabbing shiny things for his nest." Opening the door near the kitchen, he adds, "He likes anything rich — food, wine, gems —"

"But that's not how a prior should —"

"Whist!" says Nigel, putting a hand on my shoulder as a figure rounds the corner toward us.

The tall figure bows his head as he passes, glowering at me. "Brother Nigel."

Nigel bows his head, too. "Brother Bernard."

When the echoes of Brother Bernard's footsteps are gone, Nigel sighs. "It's true, I dropped one pitcher of wine — but only one. The prior claims there were several more and I dropped all of them. I have no way to prove otherwise. It's his word against mine." He rubs his eyes. "It's like that with everything. He tells everyone that I've miscounted. He thinks me as dim as my eyes." Nigel rubs his eyes again but his voice is resolute. "I may have poor eyesight but I see more than he thinks. I'm not a fool."

I swallow hard. I know what it's like to have weak eyes, and to be thought a fool. It makes me angry for Nigel. "Surely there are others who know the truth. Why don't you tell anyone?"

We hear the rise of voices chanting from the church as we enter a large room with long tables.

Nigel shuts the door behind us before he speaks again. "Brother Bernard, whom we just passed, is very close to the prior, as are several of the monks here. I don't know who I can trust." He picks up the knotted end of his belt, tugging at it as if to undo the knot. "I can only think that there are many of us in that position. We may suspect the prior but we dare not speak about it lest we speak to one of his men." He grimaces, and his Adam's apple bobs as he swallows. "The prior is harsh with his punishment."

"So I've seen." I tell Nigel about the night before, when the little boy came for food and was sent away. "The kitchen is laden!" I say.

"True, but we have a lot of monks to feed. And the bishop at Durham is demanding more and more from us, as is his right. There are far more monks and parishioners at Durham to provide for than there are here. So chickens, wine, pigs — even gold — disappear fast." He looks toward the door and around the room as if the walls themselves might have ears. "Also, the prior claims that the villagers are shorting us on their tithes and that I miscount our supplies because of my poor eyesight."

"He's lying," I say again, and this time Nigel does not reprimand me.

He sighs and sits on a wooden bench, putting an elbow on the table and propping his chin in his hand.

I begin to notice the room now that my eyes have adjusted to the light coming through the high, narrow windows. "What is this room?"

"The dining hall," Nigel says, running his finger along a grain of wood in the table.

I remember the bread and cheese I have for Nigel from my breakfast and put it on the table in front of him. He hesitates and looks back at the door.

"It's a dining hall, after all," I say, and he smiles, thanking me for the food, as well as Our Savior, before eating it.

A flicker of color catches my attention and I walk to the far end of the room. What I find there, on a separate table, perpendicular to the others, is a box the size of my hand. It's pure gold. I've never seen anything so bright! In addition, there are large red and green stones on top of it that look like the stained glass in Carlisle Cathedral.

I reach out my hand to touch it.

"No, no, you mustn't open it!" Nigel says, his mouth full of food.

I draw my hand back. "What's inside?" I can't imagine what could be more valuable than the box itself, all gold and jewel-encrusted.

"It's a reliquary. It contains a fragment of bone from St. Nicholas of Myra. It's holy."

"St. Nicholas?" I turn to Nigel. "Isn't he the patron saint of the poor?"

"Yes."

I cross my arms. "Well, then, I think he'd rather see the villagers be given food than have more jewels added to his reliquary."

Nigel smiles grimly. "I agree."

"Why don't you leave this place?"

"It's not that easy. I've made a commitment. And," he says, brightening and rising from the bench, "there's a particular reason I want to stay."

I follow his tall, willowy form through the cloisters and up the stairs to a room that's as large as the dining hall, but it has wider windows and feels much brighter. There are lots of tables and benches, too, only they're small and extend from the outside walls, each set of two tables having a bench, so they form little alcoves, with the windows shedding light on each table. And there are books and scrolls everywhere, on the center table and on many of the smaller desks by the windows.

"This," says Nigel, "is the library. I hope to be a scribe, despite my eyesight. Now all I do is inventory, and not very well, if you believe the prior."

"I don't," I say quickly.

He smiles. "I use this reading stone to see the letters." He picks up a rounded lump of glass, sliding it across a manuscript and leaning down to stare at it. I do the same, and see that when you look down through the glass, the letters appear larger.

"It's hard to scribe like this, however," he says. "Brother Ignatius got approval to order spectacles for me but the prior claims they were stolen by some village boys." Nigel shakes his head. "Why would village boys want spectacles? They couldn't sell them, because people would know immediately that they were stolen, being too expensive for any peasant to buy. They're sitting on the nose of some knight or his lady."

I feel my jaw clench. Even Father Fraud is not this bad. How could you take someone's eyesight away from him? I know what it's like to have trouble seeing. Especially by the end of the day — or even the beginning of the day if it's cloudy and gloomy — it's hard to focus on letters.

In the far corner I see another box with jewels on top. Although it's only wood, it does have gold corners and is much larger than the one in the dining hall. I point to it. "Another reliquary? Shouldn't these be in the chapel?"

"We have two in the chapel already," Nigel says.

I shake my head again.

"I know," Nigel says sadly, but then he brightens. "I brought you here to show you something special." He walks to one of the desks by the window and reverently touches a manuscript that lies open. "These are the chronicles that have been kept since 1272, a history of our area. This is what I want to write, not" — he crosses himself — "copy gospels."

"Why?" I ask him.

"Because it's real. It's modern. It's what's happening now. I want to write down the events of the day so those in the future can be informed. We're Augustinian monks. We search for the truth."

"The truth about what?"

"Well . . . everything. The truth about life. Look here." He points to a passage. "Do you know of the event at Windsor two years ago, when the king had hundreds of knights and ladies for a tournament at great expense?"

"I've heard of it."

"Brother Ignatius didn't think much of it, so while he reported it, the way in which he reported it — saying a lot of money was spent as is befitting the nobility — leads one to question why such money is spent. Yes, they're nobles, but must they spend it all on games when so many are sick and hungry?" Still smiling, he says, "I'd like to have that power, the power to make people question."

I shrug, thinking that a bow and arrow are much more power than mere words. On the desk opposite, I see a manuscript with many pictures, little houses and churches scattered across it. I move around the desk so I can see it more clearly. "What's this?"

"A map," Nigel says. He points to a blue squiggly line. "That's the River Irthing, and this one, east of here, is the North Tyne."

"And all the little houses, are they towns?"

"Yes, and the large castles indicate cities. The cathedrals are, well" — he laughs — "cathedrals." He taps a small building with a cross. "That's us, Lanercost Priory."

I stare at the priory, looking at the city pictured to the left of it, which is labeled *Carlisle*, where I came from. I also see Penrith, below Carlisle, and start to appreciate how far I have come.

I point to a funny jagged line, like a row of little square baby teeth with gaps in between them. "What's this?"

"Why, that's Hadrian's Wall."

"Hadrian's Wall," I whisper. I let my eyes drift north of Hadrian's Wall into Scotland. Unlike the many cities, towns, priories, and cathedrals dotted all over England, Scotland is a virtual wasteland. It has some cities, like Edinburgh and Glasgow, but north of them is much darkness, and north of the darkness lie giant hills many times the size of ours. It's a mysterious and frightening land. No wonder the Scots are savages.

"Do you know where we're fighting the Scots now?"

Nigel shakes his head. "War is unpredictable, so who

knows? We think King David means to attack Durham Cathedral and then York, so the Scots will be headed south over Hadrian's Wall, toward Durham. Lanercost Priory could be in their line of fire, but we're hoping they'll head in a more easterly direction. Other priories, like Hexham, which are in a more direct line, are in danger."

He stops and looks at me. "Young Badger . . . you're not thinking to follow the battle, are you." He says it as more of a statement than a question.

"You'd be surprised what a master I am with the bow," I say proudly. It's a mistake.

"The battlefield is not the place for a boy," he says sternly.

He's like all the others. So I tell him instead the story of going to retrieve Hugh from battle and bring him home. It doesn't ease his brow much. I think monks, even those who are not quite monks yet, can sniff out a lie at a hundred yards, much like dogs can sniff out meat.

"Would you like us to send a message to your father that you're well?"

I wrestle with that. If Father knows I'm at Lanercost now, will he be able to figure out where I'll go next? And track me down? Yet, he's worried, I know. Then I realize how I can satisfy both of us. "Yes, you may tell him that I'll continue west to Carlisle to look for Hugh." In truth, I'll go the other way, but no one needs to know that, least of all Father. I offer a quick prayer of forgiveness for the lie.

Nigel looks at me askance and I try to distract him. "What's that desk with the high chair?" I ask, running over to the chair and jumping on it.

"Whist!" he says. "That's Brother Bernard's desk, the prior's right-hand man."

I grab a scroll, unwind it, and start to read.

"Badger!" he says, alarmed. "You should put that down." He tries to grab it but I twist away from him, still standing on the chair, and read quickly, fairly spitting out the words. "Accounting of Lanercost Priory by My Lord Prior Osmund!"

Nigel looks at me, stunned. "You read — and very well." Then he frowns. "An accounting? What is this accounting?"

I shrug, looking at the columns on the page, a long list on the left of food and wine and jewels, a column with numbers, then a column with names, and a column on the right with money amounts. I'm not exactly sure how to read it, so I just call out the first things I see. It's hard to read because Nigel is bending down over it, squinting at it.

When I read the word *Spectacles*, and *2 pounds, 10 shillings*, we both stop and stare at each other.

"Spectacles," I repeat. "Your spectacles?"

"Ockham's razor," Nigel whispers, staring into the distance.

"Ockham's razor? What's that?"

Nigel's eyes are still wide. "William of Ockham used the theory so much that it is named after him. It states that when confronted with a problem it is wisest to use the simplest explanation unless a more complex explanation proves correct." He looks at me and speaks faster. "The prior has been feeding us a line that the bishop is requiring more, the Scots are stealing our supplies, the villagers are giving less — it's all lies! He's simply embezzling, taking the goods and selling them to make money for himself. That's how he manages to have such finery."

In the silence, the door to the library bangs open. I don't know who is more shocked, Prior Osmund or us!

chapter the twenty-first

In Which I Meet a Knight!

NIGEL LETS GO OF MY ARM AND BOWS TO THE PRIOR. I TRY to bow, but as I'm standing on a chair it's but an awkward dip, like Bessie when she drinks water from the stream.

Prior Osmund marches over to me and his eyes bulge when he sees the scroll in my hand. Snatching it away, he fairly screams, "Give that to me! Ignorant shepherd! What are you doing with this?"

At first, I don't know what to say, and I'm struck dumb. Nigel's words linger in my ears: *Ockham's razor.* I decide to use it. The prior thinks I'm a mere shepherd boy so I won't give him reason to believe anything else. I must keep it simple. I smile eagerly. "I'm reading!"

I see Nigel's eyes widen behind the prior and his head shaking a vigorous no.

The prior blanches before his face turns a blotchy red. "What?" He says the next words slow and roiling and threatening. "What does it say, boy?"

"It's a psalm!" I say brightly, and stupidly. "We have them at our village church, too!" I smile, even more brightly and stupidly. "The Lord is my shepherd!"

The prior's face relaxes into a superior smirk and he clutches the scroll to his chest. "It's like a psalm, yes. Now run along and do not be touching things you can't begin to comprehend. And, Brother Nigel?" He scowls and I hold my breath for Nigel. I don't want him punished again. "You know better than to let vagabonds in here. Don't let this boy out of your sight!"

Nigel scurries to the side of the prior so he can see him, and bows. "I am deeply sorry, my lord. The boy is exuberant and . . ." He gives the prior an apologetic smile and shrugs, holding his palms upward in supplication.

The prior cracks a smile and mouths a word to Nigel. I have heard that word so many times, I can read his lips: *addlepate.*

For once, it's a useful name. I want the prior to think I'm simple, so I continue to smile at him as Nigel takes me by the hand and pulls me toward the door. I even wave and make an awkward bow and call him "sire" as we step out of the library. Though he harrumphs and rolls his eyes, he seems pleased at the title.

I start reciting the psalm about the Lord being my shepherd, loudly, so the prior can hear. Nigel shushes me and I ask why, also loudly, so Nigel must shush me again.

When we reach his cell and he closes the door behind us, we stare at each other a moment before we both cover our mouths so we can laugh, albeit quietly. I'm still laughing when Nigel shakes his head, although his tone is only half reprimanding. "You, young Badger, should be in an acting troupe."

I grin. "It's all thanks to Ockham's razor!"

He looks at me quizzically.

"I gave the prior the simplest explanation. He expects I can't read so I didn't need to come up with any story. I wager that when he saw us, me standing on the chair, you holding on to my arm, it looked like I'd been running and jumping around like a simpleton and you were trying to catch me."

"*Simpleton* is the last word to describe you."

"True," I say, "the correct word is *addlepate*." And we laugh again.

But I feel like an addlepate when Nigel asks me to list all the items on the scroll, the quantities of each, and the amount of money attributed to every one of them.

"I have no idea," I say.

He looks at me in disbelief. "Surely you must."

"Nigel, I simply read it. I can't remember it."

"You can," he insists. "You said ten flagons of wine, twenty shillings; eight chickens, ten shillings; two pots of honey, six shillings."

Now I look at him in disbelief. "How do you remember all that?"

He seems surprised by my question. "It's important information." He sighs. "Understandably, it's not so important to you. Maybe that's why it didn't stick."

"It didn't stick because it was a whole scroll of information.

Do you think I can make a picture of all that and store it inside my head? That's why there are scrolls!"

"But if we don't have the scroll?" He opens his palms as if to emphasize that, in fact, we don't have it. "That's why it's good to remember." He repeats the items I read out.

Now I'm curious, because I wonder how he still remembers the list. "How do you do that?"

"Loci."

I remember my Latin from Father Fraud, or at least, I think I do. "Places?"

"Exactly. I simply walk around the rooms in the priory, depositing the chickens in the kitchen, the wine in the horse trough, and two pots of honey poured over the prior's head."

We both laugh at that.

"But how did you think that up so fast?"

He shrugs. "I do it all the time. There's a lot to learn when you join an order. Rules, history, remedies for all maladies — Brother Ignatius taught me the loci method and made me practice so much it's now how my mind works. Also, since I can't see well, I have to, as you say, make a picture and store it inside my head."

"That's amazing."

"No, anyone can do it."

"Ha! I'd get lost walking around this place so it wouldn't help me remember a thing."

He shakes his head. "You pick a place you know. Your village, any place where you can picture items at different spots and then walk that path in your mind."

I'm picturing putting the chickens in our church but I've already forgotten how many there are when Nigel smacks his hand on the wall, making me jump.

He swallows hard, his Adam's apple bobbing in his throat, like he is choking. "I want to stop Prior Osmund!" he hisses. "I don't want him to get away —"

A shout from the hallway stops Nigel, and we both look to the door when we hear more shouts and running feet. Soon we're in the hallway joining the body of monks running toward the courtyard.

"What is it?" Nigel asks.

"Herald," someone answers, out of breath, "with news of battle!"

We run into the courtyard and see a dark-haired knight brushing his horse, a beautiful, dapple-gray courser bigger than any horse I've ever seen. He's taller at the shoulders than even this knight, who himself is a tall man.

Prior Osmund is already there, talking to the knight. I notice he has lost his gold chains and his rings! "And so we're limited in our supplies," the prior says with a heavy sigh.

The knight looks to the monks, as if for confirmation, but most of them avert their eyes. His eyes land on mine and I hold his gaze. I cross my arms and frown. His eyes linger on me a moment more before flitting over the prior and back to his horse, whom he continues to brush. "That is indeed distressing news."

"Do not worry, Sir Knight," the prior says, "we'll find sustenance for you."

"I am well fed," the knight says, an edge to his voice. "It's the villagers and your monks for whom I worry."

The prior bows his head and clasps his hands. "We are privileged to suffer in the name of Our Lord."

The knight's face is in shadow but I'm sure I see him roll his eyes. I can't help smiling. I like this knight.

As we return to Nigel's cell and the monks whisper about the possible impending attack, I ask about the knight. "Is he one of the prior's?"

"I've never seen him before. He must be a free lance. He doesn't even travel with a squire."

"Maybe you or Brother Cuthbert could talk to him! Tell him about the prior!"

Nigel shakes his head. "This free lance may want to trade with the prior, too."

"No, Nigel, I can tell he's honest!"

But Nigel won't budge. "It's too risky for any monk to approach him."

Too risky for monks, perhaps, but not for me.

That night, when the brothers go to chapel again — St. Jerome's ears, it seems to be all they do at this place! — I wait outside the dining hall for the knight to finish his meal. Still, I hide behind a pillar because I don't want any of the bad monks to see me.

As the knight walks by, I hiss, "Sir Knight!"

He stops. "A miracle," he says quietly, "a talking pillar."

I step out from behind the pillar. "No, sir, it is I, Adri — I mean . . . the Badger."

I see him press his lips together, I think to hide a smile.

"I have important information."

He is so tall and gaunt, but his face is kind as he looks down at me and nods. "Speak."

"The prior is the one stealing the supplies. He sells them to knights so he can buy jewels and rich foods and wine for himself."

The knight raises his eyebrows. "That's quite an accusation."

"It's true! I read a scroll on his desk —"

The knight startles, either because he doesn't believe I can read or he can't believe my impudence.

I hurry on and tell him about the chickens, wine, honey, spectacles, and how the accounting lists the person who paid and the amount. "The villagers can barely survive and yet he takes more. In the name of God."

"In the name of God," the knight fairly spits out. "Can you get me this scroll?"

I can barely choke out the words. "You mean . . . steal it?"

"It's hardly stealing, given what he's done."

It seems we both realize at the same time that the sound of chanting is replaced with footsteps as the monks are leaving the chapel and heading toward the cloister.

I dive behind the pillar again, just in time, as the prior calls out to the knight.

I can see the knight, who rubs his mouth, hiding his lips but not his words. "Meet me here at Lauds," he whispers, "with the scroll," and he walks away.

I return to Nigel's cell, wondering what I've gotten myself into. I close the door behind me. "Nigel, when is Lauds?"

Nigel yawns and rubs his eyes. "The prayers just before dawn."

"Does everyone go? Even . . . the prior?"

"He usually makes it to Lauds." Nigel smiles wryly. "Matins is too early for him."

"Will you wake me up before Lauds? I need to be on my way."

"So early?"

I shrug. "You said yourself that I should move fast because of the fighting."

He sighs and agrees.

I feel guilty for misleading him. I know he wants me to move quickly away from battle, and I'll be moving toward it.

But first, I must steal a scroll.

chapter the twenty-second

In Which I Become a Knight, Almost

WHEN NIGEL WAKES ME, IT'S STILL DARK. HE BEGS ME TO beware of thieves and even those who say they're pilgrims, because their purpose is not always good. He's still talking when the bells call the brothers to Lauds and feet hurry past in the hallway.

"I'll be careful," I assure him.

Nigel smiles. "I must go to chapel. It doesn't take much for the prior to find fault with me." He pauses at the threshold. "Godspeed, Badger, my friend."

I go to shake his hand. "It's actually Adrian. Just don't tell anyone."

Nigel smiles and bows his head. "I give you my word, Adrian."

When he closes the cell door and I'm left in the dark alone, listening to his lone footsteps grow softer, I think of the punishments he has already suffered at the hands of the prior. I don't want him to be blamed for what I'm about to do and be punished again.

170

I think for a moment then pray the good knight will wait for me as I scribe.

Dear Nigel,
I am sorry to abuse your friendship. I am not a shepherd boy but a spy. May you and God forgive me! The prior surely will not. You will know why soon enough.

—the BADGER

I leave my pen on the parchment as a gift for Nigel. It's no use to me where I'm going. All I need on the battlefield is my bow.

I glance through the narrow slit of a window in Nigel's cell and I'm stopped dead. The sky is bright red. I know it'll fade in moments to an orange hue and then pink, then dissolve altogether into the pale blue we know as the sky, but for this moment it's red. Bloodred. The rhyme comes into my head . . . *Red sky at night, shepherds delight, red sky at morning, shepherds take warning.* I shiver, from the thought or the chill air or both.

The monks' voices rise in chant, reminding me that I must move, and quickly.

I open Nigel's door quietly and enter the empty corridor. With the monks' singing masking my footsteps and the dawn glow lighting my way, it's easier than I thought to slip up the stairs to the library. I walk softly to the prior's assistant's special desk . . . it's empty! I look for the scroll on the floor underneath. Not there! I check every other desk with no luck. I look on the floor, in every corner. Where could it be?

Think, addlepate! I tell myself. My eyes scan the room, looking over every desk and under every stool, past the windows, past Brother Bernard's special desk and chair, past the reliquary, past the — wait! My eyes move back to the reliquary.

In my head, I hear Nigel's voice. *No, no, you mustn't open it!*

Ockham's razor! The reliquary is the simplest place because no one would dare open it. I run across the room, hesitating only briefly before raising the lid. . . . I knew it! I grab the scroll and make for the door, but then hear something — or rather, the lack of something. There is no singing anymore. Lauds is over!

I must get to the knight quickly but I hear footsteps on the stairs! I run to the windows that overlook the courtyard, step on top of one of the desks, and hoist myself to the windowsill. I position myself so that my feet will hit first when I drop to the ground. Still, it's a long way and I catch my breath, but what disturbs me more is the sight of the knight, already on his horse, heading for the gate.

"No! Wait!"

Monks are stepping into the courtyard, looking up at me and pointing, some crying out not to jump and others, just as loudly, telling me to get down at once.

"Stop! Stop!" I scream at the knight, waving the scroll in the air, while some monks, thinking I'm yelling at them, shout at me for daring to give them orders.

Thankfully, the commotion causes the knight to turn his head and, when he sees me waving the scroll, he slows his courser, turning him to head back toward me. Suddenly, the knight stands in his stirrups, letting out such a war cry that his horse flies like lightning toward me. I'm surprised, but pleased, until I see why.

Prior Osmund is in the courtyard, heading toward me. "Stop that thief!"

I crouch on the ledge, safely out of reach, but even as I think that, the door to the library opens and Brother Bernard runs in, with several monks behind him. They'll get me one way or another. I close my eyes, not wanting to know my fate, and cling on to the windowsill as I hold the scroll as far down as I dare so that the knight can grab it.

But the knight doesn't grab the scroll — he grabs me! I feel myself wrenched from my perch and open my eyes to see land rushing past below me, horse hooves flying, reins flapping, and the horse's mane in my face. Just as suddenly, the knight pulls me upright and I am propped in front of him, my legs straddling his horse, riding for the first time in my life. I scream and let loose of the scroll. The knight seems to hold me, the scroll, and the reins all at once, and my addlepated brain is wondering how he can have three hands.

"I didn't mean to scare you, boy, but I couldn't leave you with the prior once he saw you had the scroll. He's not a man to be toyed with, and it's I who put you in danger."

Although I hear and understand him, I can't answer because I'm too distracted by the pounding of the horse's hooves and the world racing by, as if I'm an arrow shooting through the air. The wind rushes into my open mouth. My hair whirls about like I'm in a storm. Trees fly past. I'm mesmerized.

When I feel the knight turn in the saddle and look behind us, I grab on to the horse's mane because the knight's twisting threatens to unbalance me. I can feel the heat and sweat of the horse as my hand brushes the animal's neck. I notice that he snorts and breathes heavily. When the knight turns back again he pulls gently on the reins and speaks softly to his horse, calling him "Lightning," which I think is an apt name.

To me, the knight says, "We're in luck! The prior does not appear to chase us."

I should feel relieved that we're not pursued and that the horse is no longer flying, but all I feel is wild bouncing in the saddle, much bumpier than before. I had always thought a knight to be so fortunate to glide along on a noble steed. Instead, it's nothing like gliding. It's sore and painful to the crotch. I wriggle around to try and save my privates. I'm more worried about them right now than the prior.

The knight laughs, but not meanly. "You're not used to riding. We'll slow down soon. For now, we must continue to put distance between us and Lanercost."

I wonder what he means by "soon," because it seems forever that we bounce along, sometimes on the road, sometimes cutting across a fallow field, sometimes uphill, which is unsettling, or downhill, which is far worse because it feels like I'll be pitched right over Lightning's neck. My stomach is so jostled that I am, for once, grateful that I haven't eaten, or else I'd be puking.

Finally, we slow down until Lightning is only walking. I sigh as much as the horse.

"I am Geoffrey de Molay," the knight says. "I currently serve my liege, the bishop of Durham. What's your real name, boy, and who are you? Obviously not a lost shepherd."

I decide I can trust him enough to tell him the truth. "Adrian Black, son of John the bowyer, of —"

"Ah, that would explain the bow and quiver that have been poking me for the past hour."

"Sorry, sir."

I look at the weaponry attached to his saddle. He has everything a knight could want — bow, shield, fine sword. But no permanent liege. "Why are you a free lance, sir?"

He takes a deep breath and lets it out slowly. "My great-grandfather was a Knight Templar."

I can't help flinching. "The Knights Templar? Weren't they . . ."

"Disgraced and disbanded? Yes. That's why I don't give my allegiance to any one group. Perhaps the Knights Templar did turn bad, perhaps not, but being a free lance allows me to give my liege to whatever group I feel is worthy. And affords me much travel. Where's your home, Adrian?"

"Ashcroft, near —"

"Ashcroft! You're quite a distance from home. Why?"

"I'm looking for Hugh Stout, my friend who's a soldier. I mean to join him in battle." I brace myself for his laughter, but it doesn't come.

"I see. And along the way, you're holding priors accountable for their sins?"

"Sir, I —"

"Don't worry. I've long distrusted that man and I'm grateful to you for uncovering his crime. You have done a man's job, and a noble deed."

I'm glad I'm seated in front of him so he can't see me grinning. A *man's* job! And a noble deed!

I stop grinning when Lightning's head suddenly dips down and disappears, and I fear I'm going to fall off the front. I clutch on to his mane. When I look down, I see the horse is merely drinking from a small creek.

Behind me, the knight jumps off Lightning and stretches. Looking back at me, Sir Geoffrey seems surprised to see me still on the horse. "You may dismount."

I'm not sure how, but I slide awkwardly off, my legs all wobbly.

Sir Geoffrey kneels beside his horse and drinks from the same water, albeit upstream. He turns to look at me. "Aren't you thirsty?"

I realize then that I'm parched and stoop down to drink as well. When I'm done slaking my thirst, I turn to see that he has pulled out the scroll and is reading it.

He shakes his head, his mouth twisted as if he has eaten rotten meat. "What does he use all this money for?"

"He buys himself jewels. He took all his rings off before you saw him."

"Not all of them. There was still one stuck tight on his right index finger."

"Maybe his fingers have grown too fat."

"Along with his stomach," Sir Geoffrey adds, "and his

head. Man of God, indeed!" He picks up a stone and throws it into the water and it skips four times. His dark eyes are deep pools. "I really wanted to be a monk myself."

"A monk?" I stare at him stupidly because I can't imagine him as anything but the grand figure of a knight that he is. And why would anyone rather be a monk than a knight?

He smiles sadly. "But, it's my lot. I was the one sent to be a squire. My brother, who is better suited to be a knight, has just started as a novitiate."

"Does he like it?"

His smile grows more impish. "He hates it. Absolutely hates it!" Losing his smile, he shakes his head. "Destiny. It's both a friend and a curse."

I wonder at Nigel's destiny and ask Sir Geoffrey what might happen to my friend. "I scribed a note, saying I'm a spy, and making it sound that Nigel had no idea. He really didn't have any idea that I was going to steal the scroll, only what it said."

He pats my shoulder twice. "You are, indeed, clever. And brave." He looks me in the eye and stares for a moment. "Maybe it's you who should be the knight." Rolling the scroll back up, he adds, "I suspect Nigel will be fine. And, once the bishop sees this scroll, the person who will be in danger is the prior."

"And Brother Bernard and the others who support him?"

Sir Geoffrey nods. "The bishop will look into all of it." He secures the scroll to his saddle. When he takes out meat pies from his saddlebag, my mouth starts watering.

He hands one to me and I eat hungrily. He laughs. "Maybe you would make a good shepherd, given how much you like mutton."

"Never has a mutton pie tasted so good — not that I get them often, but this is the best one I've ever had!" I take another overly large bite.

"I think it's partly your age," he says.

"I'm thirteen," I say defiantly, even though my mouth is full.

"Exactly. Lads your age are growing fast and would eat leather if it had enough gravy on it."

I swallow. "Oh. People always think me younger because of my size."

"You're too wise and traveled for a young boy." The sun is behind him and he looks past me. "Still, I would think your family might like you home."

I stop eating. "I can't, sir. Not yet. I have to find Hugh." I look toward what must be north and point. "Is that where the battle will be?"

He nods. "Likely."

"Are you going?"

He nods again. "I must get to Durham, but I'd like to see how far the Scots have come and do my part to send them back. Then I'll report to the bishop at Durham, both on the battle and" — he pats the scroll — "the wicked prior."

"Can I . . . ride with you?"

He sighs. "I can't make you go home. You're making your own way now."

My chest almost bursts with pride.

"However," he adds, "you're still too young for me to take you into battle."

"But —"

He holds up his hand. "I can't even say for sure where the battle is. The Scots may have crossed Hadrian's Wall already, or at least be headed there. Tell me what this Hugh Stout looks like, and I'll keep an eye out for him and tell him that his brave friend Adrian — the Badger" — he winks — "will be waiting for him at Housesteads Fort, a likely crossing place for the soldiers on their way to Durham."

I describe Hugh but tell Sir Geoffrey, "I'd rather go into battle now."

He smiles and points east. "Housesteads is that way, about five miles. You may see me there soon if I don't find the fighting. That's where I'll cross." He pats his horse, looks at me, and stops. Slowly he opens his saddlebag and takes out a soft black cloth, unfolding it. He hands me what looks to be a coin. "You should have this."

It's a medal stamped with a special seal: two knights riding one horse.

"It was my great-grandfather's," Sir Geoffrey says. "That's the insignia of the Knights Templar. No matter what the truth is about them, it has always brought me good luck."

"Shouldn't you keep it, then?"

He mounts his horse and smiles down at me. "But I'm a free lance and protected by the bishop. I give it to you to remember this day." He points to the image on the coin. "You are the second knight, Adrian." Patting the scroll again, he says, "Thank you for your service to God and the king." He even nods his head to me in a little bow, as if I'm truly a knight!

I return the gesture, bowing lower, of course, because he's the real knight.

I watch him ride north, beyond Hadrian's Wall, and disappear over the hills. I clutch my medal and stare into the gloomy land of the Scots beyond the wall, part of me wanting to cross it, and part of me glad not to.

chapter the twenty-third

In Which I Hide in a Latrine

WALKING IS DIFFICULT BECAUSE MY CROTCH IS SORE FROM riding. I have to walk with my feet wide apart, as if I still have a horse under me, to avoid chafing. I imagine Bryce, and William and Warren, and Simon — anyone, really — laughing at my strange walk. I, however, am not finding it amusing. At least it's a dry, sunny day so I don't have to slip and slide over muddy paths. That would be painful.

I'm also glad the day is clear so I can keep a wary watch on the other side of Hadrian's Wall in case any wild Scots attack me unaware. I pass the rubble remains of Roman settlements and it's not long before I reach the sprawling ruins of Housesteads Fort. It was almost as big as our village and makes me wonder what the Roman soldiers were like over a thousand years ago and how different they were from us today.

I know one way we're all the same, though, and I head to the far corner of the fort ruins to see . . . the latrines! I smile when I think of Nigel, and I can picture exactly how the soldiers would've sat around the huge vault with its stone channels that flushed water in and waste out. I peer down into the latrine to see how deep it is and a glinting catches my eye. Awkwardly, I lower myself into the latrine, which hasn't been used for centuries, so it doesn't even smell. In the corner I look to see what caused the shining, and it takes me a moment to find it. Aha! It's a coin, but not like any coin I've ever seen. Although it's worn, I can make out a man's head on one side and what looks like someone sitting on a rock on the other side. There aren't any letters, or they've all worn off, but I think the coin is Roman! I put it in my pouch along with the medal from Sir Geoffrey.

I have to find some rocks that stick out from the wall before I can boost myself high enough to grab the edge of the giant privy and crawl out. The clinking of the coin against Sir Geoffrey's medal makes it worth it, especially since I don't have any real money anymore. I sit on the edge of the latrine to catch my breath and realize that I haven't used my money to buy food for Hugh or me. The fish I bought went to stave off Simon's wrath, and the last coin saved Henry's knife. I wonder now what I was thinking — that I'd just go shopping for food and then go next door to the battlefield?

Thinking of food gets my belly rumbling, so I walk to the woods nearby in search of game. I want to stay in sight of Housesteads in case Sir Geoffrey comes, hopefully with Hugh! I'm so heartened by that thought that I start to sing. *There's no one around so I won't hurt anyone's ears*, I think to myself, smiling, because that's what Hugh says about my singing. The wildlife must hear me coming, though, because I see nothing but a few squirrels, and they're quick, quicker than I am with my bow. I start practicing my archery against a birch because, obviously, I need to. It feels good to nock-mark-draw-loose over and over, letting the arrows fly until I hit a sweet rhythm.

As the sun goes down, my belly reminds me of my hunger, so I scrounge until I find some apples on the ground. They're mostly rotten but there are good bits, and I wolf those down. I hurry back to the fort to see if anyone is coming.

Before long, I see a group of riders! I'm about to start jumping to get their attention when I see the lion rampant on their flag and dive behind a rock. It's the Scottish Army! Or at least half a dozen of them. And they're riding straight for me! I can't stay behind this rock because it only gives me protection from one side. I'm on a barren hill in plain sight.

Ockham's razor! Think! What's the most obvious answer, the only place where I can't be seen on this wide-open hill? The latrine! I crawl to the corner of the fort and drop myself in the ancient privy even as I hear the horses' hooves and the men's voices. Please, God, let them not have seen me!

I push my back against the wall of the latrine and hope the overhang will hide me well enough now that it's dusk. In my head, I thank Father for the millionth time that he returned those stupid pointed shoes, which would now be sticking out so much they'd give me away. If I live to see Father again, I'll thank him to his face.

I hold my breath as I hear the horses' hooves and the jangling of swords and pots and who knows what else on the saddles. The men dismount and their voices get louder because — St. Jerome's bones! — they're heading this way.

"He's barely more than a lad and he puts many a man at risk in his rash judgment and haste!" a gruff voice bellows, and I shrink back even more, imagining how large he must be.

"Aye, many a man who has family and farm to care for," another man adds.

There are grunts of agreement and I wonder who they're talking about.

"But," a younger voice says, "he was pressured to by the king of France. Do ye not think it's wise to keep France as a friend? What about the Auld Alliance?"

Another man snorts. "The Auld Alliance! I dinnae see France rushing to our aid, so why should we rush to theirs? Nay, the timing was no' right for this type of attack."

"Why not?"

"Daft boy!" the gruff voice says. "Do you truly think that King Edward would take his whole army to France? Say what you will about him, but the man is no fool. Would he leave no men behind to defend his own kingdom? Of course not. England may be weaker but how weak? Weak enough for us to take over? I think not."

I realize that they're talking about their King David and his ill-reasoned decision to attack England. The gruff-voiced man is right about that! From what they say next, I know that this is an advance team and that King David intends to lay waste all the way down to the border and across it.

"After tomorrow's battle," the gruff voice says, "they can come south using this route. I dinnae see any English soldiers here. They're likely waiting at Durham."

"I wish we'd taken out more of their longbows," a whiny voice says. "They're lethal. I'm glad I got one of their archers, at least."

There's a roar of laughter. "Aye," the gruff voice says, "a lad who was younger than Rory here."

"With long fair hair like a maid!" the young voice says.

I fight to keep the bitter bile in my stomach from coming up. A longbow man who was a boy with long fair hair? Could it be Hugh? I pray to Our Maker and all the saints that it was not Hugh.

"A tall, good-looking lad, though," a man says. "There's a girl in love with him back home and she'll be heartbroken."

I think of Bess as several soldiers laugh until a sharper voice cuts in. "Poor lad kept looking at the man beside him, his father, I'll wager."

His father? It must be Hugh, then. My legs almost buckle. I want to wail. I want to scream. I no longer care what they do to me. They killed my best friend! How much worse could they do? I reach behind me for my bow. I can hit one of them before they get me. I hope I hit Hugh's killer, but if not at least I'll cut down one pagan!

"It's not my fault the lad had no skill as an archer," the whiny voice says, and I freeze. "He could barely hold the bow, never mind shoot an arrow. They should never have let him on the battlefield."

It wasn't Hugh! I praise God even as I ask Him to care

for the family and girlfriend of the boy who was shot. I can't keep a sigh of relief from escaping my lips, but the soldiers don't hear for all their jeering at the whiny-voiced man.

"Shall we camp here for the night?" a soldier asks.

Please, no! I can't stand like this all night, stiff as a statue, my back pressed against the stone wall.

"What?" the gruff voice says. "On the top of a hill where everyone can see us?"

"Not if we're lying low among the ruins."

"Ruins, they are, and not much of anything to hide us. Nay, we must move on."

There are groans and grumblings but the gruff-voiced man seems to be their leader. "What are you doing?" I hear him say.

A man laughs. "These were the latrines. I'm going to relieve myself!"

I push my back against the wall and turn my head so my cheek is pressed against the stone and clench my eyes and lips tight shut as the piss rains down. Fortunately, I am spared from both piss and capture, as the soldiers mount their horses and ride south.

When I'm sure they're far away, I climb out of the latrine. I look down the hill where they rode off, taking them into England and everything familiar to me — my village, my family, my home. I turn and gaze north across Hadrian's Wall, into the unknown, darkening woods, remembering the map of Scotland at Lanercost Priory. With heart pounding and legs trembling, I pick my way over Housesteads ruins and stare at Hadrian's Wall.

I climb to the top of the wall and take a deep breath. I pray to be noble like Henry and smart like Nigel and brave like Sir Geoffrey, and Hugh, wherever he is. As I crawl across, I lose my footing and tumble over the other side, scraping my cheek on the stone and drawing blood. A cry escapes my lips, followed by an eerie silence, and I feel exposed, as if the whole world knows I don't belong here.

chapter the twenty-fourth

In Which I See My First Battle

ONCE MORE I'M GRATEFUL TO NIGEL AND WHAT HE taught me because I use his loci trick to remember my route through these pagan Scottish woods so I can find my way out again. I pass a gall on an oak that looks like Father Fraud's fat face. That represents the church, at the south end of our village. The tree roots that resemble arrows, pointing north, are for my home and shop at the north end of our village. The three pale rocks huddled together like sheep stand for the field of sheep where I pretended to be a shepherd my first day on the road.

Before it's completely dark, I stop and make camp by a stream. I manage to kill two rabbits. The practicing I did in the woods must've helped my aim. One rabbit is very small but the other is larger. It's good I got two because the scrawny one has little meat. I almost wish I hadn't shot the small one. His scared eyes make me think of the boy those soldiers talked about, the one I thought was Hugh, until they said he wasn't a skilled archer. I wonder how the boy felt at that last moment before he was shot. I think about how Hugh gives a blessing to the creatures he kills, thanking them for providing him sustenance, which I always thought strange. I've never before felt the need to say a prayer like that, but I do now.

I make a fire and cook the rabbits, skewering them on sticks. The light and heat give me some comfort. I'm not much worried about being seen because soldiers will be gathered north of here for tomorrow's battle. I'll rise early to find the fight.

But first, I eat both rabbits because I'm famished, sucking the skewers when I'm done. I don't even feel sick from all that meat, only gluttonous, but I don't care. I need to be fortified because tomorrow I'll take part in my first battle. For God and country.

I'm awakened early by a noise that's like the entire Scottish army invading my camp. I grab my bow, my eyes still blurry, and dive behind a tree. I come face-to-face with a squirrel that's as frozen as I am, but only for a moment. He bounds off, crashing through the dead leaves, and I wonder how a creature so small can make so much noise.

Still, I'm grateful to be up early as I hurry northward to find the battle, even following a ready-made path through the woods at one point. I wonder if the path is leading me the right way. By the sun, I know it's north.

By midmorning I hear men's voices and the clashing of swords! I grab my bow and load an arrow. Following the sound, I climb a steep wooded hill, and when I reach the top I see the glorious battlefield. Panting, I stand there, mesmerized.

Below me, English longbowmen are stationed in groups around the field and I hear constant shouts of "Nock, mark, draw, loose! Nock, mark, draw, loose!" as they let loose volley after volley of arrows. The arrows hit their targets, even finding men with no armor, not even padding, so the arrows cut into their bodies, sometimes going through their chests and sticking out their backs, or skewering arms or legs like the rabbit on my stick. I am frozen.

"Nock, mark, draw, loose! Nock, mark, draw, loose!"

Men fall with each volley, amid shouts and groans, horses twisting and turning, swords clashing against shields, against other swords, against men.

"Nock, mark, draw, loose! Nock, mark, draw, loose!"

More arrows. Men pierced with arrows bleed around their wounds or sometimes out of their mouths. But sword fighting is even worse. Men slashed with swords spew blood from their wounds, so that clothes and faces and earth and air are sprayed with the life — no, the death — of men. Worst of all are the pickaxes that chop up men like animals in an agonizingly slow way that leaves men screaming for mercy, and yet there is none.

"Nock, mark, draw, loose! Nock, mark, draw, loose!"

My stomach and face are twisted into a knot. I'm shaking, yet I can't stop watching, though I've seen enough. I can't make myself go onto the battlefield. I don't know if I could even hold my bow steady, never mind hit a target. And what target? A man's chest? So I can watch him die like the rest of these men? I clutch my pouch with Sir Geoffrey's medal, but I wonder if God Himself could save anyone from this hell.

I stand there, hearing men scream in pain as they are cut down by arrow, sword, and ax. I don't even know which side is which, since it looks like a mass of bodies and blood. My bow hand grows stiff, as I stand at the edge of the woods, cowering against a tree.

I'm relieved when I finally see Sir Geoffrey and Lightning on the battlefield. I even start to wave, although I don't expect him to wave back. He doesn't notice me, but seeing him gives me strength. He said I was brave, brave enough to be a knight like him. I take a deep breath, force the bile back down in my stomach, and start down the hill to the battle.

But while I'm making my descent, Sir Geoffrey is struck down, an arrow piercing his neck, and he falls from his mount. Lightning notices right away, turning in confusion, but there's nothing he can do. We both watch in horror as the Scottish savages heave swords and axes at Sir Geoffrey's writhing body.

Suddenly, my own body lurches violently and I crawl into the underbrush, where I retch, my body convulsing over and over as if I, too, am being torn apart. I can see the chunks of rabbit in my vomit and I think of the poor defenseless rabbit that had no weapon at all against mine, and I retch some more.

I lie there, sick and stunned, for I don't know how long. When I realize that the fighting noises have died down,

I look over at the battlefield toward Sir Geoffrey's body. Englishmen are burying him, or the parts of him that are left. When they're finished and gallop off, heading south, I make my way over to the burial mound.

Kneeling by his makeshift grave, I think of how Sir Geoffrey wanted nothing more than to be a monk and instead he ended up here. *Destiny,* he said. He called it both a friend and a curse. I think it's only a curse. Destiny dictates that Hugh remains a peasant though he's brave and strong and at fifteen could be a squire, if he'd been born a noble. Destiny is what makes Henry a street boy, though he's as good as any noble. Destiny is what makes me puny and useless. I look down at the grave. If this is what destiny brings, I don't want any part of it.

I pull out the medal from Sir Geoffrey and am about to place it on his burial mound when I hear a voice behind me.

"What is that, boy?"

I whirl around to face a leper and stagger to my feet so I can keep five steps away from him. He has several leather pouches slung over his shoulder and two swords in his belt. He's scavenging the corpses!

"How dare you?" I scream at him. "Stealing from brave soldiers?"

"Calm down, boy. It's not as if I can work in a field or learn a trade. What would you have me do? I'm cast out yet I'm still a man, struggling to survive."

"Well, there's nothing here for you!" I yell at him, I'm so enraged.

"Except that coin," he says, staring at my hand.

I grab my bow and load an arrow so quickly I surprise even myself. The leper is truly surprised. He backs away, then turns to hobble off as fast as he can, calling over his shoulder, "How else am I to care for myself? Have mercy!"

I don't shoot him but I feel no mercy.

Turning back to Sir Geoffrey's grave, I decide to scribe something instead, since the medal will likely be stolen.

I use my finger to scratch into the cold earth, choosing something from the Bible since he wanted to be a monk:

Thou shalt not kill.
Godspeed, Sir Geoffrey, valiant knight and friend.

My throat is raw as I leave Sir Geoffrey and head south. God's eyes help me find Hugh — and God's heart help me find him alive.

chapter the twenty-fifth

In Which I Have an Unexpected Encounter

I AM COLD AND WEAK AND MISERABLE. I WALK AS IF IN A trance. I reach the place where I set my fire and cooked the rabbits, the last time I used my bow, and I curse myself for not using my bow on the battlefield. Could I have saved Sir Geoffrey? If I'm a master archer, I should have. Why didn't I?

If it weren't for practically stumbling over the rocks that look like sheep, the tree roots that look like arrows, I'd be lost. I come to a stream and walk right through it instead of looking for a better place to cross. When I look down at the water and see my reflection, it's shaking as if shivering from fright. It doesn't look like a master archer. It looks like a small, scared boy. Useless. And that's how I feel.

Without stopping, I walk on. I can't eat, the battle scene playing over and over in my head. It's growing darker and colder and the rain begins. I'm dangerously close to crying, again. I can't even tell if the wetness on my face is rain or tears.

But I continue to step one foot in front of the other, putting distance between myself and the field of blood, looking for Hugh. I come to Hadrian's Wall and cross back into England. I can't believe that just yesterday I was here, finding trinkets and shooting trees, playing like a child when there was war and killing close by. I don't feel like playing anymore.

When it's completely dark, I tread carefully, both because I keep tripping on the wet leaves and mud and because I don't want to come upon the wrong encampment. Yesterday, at Hadrian's Wall, the worst I feared from a Scottish soldier was his piss. Today, I know better. A pagan Scot will not think twice to cleave in two a man, a boy, a knight, a friend. I shudder, thinking of both Sir Geoffrey and Hugh as I walk through the night.

A small campfire is ahead, and the sounds of men talking and eating. If they're English soldiers, I want to make myself known and sit with them, telling them what I've seen, sharing the horrors of war. I creep closer and peek through the trees, in case they're Scots. But their accents are too familiar. So are the smells of food, and I'm about to walk into their camp when a voice stops me.

"Don't aim for their padding, you fool. Cut an arm off! That'll stop their blow!"

"Right!" says another. "Or torture him so much he'll commit suicide and take himself to hell."

There's much laughter as more men join in, discussing the best forms of mutilation. I can't believe my ears. They're Englishmen but they talk like pagans!

I move on. After some time, I hear a howling and then grunting, and I force myself to believe it's wolves because I'd rather be torn to shreds by God's creatures than by pagan Scots.

I remember to arm myself, my arrow ready to fly once I can pinpoint where the commotion comes from. I can see almost nothing and am as likely to hit a tree or bush as the grunting beast. I take a step forward and a twig snaps under my foot.

That's when I hear a voice and realize it's not animal but man — no, two men.

"Whist!" a voice says.

"I dinnae think —" the second voice says, definitely a Scot!

"Whist!" the first one commands again.

There's a growling cry and the breaking of branches as something moves toward me. The pagans are charging at me!

I draw back my bow and shoot an arrow.

It hits its mark because I hear a cry of pain.

"Stay back!" I command. "I'll kill you both!"

"No — A-A —" One man struggles to speak.

I don't know what he says, nor where the other man is. "I warn you! Stay back!" And I load my next arrow.

"Adrian?" The voice is weak and soft and pained, barely able to breathe. But I know that voice. It's Hugh's.

God's heart! I've shot my best friend!

chapter the twenty-sixth

In Which I Find Out about Hugh

"HUGH!" I CRY, SHRILLY.

There's no answer.

I try to reach him but trip in the darkness, falling over a groaning body. I shake him, yell at him, try to pull him up, at least lift his head and finally realize he's facedown. "Hugh!" I scream.

"Stop!" Hugh cries, but not from this body, rather behind me.

I jump up, backing away from the body, falling in the mud. "Where are you? Are you shot?"

"Here. No. Your arrow missed us both."

"What's going on? Who's . . . this?"

"A fallen soldier."

My mind finally catches up with what's happening. There were two men. And one of them was a Scot. "A fallen . . . Scottish soldier?"

There's no answer.

I still can't see Hugh. Again, I ask, "What's going on?"

Hugh's voice is weak, exhausted. "What are you doing here, Adrian?"

"I came to find you, to help you."

"But I —"

"I know you said not to, but —"

"What about your father?"

I shrug, although I know he can't see me in the dark.

"What about Bess?"

"She's fine."

The man on the ground groans and I feel Hugh brush past me to kneel at his side. I simply stare.

"We need to get him back to my camp."

"Hugh! He's the enemy. Let's get out of here. Fast!"

"No!" The loudness of his voice surprises me.

I think of the English camp I just passed. "Do you know what our own soldiers will do to us if we help him?"

"I know," Hugh says in such a dark voice that I wouldn't know it was Hugh if I weren't already convinced of it.

"Why are you doing this?" I whisper.

"He was stopping his own soldiers from killing an English boy and was hit by their ax on the head and, here, on the shoulder." I can't see in the dark but I know Hugh is examining him. "Then, behind him, an English soldier shot an arrow in his arm." Hugh's voice cracks. "He was just trying to save the boy. We have to get him to my camp."

I hesitate, stalling for time. "Your camp? You have a camp?"

"Yes. It's not much, just a place for a fire and branches to cover me from the rain, but there's more shelter than here."

"You're alone? Why aren't you with the other soldiers?"

"They don't accept me as one of their own. Nor I, they," he mutters, or at least it sounds like that's what he says. "I'm still looking for Father. Once I find him, I'll join the men of our village."

I'm glad Hugh can't see me shudder in the dark. From what I've seen today — all those men killed — Hugh may no longer have a father.

"You said you came to help me," Hugh says, his voice worn out.

"Yes, but not for . . . this!"

"Please, Adam?"

Why do I always weaken when he calls me his dead brother's name?

With difficulty, we drag the man for what seems like forever. Several times I almost ask Hugh how far his stupid camp is and can't we stop, but I don't want to sound weak and sniveling, so I keep going. Mostly I stay quiet because I don't want to be caught by any of our countrymen.

I know because of his training from Grandmother that Hugh can't just let the man die. And maybe my friend's mind is confused by the horrors of groaning, dying men. My brain is a bit addlepated, too. It must be, because I'm helping him. But when we finally reach Hugh's camp and he starts a fire, I try to reason with him.

"If he's badly wounded, maybe you should just kill him."

"What? But . . . he's not even on the battlefield."

I think about what the Scots did to Sir Geoffrey. "He's the enemy."

"I'm not truly a soldier."

"But it's a mercy killing if he's going to die anyway."

Hugh stares at the man. "I believe I can cure him."

I stare at Hugh. "Do you know what you're saying? He's a wild Scot!"

"Does he look wild to you?"

I look down at the man. "Well, no, but that may be because he's wounded."

Hugh sighs, opening his medicine pouch. "Or because he's an ordinary man like our own fathers." Hugh starts toward him. The man lets out a cry and his arm shoots up, and we both back up a step. Though the arm falls back to earth again, I can't help but notice how large the hand is. I can't take my eyes off it. The man is a monster. And he's muttering unearthly, frightening sounds.

It's only when Hugh moves toward the monster that I stop my frozen staring.

"Hugh! What are you doing?"

Hugh is already kneeling by the man. He hesitates for just a moment, but continues taking herbs out of his bag.

I cover him with my bow, shakily. I pray that the monster is wounded enough to be incapacitated because I'm shaking so much I couldn't hit a creature the size of Bessie even if it were right in front of me. The only reason I don't shoot is that I'm just as likely to hit Hugh as I am to hit the Scot.

"I think you can put that down," Hugh says. "I need your help."

When I draw closer, I see not only how large he is, but also his hair color. "Look how red his hair is!"

Hugh doesn't answer, but keeps working on him.

"Uncle says the redder the hair, the wilder the Scot."

Hugh snorts. "Your uncle is an ale-head."

That I can't argue. "Still, it doesn't mean that everything Uncle says is wrong."

"How many Scots does he know?"

"What difference does that make?"

"How many?" Hugh insists, his voice raspy.

"None."

"I know one," Hugh says, turning to look up at me, "and I've never seen a braver man."

Maybe this Scot wasn't brave to try to save an enemy boy in the middle of battle. Maybe he's an addlepate, and I tell Hugh that. "Addlepate and pagan is not a safe combination."

"It's safe because he didn't want to kill a boy our age, certainly not as young as you. You don't need to be scared of him."

"I'm not scared!"

"That's what it sounds like to me."

"Well, maybe you need a poultice for your ears because you're not hearing right!"

"Fine, then help me. Put your hand on his wound."

I look down at the soldier and see the blood oozing through the slash in his leather armor.

"Put your hand on the cut while I make a poultice!"

I see the man's chest rise and fall, and hear his moans and, maybe because it's dark, I can't see the full paganness, and I pretend he could be any man from our village, so I do what Hugh says, holding my hand over the bloody gash. But I'm not happy about it, and my stomach is churning. I thought I'd have pagan blood on my hands from killing one, not by trying to heal him. I thought I'd prove to everyone that I'm not the one they should fear, but the pagan Scots, and that I'd save them from the pagans. I feel like a traitor to Sir Geoffrey. I want to retch.

Hugh works on the Scot for what seems like an hour. My friend has always been serious about herbs, but never quite like this. Something has come over Hugh and it's a frightening thing. He seems to have forgotten which end of the arrow is the point and which is the goose feather. Yet he seems possessed and I dare not cross him.

After we move the soldier closer to the fire, the rain that had died down starts again and the wind picks up.

Hugh eyes my cloak. "May I borrow that to cover him?"

"What?"

"He's ill. He's shivering. I need —"

"No!" I'm sure my mother wouldn't want her cloak used in such a way.

After Hugh builds a lean-to of branches to protect the fire so it won't go out, he shields the man from the wind with his own body. I sit huddled against the trunk of a tree, trying to stay warm and dry but feeling wretched, as much from my selfish behavior as from the rain.

It's not the reunion I pictured. Maybe Hugh and I have both seen too much. The horrible death of Sir Geoffrey is enough to make me never want to see a Scottish soldier again, never mind heal him. I know Hugh is a healer at heart. He has knowledge and patience like Nigel. He's noble like Henry and Sir Geoffrey. He's my best friend. But right now, I can't even stand to look at him.

chapter the twenty-seventh

In Which I Decide Hugh Is an Addlepated Fool

BY THE LIGHT OF DAY, I CAN SEE THE PAGAN-NESS IN THE soldier. What I thought was dirt on his face is a grizzly beard. His shirt and leggings are coarse and ripped. His hands and feet are the size of a bear's. The man even smells foul.

Hugh is already tending the fire and cooking something over it. My mouth waters since I didn't eat at all yesterday.

I stretch and walk over to the fire. "What are you making?"

"A poultice for him," Hugh says, nodding his head toward the soldier.

"The one pot we have for cooking and you're using it for treating the enemy's wounds?"

Hugh looks at me darkly and rises from the fire. "I'm going to find garlic," he says, grabbing his pouch and striding off into the woods.

I feel angry and resentful, and also starving. I think about calling some choice words after him, but he's already disappeared. When I hear an unearthly noise behind me, I turn and see the large pagan soldier sitting up and growling like a beast, his piercing blue eyes glaring at me as if I'm the cause of his injuries.

All I feel now is fear. He's struggling to his feet, keeping his eyes on me. He means to hurt me! My bow is over where I slept, behind him. A quick glance around the camp shows me a few sticks and tiny acorns. Even David couldn't fight this Goliath with acorns. There's not even boiling water in the pot to throw at him. It's Hugh's soothing poultice. If I pitch it at him it might only serve to heal him.

My only option is to run, which I do, fast. I want to catch up with Hugh but after only a few dozen paces I realize I have no idea which way he went. I jump behind a tree to give myself a moment to think. Panting, I peek around to see how close the soldier is.

I don't see him at first. And then I notice the lump on the ground, about where he was sleeping. And he's silent.

Now I look around quickly to see if Hugh is anywhere nearby, possibly laughing at my hiding from a wounded soldier who is collapsed in a heap at our camp. I straighten myself up and try to put on an air of dignity. After all, I was only acting wisely. He might've been dangerous. He still could be. I tread slowly and carefully back to our camp, never taking my eyes off the soldier lump.

As I draw close, I hear the soldier muttering something. "Mee-ree, Ku-hin."

The second part sounds like "cut him" and the first must

be a pagan battle cry! Maybe he was calling for reinforcements to come and cut, or kill, his enemy!

Moments later, I hear Hugh returning, and I'm silently grateful that I'm back in camp and not behind that tree.

Hugh drops his pouch and runs to the soldier, kneeling next to him. "What happened?"

"He made some pagan battle cries — I think he was trying to come after me — and then he collapsed."

Hugh gently pulls the giant onto his back, straightening out his arms and legs. "He was probably wanting help."

"I don't know about that. He was saying things that sounded more like an attack." I try to imitate the words, including the ones sounding like "cut him."

Hugh only shrugs, still tending the man. "Maybe it's names of his family."

"What? Pagans call out the names of their family when attacking in battle?"

Hugh looks up at me. "He's not attacking in battle. He's a sick, wounded man, lying in pain, looking for comfort. Grandmother says the most frequent utterances of the wounded and sick are the names of their loved ones."

"MEE-ree? Who is MEE-ree, then?"

"Mary? Marie? Mairi? His wife?"

"He didn't say 'Ma-ry.' He said 'MEE-ree.'"

"He's a Scot. Their speech is somewhat different."

"And 'cut him'? What name would that be?"

Hugh smirks at me. "Maybe you misheard and it's you who needs a poultice for your ears."

I snort.

"Adrian, they call their babies 'bairns' and name their bread 'bannock.' Haven't you heard these terms before?"

"I've heard of Bannock*burn* before." I glare at him, reminding him of the battle in our grandparents' time when Robert the Bruce attacked and defeated the English, ending in Scottish independence.

He is clearly uncomfortable with my reminding him of that. After all, his own grandmother's brother was killed in that battle. Grandmother has no love in her heart for the Scots and would likely think Hugh a traitor for protecting one.

But Hugh says nothing, taking the poultice from the fire and pulling garlic out of his pouch. The way he dresses the man's wounds both fascinates and annoys me. It's as if he doesn't see the face of his patient, only the wound that needs treating. He's both scientist and healer. His eyes are sharp, all-seeing, all-knowing, yet his face shows compassion and care, even pain, wincing with his patient. I respect his ability but I'm still angry that he's using it on the enemy.

I slump down, partly from defeat and partly because I'm famished. When I see Hugh take hawthorn berries out of his pouch, mash them into a mush, and try to get the man to eat them, I shake with rage.

"Bad enough we're sheltering and healing the enemy, but you want to give him our only food? What's wrong with you, Hugh Stout?"

Hugh's eyes widen. "I'm simply doing what's necessary for the herbs to work. Rest, warmth, and sustenance." He adds, "You may have some berries, too," but I sense reluctance, as if he'd rather I leave them for the Scot.

He hands me the pot, now empty. "I'm done with this. Why don't you fill it with water? There's a stream straight back that way." He points behind me. "Also, if you'd like to bring us a rabbit or a squirrel, we could have a real meal."

"All of us, you mean?"

"He won't eat much," Hugh answers, "but a little broth would do him good."

I grab the pot and my bow and storm into the woods. I swear, loudly, that I will eat heath pea, that bitter vetch, to stave my hunger for several more days before I'll kill a rabbit and give the enemy some broth.

But hard as I search, heath pea doesn't exist in this wretched place. It's not my fault. I'm craving food so much I kill several squirrels.

I feel better after eating. I don't hate the Scot or Hugh so much, although I still don't like them. I rapidly lose even that goodwill when Hugh tells me he's going to find the battle and look for his father, and has the nerve to say that I must look after the soldier.

"Me? I'm supposed to be going into battle with you!" In truth, after seeing what battle is like, I'm in no rush to go back. But I don't want to stay with this pagan, either.

"Adrian, I really want you to go home, but we'll talk about that when I get back. If you want to do something useful, go hunt more food. We could use that. But, please, if you leave him, cover him with leaves so no one finds him."

When Hugh is gone I spend much time kicking the acorns around camp, not caring if I hit the pagan, wishing he were a pig who would eat the acorns then move on to the next batch and leave us alone. Eventually, I go out hunting, after sprinkling a few leaves on the stupid pagan.

When I return with squirrels, I see that the soldier hasn't moved. I put my catch up in the branches to keep it away from scavenging animals. When I turn around I notice for the first time that the man has a pouch around his waist. What does a pagan carry with him into battle? I have to know.

I walk stealthily to the soldier, whose breath is even, and he appears fast asleep. Still, I stand next to him for a while staring at the buckle on his pouch before kneeling silently at his side. With trembling hands, I reach out and begin to unbuckle his pouch. It takes me ten times longer than usual because I don't want to give the pagan a hint of what I'm doing.

I have it almost open when the breath catches in his throat and he takes several gulps, his head turning toward me, and I dare not move my hands from the buckle lest I make a sound. I stay still as a rabbit in plain view, hoping not to be seen.

When his breathing evens out I start, very carefully, removing the items from his pouch. There are some hard, flat oaten loaves, and I'm angry that we are feeding him when he could be feeding us! There's a leather flask that I open and sniff and nearly fall over at the acrid smell that burns my nose. It's some kind of sour ale. I put it on the ground next to the hard bread. Next, I pull out a thin whistle with six holes. What, is he a minstrel? I give it a soft blow and it squeaks. I freeze but the soldier doesn't move. There's also a crudely carved stick of wood that may be a weapon or, more likely, some pagan ritual item. I hold on to it lest he try to use it against us.

The best find by far is a knife that may be short, but is thin and shiny and lethal. The grip feels good in my hand. It'll be better than mine for skinning the squirrels. I shudder at what else this knife might have skinned.

But I have no time to think of that because a huge hand grabs my wrist like a vise. "That's my dirk!"

chapter the twenty-eighth

In Which I Wonder If I'm the Addlepated Fool

I DON'T KNOW HOW LONG WE FREEZE THAT WAY — THE Scot holding my wrist and I holding his knife — while we stare at each other. I only know that at some point Hugh appears. The Scot loosens his grip on my wrist but I hold tight to the knife.

"What is going on?" Hugh says.

Neither the Scot nor I answer.

Hugh crouches beside us and says again, "What's going on?" sounding accusatory while he looks at me — *me!* — instead of the Scot.

I look at the ground and see the flask and oaten cakes. "Look! He has food. And" — I glare at Hugh — "a knife. I'll hold on to this."

"What else do you have there?" Hugh asks, pointing at the wooden carving.

"That," the man says in a thick Scottish accent, "is from my son . . . Colyne."

Hugh looks at me as if to say, *I told you he was talking about his family.*

But we both say nothing and continue to glare at each other.

"He" — the man stops, cringing in pain — "made it for me himself, the wee bairn. It's a —" He stops again, gasping and crying out this time.

"Stay still," Hugh says, kneeling over him.

I clutch the Scot's knife, glad it's in my hand and not his.

"You're wounded," Hugh says, "and shouldn't be talking."

"Aye," the man breathes, closing his eyes, and for a moment I think he's dead. I even hope that he is.

But Hugh isn't reacting so he must still be alive. When I see the man's chest moving, I know he's breathing.

Finally, Hugh stands and turns to me, his face in a frown, which deepens as he sees me clutching the wooden carving. "Why are you so scared of him and his things?" he hisses. "It's simply a carving from his son."

"If we can believe what he says," I say.

Hugh shakes his head, muttering about St. Someone's bones, and it startles me because he never curses and because I'm reminded that I still have Bess's St. Aldegundis token that I should've given him already. I still grip the knife in one hand but put down the boy's carving and use my other hand to undo the medal from my tunic. At that moment, I realize that the boy, Colyne, was simply giving his father what Bess gives Hugh: a remembrance, and hopefully a talisman of safety.

I hand the token to Hugh. "Bess wanted me to give this to you."

Hugh says nothing, slowly taking the medal and shaking his head at me.

I'm suddenly feeling very small and not full of fire and venom.

The Scot speaks weakly. "Don't be angry with your friend, laddie. He's only trying to take care of you."

I turn on the soldier. "And how is helping *you* taking care of me?" I snap.

The soldier opens his eyes and looks at me. "I was speaking to the other laddie. You took my knife to protect him, to keep you both safe." He closes his eyes again and groans, his voice barely audible. "I understand that. So should he."

I steal a glance at Hugh, who is looking at the ground, just as when Grandmother chastises him. I don't know how to feel, grateful to the enemy soldier for standing up for me and trying to have Hugh see reason? Or angry that he dare take my side on anything?

It's quiet except for the ragged breathing of the soldier.

Hugh finally breaks the silence. "I'm Hugh Stout of Ashcroft, near Penrith, and this" — he nods toward me — "is my friend Adri —"

"The Badger," I say firmly, though Hugh's face scrunches in confusion.

I lean toward him and hiss, "You shouldn't tell the enemy our real names."

He simply shakes his head at me and turns back to the Scot.

"I'm Donald Stewart of Linton." The soldier takes another breath, his eyes now open. "I'm grateful to you lads for my very life."

"It wasn't me," I say defensively. "It was all Hugh's doing."

"Hugh, lad" — Donald stops to take a labored breath — "why did you save me?"

"Because you could've killed that boy on the battlefield and you didn't. You risked your life picking him up and carrying him to safety. And you were shot while doing so." Hugh stares at him. "Why did you do that?"

Donald begins to chuckle but stops, gasping with pain. Tears run out of his eyes but he ignores them. "I'm a wee bit of a fool, I am. The lad's face reminded me of my son's. I wanted him to go home, be safe." He tries to turn his head to look at us better. "Why are you laddies here? You should be home and safe as well." He looks so concerned for us, even though he's the one injured, that I feel my first pang of conscience that he may not be a brutal pagan.

Hugh's eyes are downcast. "I'm looking for my father." His voice drops to a whisper. "He needs me." When Hugh turns his head to me, his voice is suddenly sharp. "I'd like to hear Adrian's answer."

"I came to help you!" I say, sounding far too much like a petulant child. "I —" I want to tell him of all that I've been through — a near flood and losing my food, surviving the streets of Carlisle, trying to bring a wicked prior to justice, the death of Sir Geoffrey — but I know it will all pale compared to the battlefield, and battle is something I've only seen and not been through. I throw the soldier's knife on the ground and storm off into the woods. Hugh does nothing to call me back.

I sit down on the bank of the stream, throwing stones in the water for a long time before Hugh sits down beside me.

He doesn't look at me but says, "I'm sorry I've been so angry with you. I just don't want you here."

"Thanks," I say, hoping he hears my sarcasm.

He sighs. "I mean, I've seen things I don't want you — or anyone — to see. I want you to go back."

"I can't go back." I look at Hugh. "It's too late. I've already seen things I wish I hadn't." His eyes are sad but I want more than sympathy. I want respect.

My words tumble out. "A knight — Sir Geoffrey de Molay — and I were trying to expose the embezzlement of the prior at Lanercost, who was cheating the villagers for his own wealth."

Hugh's eyes widen because we both know that this is a man's business, and not something either of us has done. Until now.

I go on. "I stole a scroll, proof of the crime, and rode with Sir Geoffrey to the point at Hadrian's Wall, where he went north and I went to Housesteads Fort, to meet the soldiers as they came south. But when I spied on some Scottish soldiers, I heard about the battle — and someone I thought might be you. I decided to go over Hadrian's Wall myself."

Hugh looks even more amazed, shaking his head, not in denial or reprimand, but in awe. And respect. I'm satisfied now but I still tell him of Sir Geoffrey's death. And it dawns on me, for the first time, that the prior may not be brought to justice because who knows what happened to the scroll? That was the only proof we had! I feel, again, like I've let Sir Geoffrey down. He wanted the prior to be caught; now he'll be free.

Hugh tries to reassure me, telling me that his fellow soldiers will have taken his horse and saddlebags into their protection, and when they see he was a free lance for the bishop of Durham, they'll deliver the scroll safely. I pray that's true.

Hugh goes on to share the many battle scenes he has witnessed. The deaths sound much like those I saw in Sir Geoffrey's battle. I feel ill again. We both stare at the stream for a long time.

Finally, Hugh asks, "How did you spy on the soldiers at Hadrian's Wall?"

I can't help but smirk. "I hid in the latrines." When I tell him the story, we both laugh.

After our laughter dies, Hugh says, "I know you don't agree with saving Donald."

"It's a traitorous act, Hugh."

He nods. "That's another reason it's too much of a risk for you to stay. I'm the one who has done wrong. You haven't. I don't want you punished for my rash act."

I shrug. It wouldn't be the first risk I've taken on this journey. Besides, I'm beginning to wonder if saving Donald was such a rash act after all. "Donald . . . well, he isn't what I thought a pagan Scot would be."

"None of them are. That is," he adds, "some of them are ruthless, but then some of our English are, as well." Hugh turns to look at me and his blue eyes are piercing. "Adrian, when I pulled Donald into the woods, keeping an eye out in case our own English soldiers came after us, I realized for the first time that they were as frightening as the Scots." He shakes his head as if in wonder. "It all depends which side you're on."

"Yes," I say, "and you — and I — are in the middle." I emphasize *and I*. At first, I think Hugh is going to argue because he opens his mouth. No words come out, however, and after a look of resignation settles on his brow, he smiles.

"It's good to have you here . . . *Badger*."

We embrace for the first time since we were mere playmates whose biggest enemies were Good Aunt and the unholy trinity.

chapter the twenty-ninth

In Which I Become a Scot!

THE NEXT MORNING, HUGH COOKS UP SOME BROTH AND tries to get Donald to eat.

"Nay," he replies and, with his good arm, holds out his pouch that I found the food in. "You eat."

I take it, pulling his oaten cakes out of the bag and chomping down on one.

"Not all of them," Hugh hisses. "Save some for him. He'll need that when he goes back to . . ."

He doesn't say "battle," but we both know that's what he means. We look at each other briefly and then look away. Donald might be all right here, as a wounded man, but as a pagan soldier, fighting against Hugh's father . . . that's a very different story.

"You're both growing lads," Donald says. "You need it more than I do."

We're conflicted and say nothing. Hugh finally takes two of the oatcakes and puts the rest back in Donald's bag.

218

"Nay, you have already done so much —" Donald's voice breaks and he continues in a whisper. "How can I thank you?"

"By being a good patient," Hugh says. "Now drink."

Donald knows he's defeated and follows Hugh's orders, but then tries to sit up. "I must leave."

"You're not supposed to move!" Hugh says.

Donald struggles again to get up but it's obvious that he won't even be able to stand, much less walk. "I must" — he takes a ragged breath — "go back to battle. You lads . . . must go home. You'll be in trouble . . . for harboring the enemy."

He's right about that.

Hugh puts down the bowl of broth. "Adrian, I was awake half the night thinking . . . you need to go home."

"What?"

"It's not fair of me to drag you into this."

"It's my choice!" I answer. Even though I'm not sure I can ever go into battle, the last thing I want to do is go back to my village and prove to Father, and everyone, that I can't take care of myself. That I need protecting. That I'm useless.

Donald moans. "You should . . . both go."

I glare at Hugh. "See? You're not supposed to be here, either."

Donald starts coughing so much he is spitting up something, so I look away because I can't stand to watch. Hugh forgets our argument as he turns into a physic again. "I'm worried about leaving him," Hugh mutters, and I see my chance.

"All right," I say, as if I'm disappointed, "I'll stay with him while you go look for your father."

"Really? You can't bear sickness."

I sigh. "I know, but I'll do it."

Hugh gives me a wry smile. "I'd be grateful if you watch him today but I'll be back tonight . . . and tomorrow, you go home." There is no hint of a smile left now.

"Fine," I say. I'll think of another excuse by tonight.

Before he leaves, Hugh fusses over us like a mother. "Here's some broth for him, here's garlic for his wounds, here's mullein for his breathing, and yarrow to stop the bleeding. I brought some extra wood for the fire. If it gets cold —"

"We're not children, Hugh!" I'm feeling foolish enough that he's going off as a man and I'm left here as a child.

"All right, but will you go find food? And don't be too loud or go too far in case any soldiers are around."

I roll my eyes. "You can go now." I don't know why he's so worried. We could see someone coming from a mile away because we're right in the middle of fairly open woods, although we ourselves can shrink down below the bushes.

Hugh nods, taking his bow and quiver from the tree, and heads east to find the battle.

Donald calls after him, "Best of luck, lad, in finding your father." His calling starts a fit of coughing, which he manages to suppress until Hugh is out of earshot.

"Maybe you should use the mullein," I tell him, taking my own bow and quiver from the base of the tree. "I'm getting some food. I'm still starving."

Donald grabs his bag with the oaten cakes and holds it up to me. "Here, eat this" — he stops to cough — "before Hugh returns and tells me off like I'm a naughty wee bairn."

I can't help grinning, but I shake my head. "It's all right. I'll find meat."

It's a bright day and I put soot from the fire under my eyes to cut the glare as I prepare to hunt for food. "If you hear anything," I tell Donald, "throw some dirt on the fire and duck under my cloak." He's already partly under the bushes and well camouflaged, as is Hugh's small pot and supply of herbs. Still, he's lying there helpless. I know that one less Scottish soldier would be good for the English side, but I'd rather it not be Donald. It's hard to hate a man who has a name, and a son.

I start to leave, but Donald's coughing grows worse. It's so bad it's frightening. I try to get him to drink the strongest medicine that Hugh said to save for last. I'm aware of breaking twigs and commotion behind me and I think Hugh has returned, hopefully to check on Donald.

But when I see Donald's eyes widen, I realize it's far too much noise for Hugh alone.

I jump to my feet, turning at the same time, so I can see the enemy.

There are three of them. On horseback. One is a knight in full metal armor. Another man has a huge sword although he's so large himself he hardly needs it. The third man isn't much older than Hugh, probably the knight's squire.

I can tell from the coat of arms on the knight's shield that they're English. My heart sinks. They could just as well be Scots, because any Englishman will be angry that I'm aiding the enemy.

The knight glares down at me, looking fierce in his great helmet with just slits for eyes. Even when he takes it off, he still looks intense in the metal armor and chain mail showing beneath his purple surcoat. "Who are you, boy? And what are you doing?"

My mouth is dry and I can't speak. I don't know what to say, anyway. I try to think fast but my mind won't work! My eyes dart to the other men, both large and strong, with chain mail and leather helmets. All I can think is that they outnumber us, even if Donald were healthy and I were actually a man.

The knight's eyes darken and narrow as he stares at Donald, then me, then spits on the ground. He will hang me for being a traitor!

The knight points at Donald. "See how these pagans have no shame? This I have not seen before, but he drags his young son into battle with him? They are barbarians!"

He thinks I'm Donald's son? His bairn, as Donald says? Ockham's razor! The knight thinks I'm a young Scottish boy! I'm not in danger of being hanged as a traitor! As much as I'm relieved for myself, I see the daggers in the eyes of all three Englishmen as they stare at Donald.

Donald tries to speak, barely able to get out a "Nay — not my bairn."

"What was that?" the knight asks.

"Whist!" I say to Donald, who's struggling to prop himself up on an elbow.

222

Turning back to the knight, I shout, "I am nae a bairn!" in my best imitation of Donald's speech. Out of the corner of my eye, I see Donald flinch.

Quickly — before the soldiers can even react — I grab my bow, load an arrow, and point it at them.

Big Sword laughs so hard he practically falls off his horse.

"My, my, what do we have here?" the knight says. "A miniature King David?"

"Maybe he prefers being Robert the Bruce," Big Sword says. "Look at the war paint under his eyes! See how they teach their pagan babes to fight? How pathetic."

Pathetic? My hands are shaking, from both fear and rage. I almost forget to speak like a Scot. "Dinnae think I cannae use this!"

The knight holds up his hand. "We will not harm you, boy, since you are so young, and we are decent Englishmen." He glares at Donald. "Run along, now. We must take the soldier as a prisoner and . . . we will provide for him."

Does he think I'm a fool? He'll kill Donald on the spot as soon as I leave. "Nay, never!"

Big Sword chuckles. "See how the boy's hands tremble like a leaf!"

"A leaf?" I fairly shout it. "A leaf it is, then!"

The knight's face is as sour as Good Aunt's. "What about a leaf, boy?"

I squint at the large oak behind them, much like the ones on which Hugh and I practice. The leaves move a fair amount in the breeze but I point at a branch with three leaves on the end, looking like a trefoil. "Can ye see yon trefoil?"

The knight keeps his eyes on me but the others look to where my arrow points. When they turn back again, the knight looks at the tree, then looks at me and smiles, his eyebrows raised.

"See that leaf in the middle? I'll split it in two."

"I would like to see that," the knight says, smirking along with Big Sword.

So, focusing my right eye, I nock-mark-draw-loose and, in spite of the breeze, I oblige.

No one is laughing now. The young squire raises his eyebrows at me and I think I even see him smile. While the men are momentarily stunned, I reload my bow and aim at the right eye of the knight.

The knight's face has no trace of a smile now, but rather a grimace. "Perhaps you should turn your bow away, boy, lest there be an accident."

"Perhaps," I say, keeping my accent steady, "ye should turn your horses away from us, Englishman, lest there be such an accident."

Big Sword laughs. "You can't kill us all with one arrow."

The knight does not take his eyes off me but speaks to Big Sword. "Brave words, my friend, when the arrow is not pointed at you. Very well, boy. We will be off."

Big Sword splutters. "But what about the soldier?"

"He'll be dead by morning," the knight replies, putting his helmet back on, turning his courser, and trotting off into the woods.

His squire turns to follow him but looks back at me and nods, like Sir Geoffrey did when he took his leave. There is something kind about this squire. He reminds me a little of Sir Geoffrey and a little of Hugh. I'm glad I don't have to shoot him.

I don't have the same feeling about Big Sword, however, who gives me a threatening leer. "We'll be back, boy," he says. "You've toyed with the wrong man. This knight is vigilant in protecting his territory. He's —" but when I aim my arrow at his evil eyes he turns quickly and practically gallops after the others.

I stand there for several minutes, my bow taut, my arrow ready, lest they decide to turn on me and charge. Finally, I let my aching arms drop and heave a sigh.

I hear a whisper from Donald. "Thank you."

I nod. He doesn't need to thank me. It's not as if I'd let him be killed. "Come on," I say, "we have to leave this place fast."

chapter the thirtieth

In Which We Have a New Camp and a New Camper

I FEEL LIKE I DRAG DONALD FOR HOURS. IN TRUTH, Donald walks a great deal of the way, but leaning on me, and he's heavy as a boulder. He keeps looking behind us. He asks me three times how Hugh will find us and three times I reassure him that I made a little pile of dirt with a cross on it, the way we mark food for Thomas the leper. I pointed the top of the cross in the direction we headed.

I just hope Hugh understands my sign.

I finally find a place near a stream with plenty of rocks and bushes to hide us, and get a fire started.

As usual, I'm starving. I give Donald some water and start covering him with leaves. "I'm going to find food."

He starts to get up. "I'm going to find Hugh."

"No! Stay here. Hugh will find us. If he doesn't, I'll go look for him." Hugh will never forgive me if I let his patient run around the woods looking for him.

Donald struggles to his feet.

"Stop!" I say, trying to push him down but, even wounded, Donald is strong.

"You have done too much already, laddie!"

"Stop it!" I tell him.

"You can't stop me!"

"Oh, yes, I will!" I yell, still struggling with him.

I hear a scream behind me and turn to see a boy, like someone in Henry's gang from the streets of Carlisle, come charging at us, throwing himself on Donald and kicking me away at the same time. I fall on my ass and am momentarily stunned until I see that the boy is pummeling Donald, who has his good arm in front of his face.

"Stop!" I yell, pulling the boy off, eventually, and tussling with him until finally pinning his arms to the ground and kneeling on his chest.

The boy is panting so hard he can't speak, so I stare at him, trying to understand his behavior, noticing the long golden hair that has fallen out of his cap, and I find myself looking into very familiar blue-green eyes.

"Bess?" I say, not quite believing myself.

"Look out for the soldier!" she yells.

"Bess?" I say again.

"Get off me and fight the soldier, you ninny!"

I try to explain about Donald but I am still stunned. "Bess —"

"Would you stop saying my name?" She pushes me off and backs away from Donald like she's a cat and he's someone who has thrown rocks at her. She picks up a rock herself and, without taking her eyes off Donald, addresses me. "Maybe Mother is right that you're an addlepate!"

Hearing that word again shakes me to my senses. "I am not an addlepate! I just didn't expect to find a girl in the middle of battle, dressed as a boy, and attacking my . . . my . . ." I wasn't sure what Donald was, although I finally say, "friend."

She seems to lose her rage. "I thought he was a Scottish soldier."

"Well, he is, but . . . he's also sort of a . . . friend."

She looks at me as if I'm more addlepated than ever, then looks at Donald, drawing her arm back to throw the rock at him.

I lunge at her. "Stop! Hugh is nursing him back to health!"

"Hugh?" She drops her arm and lets the rock fall to the ground. Her voice is soft. "Why?"

I explain quickly and she drops to her knees next to Donald as if she has clobbered Hugh himself. "I'm so sorry, sir! Please forgive me! It's just that Adrian's my cousin and I was trying to protect him. I had no idea!"

"Of course, lassie. You're a brave one, you are."

"Are you all right?" I ask Donald.

"Aye, I'm fine."

"This is Donald Stewart of Linton, and this is my cousin Bess."

Bess nods at Donald, then looks at me. "Where's Hugh?"

"I don't know," I say, but when I see her stricken face, I quickly add, "He's fine. He went off to look for his father this morning." I pause before going on. "The only thing is, some English soldiers found Donald and me, so we had to leave our camp. I left a sign for Hugh — you know, one of those crosses we leave for Thomas? Anyway, I think he'll figure it out." I look over at Donald. "He was struggling with me because he wanted to go look for Hugh but I told him he needs to rest."

Bess smiles warmly at Donald, tears in her eyes. It's hard to believe she attacked him only moments ago. She turns to me. "I saw your cross. And your campfire that was still going." I cringe, realizing that in my haste to leave I'd never put it out. "That's how I knew it was you the men were talking about."

"What men?"

"A knight in a fancy purple surcoat —"

Donald groans.

"He was talking about a small boy with a bow and war paint under his eyes."

"That *small boy* sent him running," I snap, "so I'm not scared of him."

Her face grows tight. "You should be, Adrian. He's a very powerful man." She takes a deep breath. "He's the warden of the entire Middle Marches of England."

Donald bolts upright, uttering some curse I can't understand. "Sir Reginald!"

"So?"

Bess puts her hands on my shoulders. I'm surprised to notice that she's not that much taller than I am anymore. It makes me feel more like a man. "Adrian. He said, 'If I see that child again, I'll kill him.'"

"Well, he won't see me, will he?" I sound braver than I feel.

Donald is on his knees. "It's his job to patrol these woods constantly, laddie! We will likely run into him again."

"There's a lot of woods," I say.

"He has a fast horse and a lot of men!" Donald retorts. "He's a sneak and a thief! He's supposed to stop the reivers, the thieves, but he's as bad as they are!"

"And," Bess adds, "you've made him look like a fool, so he'll be seeking revenge."

"I'm not scared," I say, although now my voice sounds small.

Donald utters some more oaths and makes me wipe the soot from under my eyes and promise to never put it on again until I'm safely back in my village.

"What are you doing here, anyway?" I ask Bess, as much to change the subject as to get the answer.

"You never came back, Adrian. You never brought Hugh. I decided to come myself."

"But you're just a girl."

She gives me a face as sour as Good Aunt's.

"I mean, you could've gotten caught. You could've been killed!"

"That lassie can take care of herself quite well," Donald says, "and you should heed her warnings about the warden because she's trying to take care of you, too!" He starts coughing, and Bess immediately grabs for my pouch.

"Adrian, where are all the herbs Grandmother has you carry for your breathing?"

I shrug. "I don't need them anymore. Not often, anyway."

She stops rummaging for a moment and stares at me until Donald's coughing grows worse.

"There's some mullein in there," I say, nodding at my pouch.

I build a fire while Bess tends to Donald. He is soon asleep, or maybe unconscious. Bess hovers over him like Hugh.

"I can't believe you saved a Scottish soldier," she says quietly.

"I didn't want to," I point out. "It's a treasonous act, and I thought we should kill him."

Bess wheels around to face me, her eyes wide. "Kill him?"

"Well, he was badly wounded. And look at the size of him — like a bear, with wild red hair."

She shakes her head. "You're always like that."

"Like what?"

"Judging people on their appearance rather than who they are."

"What? I do not!"

"Donald, because he's large and has red hair."

"And he's the enemy!"

"Lepers, like poor Thomas. You can't even stand to look at him."

"Lots of people can't!" *At least,* I think to myself, *I don't throw stones at him like Bryce, William, and Warren.*

She turns back to Donald and her voice is softer. "You said I was horrible simply because I look like my mother."

"I — I don't remember saying that." I know that I thought it a lot, though.

"It was a year ago. I overheard you speaking to Hugh."

I swallow. It's true. Now that I think on it, I've probably said that more than once to Hugh.

"That's how I knew what a kind person Hugh was, because he chastised you for saying so."

That is true, too. I've been chastised much by Hugh. "I don't think you're horrible anymore."

"Thanks very much," she says with a frown.

"I mean . . . well, I guess you're right that sometimes I'm like that."

"Sometimes? What about those stupid shoes you bought just so you could look all fancy? Really, Adrian, who cares what you look like?"

That's easy for her to say. She hasn't had to put up with looking like me her whole life. Although, I realize, she has never teased me or been mean to me like every child in the village, other than Hugh. And it wasn't because she was my cousin. Jane teased me mercilessly. She even conducted a mock witch trial of me years ago, which the unholy trinity loved. When I think about it, it was Father who came to stop it, but Bess who held his hand. She was probably the one who went to fetch him when she saw what her sister was up to.

I feel like such a fool. For being mean to Bess and for being, well, exactly what she says I am — shallow, judging people on their looks. Me, of all people! I stare at the fire for a long time, only vaguely aware of Bess bustling around camp, until she brings me some pine-needle tea and sits across the fire from me.

"Sorry," I mumble.

She shrugs. "I was mad at the way you always were. I don't think you're like that anymore, at least not so much."

"Really?"

"Why else would you be trying to protect Donald now?" She gives me a smile and sips her tea.

I look over at Donald, pale and silent. I thought I was just saving him because that's what Hugh would want. Yet, now that I think on it, I couldn't stand seeing him as a sitting duck. It wasn't right. Even if he is Scottish and the soldiers are English. Maybe I really am changing.

I suddenly realize I'm famished. It's getting late and will be dark before long. I get up and grab my bow. "I'll go get us some food." I hesitate, worried about leaving Bess and Donald alone.

Bess brightens. "Can you bring back some St.-John's-wort and marigold?"

I stare at her blankly.

"They help wounds and stop infection." She gives a shy smile. "I learned that from Hugh."

I still stare at her.

"Donald needs them," she says pointedly.

"But I can't tell one herb from another! Wait . . . you can come with me and look for the herbs while I find food. We'll put out the fire, cover Donald with leaves, and he'll be all right." She looks doubtful, so I add, "We won't be gone long."

At the last minute, I remember Donald's whistle and pull it out of his bag. "Bess, if you see soldiers or any trouble at all, blow the whistle and I'll come running."

Except for the lingering smell of smoke, no one would know there's a camp here. Donald is well hidden under the mound of leaves, and yet there's still an opening where he can breathe. Bess hesitates, clutching the whistle, but I pull her along after me.

"He'll be fine," I say, as much to encourage myself as her.

chapter the thirty-first

In Which We Face Robbers

BESS DOES NOT STRAY TOO FAR FROM ME AND I KEEP AN eye out for that warden and Big Sword, or any soldiers, for that matter. I'm so hungry I'd like to get us a deer or a pheasant or two. I grin, thinking of how Sir Reginald would feel if he knew that a "Scottish" lad was poaching from his land.

I circle the area looking for Hugh, as well. My stomach is rumbling louder now. I'm still hoping to find pheasant and am irritated that I can only find acorns. I wish the stupid bird that tweets over and over would stop, because I feel like it's mocking me for not finding a pheasant. And then I realize something worse — it's not a bird, it's the whistle! Bess is in trouble!

I run in the direction the sound was, although now it has stopped. Before I reach Bess, I hear voices. Men's voices. I curse myself.

I crouch behind some bushes and peer through them. One man has Bess by both arms. There are three men in all. We're outnumbered.

I'm grabbed from behind and let out a scream.

"Well, well, what have we here?" a man's voice says in my ear, and I realize there are four. "I caught another one, boss!" He drags me next to Bess. I steal a look at her and I see as much defiance and annoyance in her eyes as fear. I think the annoyance is probably for me as she glares at the whistle in her captor's belt.

The man who has me throws me on the ground and puts a boot on my ear. Although my face is turned toward Bess, I can only see her leggings, and I'm thankful that she's dressed like a boy.

"Apart from a whistle, what can you boys give us?" a voice says, approaching.

Robbers. And I'm stuck. All I can do is stare at the shoes of the man who steps in front of my face. I can't even lift my head to look at him. I just see the red-brown color of his shoes — St. Jerome's boots! That's the leather of Tom the cobbler. Could this be his son, the robber Pippin?

"Let us go, Pippin!" I squeak.

"Who are you?" the voice says as he looks down at me. Or, I imagine he looks down on me because I still can't see anything but his boots.

"William of Ashcroft," I lie.

"And how do you know my name?"

"I bought these boots" — I try in vain to turn my feet to show him my boots — "from your father. Your dear mother wishes you to return home!"

Pippin laughs. "My dear mother is a cow!"

"But she loves you."

"Ha! Now I know you lie!"

"No, she cries for you."

"She cries *about* me, is what you mean."

"No, sir, she regrets all the vile things she has said and done. She said" — and I use her own language to make my lie as believable as possible, and even imitate her voice — "'I would ask the devil himself to rip my own heart out, it is so black with the vile actions I myself have taken against my son.'"

There is silence for a moment before Pippin's voice, quieter now, says, "Let him up."

I steal a glance at Bess as I'm pulled to my feet. She seems all right. If anything, the man holding her has loosened his grip because she's no longer struggling and he's watching Pippin with his eyes wide and mouth slightly open.

"What else did she say?" Pippin asks.

"That it's her fault you live out on the street and steal, that she has driven you to a life of crime, that no mother should ever have done to her son what she has done to you."

"Go on."

"She wishes to see you to ask her forgiveness."

"Pah," he says, his mood changing, as he steps away from me. "Little chance of that."

I see I'm losing him and have to act fast. "Before she dies."

"Dies?" He turns to face me. "Dies of what?"

"She didn't say, but she didn't look well. Your father insisted that she sit on his stool because she's so thin and frail."

"Thin?" His jaw drops. "My mother? Thin?"

I have his interest back again and I dare not lose it. "Yes, but she refused, saying she didn't deserve to sit because of what a horrible mother she has been."

"And?"

"And . . ." What else could I say? *Think, Adrian!* Ockham's razor! He's a robber. It's money he's after. "If you'll have your henchmen let us go, I can get to the coins your mother gave me to give you."

"What?"

"Yes. She tells everyone who comes to her shop about you and how wicked she was. If it's a boy or a man who might be traveling the roads" — I don't say, *Who might be robbed by her vile son* — "she gives him a few coins to show her earnest intent." I don't have any money and I know Pippin won't be pleased with Sir Geoffrey's medal, even less so with the Roman coin from the latrine at the fort, but I go on with my story. "She gives every boy who promises to walk the roads a few coins to offer you and implore you to come home. She can't give much to any one of us, of course, because there are so many people to whom she has given coins, in hopes that her son will return."

"Why didn't you say that earlier?" His voice is calmer but still wary.

"Why?" Why indeed? "Because I wanted to make sure you were really Pippin of Penrith and not just a common robber." I let that sink in because flattery often works on those who are most impressed with themselves. "If you'll let me get the coins in my purse —"

"Let go of one of his arms!" Pippin commands my captor.

My shaky hand ensures that the medal and Roman coin make a satisfying clink. The man holding Bess hears this, as he lets go of her to walk toward me and the purse. I notice Bess silently step backward several steps, away from the men, as all their eyes are on my purse. The man who holds me grabs it out of my hand.

"Hey!" yells Pippin. "That's mine!" And he lunges toward my captor, who, God be praised, turns away from me as soon as the other men reach for him. I dash away, fast as I can possibly run, seeing Bess already well ahead of me but looking back nervously.

"Run!" I scream, and we must look like rabbits escaping a hungry hunter, as we flee for several minutes, at which point we collapse under the overhang of a riverbank, panting.

"They're not following," I say, peeking over the edge of the embankment.

She nods. "They probably know that's all we have." Turning to look at me, she says, "How did you know it was Tom the cobbler's son from Penrith?"

"By his boot leather. I was just at their stall at the market last month."

"And you saw his ailing mother, who said those things about him?"

"Oh, no. I made it all up."

Her mouth drops open. "But he believed you."

I grin back at her. "His mother said he was a dolt and she also said" — I imitate his mother's voice — " 'I'd ask the devil himself to rip his heart out.' "

Her eyes widen as a grin spreads across her face, and we laugh until we have to stop to get our breath.

"You're no addlepate, Adrian. You're brilliant. And brave."

It's hard not to smile until I remember something. "Except I didn't answer your whistle until it was too late. And now we've lost Donald's whistle."

She grins again as she pulls it out of her tunic. "I took it out of that robber's belt as he was walking toward you and your purse."

"*You're* brilliant and brave!" I say.

"I think our family is clever," she says pensively. "We may not be rich, but we're resourceful."

As we walk back to camp, I can't help feeling bad about losing the medal from Sir Geoffrey. I tell Bess about him. How noble he was. How he called me noble. And how he died. "I hate that his medal now belongs to that stupid dolt and thief, Pippin."

Bess agrees. "I suppose, though," she says, "as protection money, it saved you — saved us — like Sir Geoffrey would've wanted."

"I still wish I had the medal."

"I know," she says, "but you'll never forget him, even without a medal. And," she adds, kicking some leaves on the path, "you're lucky. Just as Sir Geoffrey said, you're like a knight. You can scribe and shoot. I only know a precious few letters and I don't know archery at all. I wish I could learn how to shoot."

"Really? But you're just —"

"A girl?" Her face turns sour. "Do you think that just because I'm not a noblewoman I don't have the strength to draw back a bow? Or the skill to hit a target?" She storms off ahead of me.

As I follow her back to camp, I think about her strength with the plow, her bravery in the face of robbers, her intelligence about herbs, her skill with Bessie, even her correct assessment of what a town like Carlisle is like, and I realize she could be a fierce archer given half a chance.

chapter the thirty-second

In Which Hugh and Bess Find Each Other . . .
and There Is Kissing

THE HERBS BESS FOUND SEEM TO HELP DONALD. AT LEAST
he is awake now. I wish I'd been able to find some food,
though, because pine-needle tea and Donald's oaten cakes
do little to satisfy my hunger.

Since it's dark, I'm now on guard for soldiers or thieves
like Pippin. I suppose I'm lucky that my bow is so small,
otherwise Pippin's men might've taken it. People assume it's
a child's toy. They have no idea what I can do with it.

The moon is full so it's easy to see anyone who might
approach. I tell Bess and Donald to sleep but they're both
too anxious about Hugh. Finally, I see someone approach
from the west and I can tell it's Hugh by his walk.

I'm about to shout but Bess beats me to it, racing toward
him. Hugh stops in mid-stride, dropping everything he's
carrying, and embraces her. Such a passionate kiss I have
never seen, or heard, and hope never to witness again. I turn
away but notice that Donald doesn't. He smiles as if it's the
most beautiful sight ever.

When they finally stop and walk into camp, Hugh turns from lovesick to almost angry. "You shouldn't have come! It's not safe for a woman alone in these woods." He looks Bess over carefully and grows even more agitated. "Where's your cloak? Why are you dressed like a boy?"

She looks at the ground.

Hugh narrows his eyes. "What happened?"

"A soldier — I got away from him."

Hugh is angrier than I have ever seen him. "Did he hurt —"

"No. I got away quickly."

"The barbarian!" Hugh says, his jaw clenched.

"Aye," says Donald, equally foul-looking. "I would kill him myself if I had a chance. I'm a husband and father, and there's no place for that business in war or anywhere else. My apologies, lassie. I am ashamed of my countrymen."

She looks at Donald and shakes her head. "Don't be," she says quietly. "The soldier was English."

She tells us the story of getting captured and how she escaped. "I told him I needed to relieve myself, and not just water but dysentery."

I can't help but make a face, and Bess laughs. "Yes, that's exactly what the man did, so he agreed to let me hang my cloak on a branch to hide myself and turned and walked away a little so as not to catch the foulness. Meanwhile, I threw my hood down the path behind, made a ruckus as if I were running away, and then hid in the hollow tree. He ran down the hill, swearing, saw my hood, and kept running."

"You're a wise lassie," Donald says.

Bess smiles but shakes her head slightly. "He almost fooled me, because he came back up the path saying, 'There you are. I see you. Come on out if you know what's good for you.' I was so stuck in the tree I couldn't move my legs, which was a good thing because it gave me a chance to realize it was a trick. He couldn't see me. He just figured I was hiding. Eventually, I heard him swear and take my cloak and, once it was dark, I finally felt safe enough to unfold myself from that tree."

"Where did you get those boys' clothes?" I ask.

Bess cringes. "I took them from someone's washing line. I feel awful about that! But I did leave them my kirtle. It was dirty but still in fine shape."

"I'm sure that boy will be very happy," I say, laughing.

Hugh takes her in his arms. "I'm so glad you're safe."

Bess smiles at him. "I told you I could take care of myself."

"I still wish you hadn't come."

She gives him a sour look.

"Don't worry," I tell her, "that's what he said to me, too. He'll come around."

Hugh is smiling. "I almost forgot. I found Father!"

We all cheer. Hugh dashes to pick up the bundles he dropped while hugging Bess. He holds up two sacks with a grin. "Food, from Father and the other men."

Soon we are sitting, eating bread and cheese and even some kind of fish I've never had before, but it all tastes more delicious than even plum pudding at Christmas.

Hugh tells us his father is fine, as is Uncle — who

managed to hurt his arm enough that he couldn't battle so had to head back to Ashcroft. I'm sure he did it on purpose but I don't say so out of respect to Bess.

"But," Hugh adds, standing up and starting to pace, "he doesn't want me to go to battle. He sent me back here so Adrian and I could go back to Ashcroft." He stops, his feet now firmly planted. "But I'm going to join him tomorrow."

Donald chokes and Bess lets out a cry, but I'm happy because I know it's what Hugh wants.

Hugh hesitates, looking at me. "Listen, Adrian? Could you take Bess home?"

Before I can protest, Bess grabs Hugh's arm. "But what about Donald?"

We all look at the ground, including Donald.

"Your father is right, laddie. You've seen he's safe. Now it's time to take the lassie home."

Hugh shakes his head. "I also came to fight beside him and that's what I'm going to do."

Bess tries to argue but she knows it's not going to work, even when she tells us the other reason she came looking for Hugh. "Grandmother is very ill and the only one to take care of her is my mother."

"St. Jerome's bones!" I say, before I can stop myself. With Good Aunt's help, Grandmother will surely die.

Hugh stalks away from camp a few paces, grabbing on to a birch branch as if to crush it.

Bess goes to him, putting her arm around his waist, and he does the same to her. They talk softly for a while, before Bess pats his back and walks him back to the fire. Donald lets out a groan and Bess shoots Hugh a worried look. He nods, as if they've spoken — it's like they're married already — and grabs his pouch, mixing up herbs with such ferocity and noise, it's as if he wishes Grandmother could hear him.

It's Bess who finally convinces Hugh that she and I need to stay one more day, to get Donald to the point where he can be safely left alone. I'm thinking it will take a lot longer for Donald to be well, but she's right to ask Hugh for only one day at a time.

But first, Hugh looks at me. "Father said that you need to be very careful, Adrian. A boy who . . . has your appearance is not safe outside of his own village. Too many people may think ill of you."

I cross my arms and narrow my eyes at him. "I keep myself covered up and I've had no problems."

"Still," says Hugh, "the people in our own village know you to be the bowyer's son. No one in the rest of England is aware of that."

So the only reason I'm worth saving is because I'm a bowyer's son? I know Hugh and his father are well-meaning, but it makes me feel . . . useless.

Even when Donald tells Hugh how I saved him from Sir Reginald, and Hugh looks at me with admiration and respect, there's still worry in his eyes.

Bess lays a hand on Hugh's arm and says quietly, "Adrian can take care of himself. He's very clever."

Despite her kind words, Bess knows how un-clever I am. I left the fire going when I abandoned camp, I didn't hear her whistle for help, and I even thought her to be mean for many years until she had to point out that it is, in fact, me who is the mean one. And it's worse than that. I always thought I'd be an archer, at least, if I can't be a bowyer. After what I've seen of battle, I never want to go back. Now I have no calling. Where does that leave me?

chapter the thirty-third

In Which I Go to Battle

I KEEP WATCH OVER CAMP. DONALD IS OUT COLD, HAVING exhausted himself arguing with us about leaving him and getting home to safety. Bess falls asleep next to Hugh and I watch him gently pin the St. Aldegundis medal to her tunic where she can't easily see it, but he'll know it's there protecting her.

Quietly, he stands up and motions me to the trees at the edge of our camp. I step over the sleeping Donald and follow him.

"Adrian," he says, but he's looking at Bess. "If anything happens . . . If I don't come back —"

"Of course you're coming back!"

"But if I'm . . . injured —"

"You won't be," I say, "you'll be fine."

"Still, I want you to look after Bess."

"She doesn't really need —"

"Adrian!" His voice is sharp and his face as serious as I've ever seen it.

"Yes, of course I will. Don't worry."

He nods, thanking me, and goes to lie down next to Bess, holding her.

I try to think of some encouraging words to tell him but I know he's right. He's risking his life. It's possible that he may never return.

In the morning, I'm awakened by Bess shaking me.

"Adrian! Adrian! He's gone!" she wails.

I look around. It's true Hugh has left. I'm sorry I missed him but I don't know why she's so distraught. She knew he was going to battle.

"Look!" she says, showing me the St. Aldegundis medal he pinned to her tunic.

"Oh, right. He wanted you to have it."

"But he's going into *battle*!"

We can hear the fighting in the distance already. Donald is awake, his eyes wide.

Bess stands up. "I'm going after him!"

"What?" Donald and I both say. He tries to get up but I'm on my feet much faster. "You can't! You're just a girl!"

She wheels around, her eyes narrowed. "When are you going to stop saying that, Adrian? You're just a boy. I can go after him as well as you can."

Donald is on his feet now, looming over us. "Neither of you will go!"

Bess hardly gets out a "But —" before Donald cuts her off.

"I cannot allow a lassie into that hell!"

"I'm going," I say, although I really don't want to.

"Oh, no you don't, laddie, you'll stay and take care of Bess. It's what Hugh would want. I'll go to battle."

"But you're not ready for battle," I tell him.

"Despite what you might think, laddie, neither are you!"

Somehow, Donald gathers his things — which, I realize, are only his pouch and his knife — and drags himself off toward the clashing and yelling of battle.

Bess and I are quiet for a while, sitting uncomfortably by the fire, not eating, not talking, not doing anything. Much as I don't want to see battle again, I can't stand staying here and thinking about what might be happening.

We hear a hideous cry and Bess cringes.

I jump to my feet. "I'm going after them."

She rises quickly. "I'm coming, too."

"Please, Bess. Hugh wanted me to look after you. If I take you into battle he'll hate me forever."

She crosses her arms, staring me down. I have to think of another argument. "What if either one of them is hurt? They'll come back here needing help. You know I can't take care of them."

She drops her arms and looks down. I take my chance while I have it. "I'll be back soon," I say, taking off at a run.

The battle is as awful as the one I saw before, only much bigger. There are thousands of men this time. I look for the standard bearers to see who's who, and quickly see that I'm in between the two armies.

The longbowmen, probably Welsh, are raining their arrows down on the Scots, who have no chance. They're trying to fight back but it's complete and bloody mayhem. The

English are definitely winning. I wish I could feel happier about that.

And I realize I didn't even bring my bow with me! Not that it would do much good. My hands are shaking too much and I feel as if I may puke any moment. I swallow the bile back down in my stomach and try to focus on what I must do — find Hugh and Donald.

Soldiers are running every which way, some wounded, some dying, all trying to escape the hell and none of them, God be praised, caring about me. I keep skirting the woods around the battle, looking for Hugh, his father, and Donald. Why can't I find them? Hugh is tall, and so is Donald. They should be easy to spot. Unless they've both fallen.

Finally, when I'm near the place where I first arrived, I see Donald. I only notice him because two men in a row fall over a large body on the ground. I let out a cry.

Donald is huge, even lying down. I pray he's still alive. Even if he's not, I have to get him off the battlefield and give him a Christian burial. A soldier trips over his body as he clashes swords with another. I must get to Donald soon or he'll be trampled.

Fortunately, he's close to the edge of the battlefield. When there's no one right next to him anymore, I say a prayer for both of us as I dash over to him, hoping I'm not trampled by a horse or hit by an arrow.

I grab his legs and start pulling and — St. Jerome's eyes! — I see a flash of armor and purple surcoat above me. It's Sir Reginald! I pray he doesn't turn in his saddle and see me. I also pray Big Sword is nowhere nearby. I put my head down fast, but not fast enough, because Sir Reginald's squire sees me. The young man holds my eyes — I swear he recognizes me — until I look down and pull Donald's legs frantically.

"What are you doing, boy?" I hold my breath, not wanting to answer, but the horse is blocking my way.

I look up, expecting to see the squire, but it's another soldier on horseback, although the squire is right behind him, still staring at me. "That's a Scot!" the soldier says. "Leave him to die, and get out of here!"

"My father tripped over him, sir," I say quickly. "I don't want another soldier getting hurt."

The squire's mouth drops open, hearing me speak without a Scottish accent this time. St. Jerome's lips! I have given myself away! I am dead.

The soldier stares at me, too, his eyes almost gentle and his voice now kind. "Acts of valor in the middle of hell. You are a brave one, lad. Carry on."

I can't help glancing at the squire because I'm sure he's about to stop me. He'll tell the soldier this is no act of valor. He'll tell him I'm a traitor. And then he'll hang me.

I hear the clanging of swords and Sir Reginald's yell. "Gawain! Your help! Now!" and the squire turns his courser and dashes to the knight.

I put my head down fast lest Sir Reginald see me, but my body moves slowly, not just from the weight of Donald. It's also because the squire's name is Gawain, and I can't help thinking of King Arthur and his chivalrous knight, Sir Gawain, who was also a healer. Squire Gawain still reminds me of Hugh, and Hugh wouldn't give someone like me away.

I send up a prayer for Squire Gawain, and then one for Donald, who coughs — God be praised! He's alive! But he keeps blinking like he can't focus.

It's only twenty feet to the woods, and when I get him there I drop down on the ground next to him. "It's all right, it's me, Adrian. I'm taking you back to camp."

He doesn't answer, only breathes heavily.

"Have you seen Hugh?" I ask him.

"Hugh . . . Hugh's," and then there are only sounds I can't make out through all the gasping, wheezing, and noise of battle before the last word finally comes out, "dead."

"What? What are you saying? Hugh is d-dead?" God's heart, please tell me I am hearing wrong or Donald is too sick to know what he says!

His eyes are closed, his voice barely audible. "Must help . . . bury body."

I hear crashing leaves and sticks behind me and I lean over Donald, trying to protect his body with my own, until I see that it's Bess, with my bow and quiver slung over her shoulder. "You forgot your —" She stops and quickly looks around. "Where's Hugh?"

Donald's eyes open briefly and he says, "Lassie . . . go," before passing out.

I almost tell her off for coming but I'm glad for her help. Somehow we drag Donald back to our camp, Bess asking all the while have I seen Hugh and is he all right and why isn't he here? I keep saying I don't know, I don't know, because I don't. And I'm not telling her what Donald said. I just keep hoping that Hugh is alive.

chapter the thirty-fourth

In Which I Learn What Happened to Hugh

THE SUN HAS SET AND THE BATTLE NOISES HAVE LONG died out. Donald is still unconscious. His condition has kept Bess scurrying for herbs and making poultices and nursing him so her mind has been off Hugh, mostly. At least she has stopped asking me about him. Now she sits by Donald but her eyes are constantly scanning the woods.

Mine are, too. We're both looking for Hugh but I'm also protecting our camp, now that it's dark. I'm aware we're susceptible to many dangers, human and animal and who knows what else. It's better than thinking of the battle. And of what might've happened to Hugh. I picture him kneeling over Donald, only in place of Donald it's his father and the reason Hugh's not back at camp is that his father was wounded and Hugh is caring for him. That's what I'd like to believe.

When I hear uneven footsteps near our camp, I rise quietly and load my bow. Drawing back, I'm ready to let loose until I make out the form of the man staggering into camp.

"Hugh!"

I run to him, ready to embrace him, but he falls to the ground and I smell the vomit on him and while Bess cries out and runs over to him, kissing him and checking him for wounds, I close my eyes because I realize what has happened.

I know, because even in the dim firelight I can tell that Hugh is not wounded but shattered. I stumbled through the woods just like this after I saw the battle that lost Sir Geoffrey. And like me, Hugh has vomited at the horror of what he has seen. That's what Donald's wide eyes and few words were trying to tell me.

I drop to my knees to join Hugh and Bess. Bess is shaking Hugh because he won't speak, so I grab her arms to stop her. "He's not wounded," I say, my voice sounding dull and far away.

"Then what's wrong with him?" she asks, struggling to be free of me.

"Hugh's father is dead."

She freezes for a moment before a moan comes out of her.

Bess takes Hugh and rocks him in her arms, for hours, but still he doesn't speak. He stares in a trance, clutching his father's leather bag. I stay awake to guard us, checking periodically on Donald to ensure he's still alive. I hear victory parties throughout the night and I don't even know who won the battle, although I think it's us. Still, I wonder how anyone can rejoice when so many have died.

In the middle of the night, Hugh lets out a cry, startling himself awake. Donald, too, opens his eyes. He stares at me for a long moment as, I suppose, the fog clears from his head, because he looks around quickly and sees Bess and Hugh, and his face grimaces in pain. He remembers what happened.

I go and sit next to him. "He's been like that for hours," I say.

"He saw it happen," Donald says.

I want to retch again, thinking of Sir Geoffrey and imagining how much worse it was for Hugh to see his own father slain.

There are tears in Donald's eyes and his voice is hoarse. "I tried to help them. I called out a warning. I was making my way over to be with him, and . . ."

His voice trails off but I know what happened. He wasn't paying attention to the battle anymore. He was focused on Hugh. That's when an English archer hit him — another injury to his right arm — and he fell, hit his head, and was knocked out.

Hugh suddenly jumps to his feet, pacing around camp. Bess follows him, trying to calm him. Since it's dark, he practically stumbles over Donald. When he looks down, his eyes grow wide, almost stricken, and I wonder, is he seeing the friend who tried to help him or the enemy he helped nurse back to health?

Bess tries to stop Hugh's wild pacing but he pushes her away as if he doesn't know who she is. He starts muttering, cursing, and he doesn't seem like Hugh at all. Bess talks to him softly but he only yells at the sky. "Why?" He keeps pacing like a sick animal and I stare at him, not knowing what to do.

Finally, it's dawn. As sick as I feel, I know we'll need food. No one else is in a condition to do it, so I must. I tell Bess I will not go far nor leave them for long. I am their only protector.

A shroud of mist hangs over everything, as if the whole world is in mourning. My eyes are having trouble adjusting to the dim light in the woods, probably because they're so tired. I end up walking into a hanging limb of a tree, yet it doesn't hurt, but is rather soft. When my eyes finally focus on it I see that it wears a boot.

I scream and jump back, slowly looking upward until I see the rest of the body.

There are two of them. Men. Hanged by the neck. Their faces bluish-gray.

"Beautiful, eh?" a gruff voice behind me says, and I yelp.

I turn to see a large man with filthy hair in a rough tunic, slicing pieces of apple with a knife and popping them in his mouth. He grins, bits of white apple falling from his lips, and raises his eyebrows at the hanging bodies.

"Wh-who are they?" I ask.

He jerks his thumb at the body on the left. "Scot." He takes another bite of apple, chews it, and then spits at the body on the right. "This one's even worse than a pagan. English, but a traitor."

I gulp. "Traitor?" My voice goes up at the end.

He narrows his eyes at me and stops chewing. "Know you any traitors?"

I shake my head quickly, gulping again. "No, sir."

He steps toward me and eyes me closely. "Are you sure?

Have you seen any pagans? Remember, treason is a hanging offense, even for boys."

"No, sir, no pagans, either," I say. My voice is steady because that is not a lie. Now that I know him, I realize that Donald, husband of Mairi and father of Colyne, isn't a pagan to me.

Thankfully, the man turns away as we hear horses approach. Wiping his mouth, he drops the apple and puts the knife in his belt. "I should get a shilling for these two," he says, jerking his head to the swinging bodies, "maybe even a shilling apiece."

I shudder, and then almost scream when I see who is coming . . . Sir Reginald!

I'm still running, and gasping for air, when I reach camp. I kick dirt on the fire. "We have to leave! Now!"

chapter the thirty-fifth

In Which We Hatch a Plan to Save Donald

BESS IS TOO WORRIED ABOUT THE HEALTH OF BOTH HUGH and Donald, so she refuses to budge. I drag branches to our camp to make as much of a den as I can, watching the entire time to see if Sir Reginald is coming. Bess starts packing so that when she finally decides we can leave we'll actually be ready.

"It's all right," Bess says calmly.

"It is not all right!" I hiss. "The warden will recognize me, and probably Donald, too, although he couldn't see him very well the last time since I'd put my cloak over him. And if he thinks someone my age can be a traitor, he'll certainly accuse Hugh of that!"

I can tell by her worried look that she knows it's not all right at all. She was just trying to be strong. And now I wish I hadn't snapped at her.

It's strange to think how much I actually care about her after all these years of snubbing her. I want her to get home safely. I look at Hugh, who still sits stunned. Donald is out cold. It is up to me.

The mist has gotten even thicker and I see it as a gift from God. Not only does it protect us from Sir Reginald possibly finding us but also it will give me a chance to do what I must.

I tug on Bess's arm and speak softly. "I have to teach you archery. You'll need to know for the way home. Hugh will be distracted."

She stops stuffing herbs into Hugh's pouch. "But you're a sure shot. Hugh told me how good you are."

"Don't you want to learn?" I say, not ready yet to tell her my plans.

It's as if she knows she has to learn fast, because she does. After dropping the first few arrows and being embarrassed, which is something many people do, she quickly gets the feel for it. She could probably shoot some food or scare off an attacker. And I tell her that.

"Thank you for not making fun of me."

"Why would I do that?"

She shrugs. "It's what my family always does."

And I marvel that she can be kind and strong in spite of her ale-head father, and horrible mother and sister.

When we get back to camp, Hugh raises his head in greeting. Bess sits next to him and puts her arms around his waist. I sit on the other side of him and put a hand on his shoulder. He nods. We don't need to say anything. He knows how bad we feel for him.

We stay quiet for a long while. I don't want to tell him about the hanging bodies. But after a time of sitting in silence, I finally say that Sir Reginald is near, Donald is in danger, and we are, too.

Saying it seems to spur Bess into action, and she finishes packing. Hugh is thinking about his father, though. He cries silently, maybe so Bess won't notice. "Why?" he keeps whispering. "Why?"

I don't know what to say. I think he's not expecting an answer, really, but it hurts to see him in such pain. I try to come up with an explanation. Did the Scots really think they could take over England? Was it so England could conquer the pagan Scots, although I know now that they're not all pagans? Is that why Hugh's father had to die? I come up empty.

Suddenly, Hugh sits up straight, as if ready to pounce. Hissing through gritted teeth, he doesn't sound like Hugh at all. "I wanted to kill them all. Put an arrow through each one of their hearts. Every last Scot." He claws at the ground like he's shredding his prey.

Bess and I both glance at Donald. I can't believe Hugh would do anything to hurt him but I've never heard him speak like this.

Just as suddenly, he slumps into a heap again.

I sit next to him, trying to be of comfort, but not knowing what to say.

"I was useless, Adam," Hugh whispers.

I don't know if he's addressing me or thinking of his dead brother.

"No, you weren't," I tell him, putting an arm on his shoulder.

He shakes his head. "My mother, my brother, my father, and now Grandmother . . ."

"You were only six when your mother and Adam died, Hugh. And," I add softly, "there was nothing you could do for your father."

I wish I hadn't said it because his face clenches in pain and he heaves several times, but I know I have to go on. Bess sits next to him and holds him.

"You're still a healer, and now you have to help Donald," I say, adding quickly, "He's still someone's father — Colyne's father — and Mairi's husband." I almost say, *and our friend*, but I don't want to push it. "He's in danger now and we have to get him home."

"Home," he repeats. "I have to get Bess home. I can't help Donald."

I squirm because this doesn't sound like my friend. He's a healer first and foremost. Even if Donald is a Scot, and technically the enemy, like those who killed his father, he's still . . . Donald.

"I have to get you both home," Hugh says, staring intently into space. "That was my father's dying wish. That is what I must do."

"But what about Donald?" I ask.

"I'll do whatever I can for him before we leave. I'll make the poultices and send them with him. But I must get you both home. And I must get to Grandmother fast. Maybe there's something I can do to save her."

I understand now that Hugh is not speaking from rage but rather from love — of his grandmother, Bess, and even me. But I can't leave Donald behind. When I look at Bess, I think she's reading my mind. Her worried eyes flicker to Donald, who is still unconscious, and back to me. And I know I must tell them my plan.

"Hugh," I say, "you're right. You have to get back to Grandmother and you have to get Bess home. But I have to get Donald back to his family."

Hugh shakes his head, as if unsure he heard me right. "You can't —"

"We can't just leave him here. It's not safe."

Hugh's face still looks pained, or maybe confused.

I try to explain it to him. "Look, you said yourself that you wanted to kill every last Scot you saw."

"But I wouldn't really have —"

"And," I continue, "you're a healer. If a healer could feel that way, what about soldiers who've seen so many killed? Couldn't they justify killing someone who seems almost dead anyway, but large enough to be a threat again if he recovers?" I shake my head. "He's in danger."

"But you will be, too!" Bess says.

"She's right —" Hugh begins, but I cut him off.

"You know he can't make the journey by himself. It must be sixty, seventy miles or more."

"Exactly," Hugh says.

"You should go with them, Hugh," Bess says. "I can go home myself."

"No!" Hugh cries. "I will not allow it!"

"I came here myself, didn't I?"

"Yes," says Hugh, softer now. "And I have much respect

for that." He takes her hand gently. "But there has been more battle since, and many vile, horrible acts — on both sides." He takes a deep breath. "When men are angry, their behavior suffers. I will not have you out in that — alone."

"That's why I must take Donald and you must take Bess," I say, as if the argument is now closed.

Hugh starts to argue but I capture his eyes with mine. "Listen. I don't want to be like Ailwin. Maybe I couldn't do anything to save my mother or baby sister, but I can help save Donald and bring Colyne his father back." I know that point will hit its mark. I can see the objection melt from Hugh's face and I know he's reminded of Adam. He nods once, and when Bess starts to protest he puts an arm around her. It calms her and we all look toward Donald, as if we're in prayer for a moment for those we've lost and those we hope to save. As for me, I'm thinking of Sir Geoffrey. I've already let one good man die. I'll not let that happen to another one.

Bess makes us a thin soup of berries and onions that she collected nearby. We eat the rest of the bread from Hugh's father, with much less gusto. She convinces Hugh to eat some, saying he won't have the energy to guide her home otherwise. It works, although I know it's Bess who's going to be doing the guiding. And I'm not worried about them, either. Bess can handle it.

Hugh looks at Donald and then at me. "You'll have to travel at night."

I don't relish that thought. The moon will be waning now, and leading a stumbling Donald in the dark won't be easy. Nor will hiding him all day while I, too, must sleep. But how else can I do it?

Bess must be thinking the same thing. "I wish there was a way to hide him. . . ."

"In plain sight," I finish. "I know. Me too."

"What about a disguise?" Bess asks.

Hugh shakes his head. "He has such a thick accent. As soon as he speaks he'll give himself away."

"He's too sick to speak, maybe," Bess says.

Hugh shakes his head. "He even looks Scottish, and dangerous, and much like a soldier."

"I wish there were some magic spell," I say, thinking out loud, "that I could use to keep people away so they couldn't sneak up on us unawares, like when I'm asleep. Some way to scare them . . . Ockham's razor!" I yell. "I've got it!" It helps to think things out loud.

Bess and Hugh are both staring at me. "What?"

"Donald will be a leper."

Bess's grin is quick to come. "That's brilliant!" She jumps to her feet. "And I can make him look like a leper. I've practiced on Jane!"

Hugh and I both stare at her now.

"I mean," she explains, "she's been getting those blemishes on her face and I've made several creams to help hide them. The first ones I tried were lumpy and made her look even worse, but all that practicing has made me an expert on altering faces!"

"Excellent!" I say as she runs off to gather the mud and other things she needs.

Hugh is still worried. "Are you going to be a leper, too?"

"No, I'll just be guiding him."

"Why?"

It's a good question.

Again, I think of what would seem the most obvious to anyone who happened upon us. Me, a boy, leading a leper to Scotland. Even if Donald doesn't speak and they don't guess he's a Scot, why would I be taking a disease-ridden man to Scotland? I smile slowly as I remember the story Nigel told me, of corpse warfare, those armies that catapulted diseased corpses into castles so the inhabitants would die. That will be my story, and I tell Hugh.

"But why would you be leading him?"

"Because he wouldn't necessarily go himself, would he? Especially not if he's Scottish; he wouldn't want to infect his own people."

"Who will you say came up with this idea?"

I think about that for a moment. What would Nigel say? I know what the prior would say — he'd probably be the one to come up with such an idea. Aha!

"I'll say the prior has sent me. He was so angry with the Scots stealing his wagonloads of goods — even though that's a complete lie — that it'll be a believable reason."

Hugh twists his mouth, uncertain.

I roll my eyes. "Priests have fought in battles since the Crusades, so it's not as if it's unusual for a prior to be involved like this. And there's something fitting about using his own lie against him."

"But why would you, a boy, be taking him?"

"He can be a postulant," Bess announces as she walks back into camp with her supplies. "I can cut his cloak into a monk's robe and make him look like a young man who wants to join the priory."

"Yes! And this could be my test to see if I'm really willing to give myself to God."

"A death sentence?" Hugh asks.

"It's not a death sentence," I tell him. "Monks are always taking care of lepers. My story will be that I'm going to tell the first Scottish monks I find that this leper needs caring for. On the way, I'll say that I'm getting him to touch as many Scots as possible, or at least their water supply. If the disease spreads among border villages, it's God's will. Plus," I add, "I know to stay five paces away."

"But how . . ." Hugh begins, then answers his own question. "I'll get some rope. We'll put knots to measure each foot. One end we can tie around Donald's waist, and you can hold on to the other."

"And we'll need a length of rope for Adrian's robe, too," Bess adds. "Where will you find all that rope?"

Hugh's face turns grim. "I know where I can get some."

I think I know what he means. The battlefield. He has to go back there again. But at least this time it's for saving a life rather than killing.

chapter the thirty-sixth

In Which I Become a Monk, Sort Of

"HOLD STILL," BESS ORDERS.

"It hurts!" I snap.

"I'm almost done."

"I know! You've plucked me bald!"

Hugh walks back into camp with the rope and his haggard face lights up. At me. I don't mind, though, because it's good to see some life in his eyes.

"I've never seen your hair so short," Hugh says.

"She cut most of it off and now she's plucking the rest of it!"

"Just the tonsure on top," Bess retorts. "You need a bald spot so it looks official. And your hair has to be very short — you know that."

I can still grumble about it, though.

"Adrian," she says, with some hesitation, "is it all right . . . do you mind . . . if . . ."

"What?" I ask.

"If I make your hair and skin darker? Some people — well, you know how they react to the sight of your pale skin and hair, and they might think you're —"

"I know, I know. Yes, that's fine. Go ahead and darken it."

She breathes a sigh of relief. I don't know why. It's not like I'd be mad at her for telling the truth, and I'm happy to have a disguise in case I run into Sir Reginald or anyone who might think I come from the devil. I can't wear my badger eyes anymore because Sir Reginald might recognize that, so maybe my darkened skin will cut the glare.

By the time Bess finishes my monk's robe, I truly do feel like a postulant. She laments the fact that I don't have sandals and Hugh offers to make some out of the leftover bits of rope, but I refuse. It's cold now and it'll only get colder as I head north. I've learned the importance of comfortable boots. I'm not giving them up for ropes.

Donald finally wakes up and is upset with our plan, at first refusing to cooperate.

"Fine," I tell him, "then I'll just squat next to you here like a sitting duck."

That gets him moving. Bess is a master at making his face up to look like a leper. She also puts mixtures on his hands and feet that look like vile growths. I can't help but cringe every time I glance at him. She even adds pustules around his eyes because she comes up with the idea that he's going blind, which is another reason he needs me as a guide. She really is quite brilliant, this cousin.

While Bess works, Hugh gathers herbs and puts together measured parcels and poultices, telling me what's what, how to prepare them, and what to give Donald when. I try desperately to use Nigel's loci method to remember his instructions. I can't write it down because I have only one piece of parchment left and I need that for the document that will hopefully save Donald and me.

Hugh sits down next to me. "I feel like I got you into this. It doesn't feel right having you take care of him, guiding him all the way back to —"

"But I want to," I tell him. "And it feels right to me. Now go help Bess."

He sighs and does as I say. It feels good to be in charge for a change.

It's late in the day when we're ready. Hugh says there's enough light to get started, at least. I know he's eager to get home to Grandmother. Also, he says Donald can't walk very much this first day. We can put a little distance behind us and then stop for a good night's rest.

It's not easy saying good-bye. Donald hugs Bess and Hugh as best he can, thanking them over and over. I don't even mind that Bess hugs and kisses me. She doesn't seem to want to go. I wouldn't want to go back to Good Aunt, either. I do feel a pang of homesickness that I won't see Father for quite a while. Father!

"Hugh, will you give Father a message for me?"

"Of course," Hugh says, giving me a hug good-bye.

"Tell him . . . I understand now what Mother meant about being a bowyer." I answer Hugh's confused look. "He'll know what I mean."

As I watch them walk off together, I know they'll be fine on their journey.

Before Donald and I go, I mix some ashes from the fire with water to make ink, sharpen a crow's feather into a crude pen, and write a letter on the back of my last piece of parchment as if I'm the prior, not the Badger this time — large, flowery, important-looking letters. And I draw a quick, rough sketch of the Mary Magdalene carving above the door of Lanercost Priory.

Please give food and assistance to this boy, who is doing a service for God and country as he leads this leper to the land of the Scots. It is but meek retribution for all that the pagans have stolen from me and for all the lives we have lost.
Osmund, Prior of Lanercost

chapter the thirty-seventh

In Which I Try to Save Donald

WE DON'T MAKE IT FAR THAT FIRST AFTERNOON, PERHAPS a mile, before Donald collapses, so I decide to make camp. He sleeps fitfully while I keep watch, thinking about where the battles might be and what route we should take to avoid them. I find myself falling asleep and jerking awake all night.

As dawn breaks, Donald groans. I change the poultice on his arm like Hugh showed me, although I squint my eyes almost all the way shut so I don't have to see, and still I almost gag. It smells putrid and is oozing green.

Throughout the day, Donald gasps for breath and looks so sickly even under Bess's masterful face painting, that for the first time I wonder if he's even strong enough to make it back home. I think about what he has done, the reason for his injuries — saving an English boy, helping Hugh — and I know that I'll at least give him a Christian burial, even if some would call him a pagan. But I pray it doesn't come to that.

I keep encouraging him to press on. I want to get us out of the English Middle March, Sir Reginald's territory, although I know it covers a huge swath of the country. The sooner we're in the Scottish Middle March, the better.

I cannot believe I just thought that it would be better to be in Scotland! I almost laugh except that Donald is starting to moan in pain again. He trips. I help him to his feet, but he slumps back down, coughing and shivering. It's so cold and damp today. Although we haven't made much progress, we have to stop.

"Here," I say, giving him my cloak as a blanket even though he protests. I also cover up his legs and feet with dead leaves. I start a fire to keep him warm and rummage through the pouch of herbs Bess collected for me, desperately trying to remember Hugh's instructions.

There's a stream not far off so I'm able to get water and boil up some herbs and make Donald drink the tea. His eyes keep trying to roll back in his head. I am feeling weak and light-headed myself, and I remember that we've had very little food. I must keep us strong or we have no hope of making this long journey. I tell Donald he can rest for now. The woods are quiet.

Even drinking the warm tea myself doesn't stop the chill, and I have to go a long way before I find any food. Still, it feels good to be doing what I do best, using my bow, and I catch two squirrels. We can have one each.

With Donald in mind, I try to find more herbs that might help him, though I'm bad at identifying them. If I can tell them at all it's by smell, especially garlic, which is supposed to help wounds, so I sniff practically everything I find until I'm sneezing and coughing and my nose clogs up and I realize I'd better stop. I can't smell anymore, anyway.

I'm heading back to camp in between coughing fits when I spot a band of English soldiers on the road ahead. They're foot soldiers, most with only padded cloth for armor, but they all have bows, maybe even made by Father. St. Jerome's bones! My brain is as clogged as my nose because I'm just now realizing something — our camp is little more than a mile away and the soldiers are heading straight for it! What if they find Donald? I'm not there to tell them to stay back, that he's a leper. And if they get up close, will they be fooled by Bess's makeup? Or will they see his red hair and shoot first?

"Stop!" I cry "Stop!" and run after them, flailing my arms and screaming. I hope Donald has heard them and at least put out the fire. I continue to scream, and cough, and wheeze, and curse — until I remember I'm a postulant, so I stop the cursing.

They stop and turn, one of them calling back to me, "Calm down, boy! What's all the ruckus?"

As they come toward me I have a moment to catch my breath and think. Ockham's razor! Why would I be screaming at soldiers to stop? Because I don't want them to find Donald, of course, because he's the enemy. The enemy! That's it!

"Sir!" I say, still out of breath and my heart pounding, more from fear, I think, than running. "Scottish soldiers!" I point behind me. "I saw them!"

The leader squints into the distance. "How far?"

"Way in the distance," I say, because I want these soldiers to go far away. "But they're not very fast," I add, along with several sneezes, "so you can probably catch them."

Now the leader squints at me. "Are you sure they were Scots?"

"Oh, yes, they spoke funny," and I imitate Donald's accent.

"I thought they were far away," one of the other men says. "How could you have heard them?" He turns to the man next to him. "I don't trust this . . . creature. Look how pale his eyes are. He's not normal."

"Whist," the other man says, "he's some kind of priest or postulant."

"Nay, he's too young for that. He's probably playing at being a monk."

The rumblings among the men about my not being "normal" are spreading. I try to stay calm and think fast.

"Which is it, boy?" the leader asks. "Are they far away or close by?"

"They're far away now, but I was hiding in the bushes when they passed so I heard them."

"What did they look like?" the leader asks.

All I can see in my mind is Donald and I don't want to describe him. I close my eyes, trying to picture the battle scene I saw with Sir Geoffrey, and then it hits me. "I don't know, sir." I hang my head. "I had my eyes closed because I was so scared."

Some of the men laugh.

"Like a kitten," a man says. "If they can't see you, they think you can't see them."

"Sorry," I say meekly. I don't even mind the coughing fit that follows because it makes me appear such a weakling.

"We thought we saw a fire that way," a soldier says, pointing in the direction of our camp. "Did you see any soldiers back there?"

I shake my head fast. "It's a leper!"

Some men groan, others cross themselves.

One man pushes his way to the front of the group. A priest. "I will go pray with him."

God's lips! I don't know what to say. Somehow, I don't think he'll believe the story of dragging a leper across the border to infect Scotland and, even if he does, he'll probably still want to pray with him.

"He's gone now," I say quickly, remembering what the unholy trinity used to do to Thomas. "I threw stones at him so he'd clear off!"

The priest grabs my arm and shakes me. "He is one of God's children, boy! How dare you be so cruel?"

I don't mind being shaken because at least the topic has changed from my odd looks and questionable story to my simply being a rotten boy.

"Come on, men," their leader says wearily.

I watch them pass with relief that turns to panic, because the leader orders his men to fan out in different directions to keep looking for evidence of Scots. *Satan's arrow, please don't let them come near our camp!*

As soon as I'm over a rise and out of their sight, I take off at a desperate speed, sprinting all the way back to our camp.

As I approach, I see that Donald has put out the fire and is hidden from view, so all's well except that, St. Jerome's lungs, I've been running so fast and the air is so cold, I can't breathe! It's as if I must now pay for the many days I've had free of problems. And I must pay a very large price, too. I collapse on the ground and my world goes black.

chapter the thirty-eighth

In Which Donald Saves Me

WHEN I OPEN MY EYES, DONALD'S FACE IS ABOVE ME. HE'S talking and fretting, like Father used to when I was younger and had such terrible wheezing fits. He has tucked my cloak around me and even put something soft beneath my head.

"Mullein," he says. "I'll fix it up right now, laddie — hold on!"

I see the blood oozing from his arm and try to tell him to lie down, but I can barely speak. He tells me to hush anyway, in between his own groans. St. Jerome's bones, we're like two wounded animals from different packs who are trying to save each other.

I close my eyes again and try to focus on breathing while I hear Donald start a fire, muttering "Mul-lein, flea-bane," like it's a chant. I don't know how much time goes by but I wonder why it's taking the water so long to boil and why he hasn't brought it to me when I realize that, although it's smoky and my eyes are stinging, I'm breathing easier. When

278

I finally open my eyes, Donald is sitting next to me, staring eagerly, as if I'm a dancing bear and he's waiting for me to perform.

"You're a scrappy wee lad, you are. What is it you call yourself? The Badger? Aye, it fits." He smiles so wide his beard seems to grow. "You're breathing easier."

I nod.

"I am, too," he says. "Hugh has much herbal wisdom."

"But you didn't even use the mullein."

"I did!"

I prop myself up on my elbow and look around me. "Where's the pot, then?"

"What pot?"

"The pot with the boiled mullein."

His face falls. "Is that what you're supposed to do with it?"

"Yes. Why, what did you do?"

"I threw it in the fire."

"What!"

Donald's face turns pink. "Well, that's what you do with fleabane!"

I can't help laughing. "It worked, anyway. I feel much better."

I start to get up but he pushes me down. "Stay still," he says, sounding like Hugh.

"No, I have to keep a lookout for those soldiers."

"They're long gone," Donald assures me. "You were out for a while."

"I have to get up. The squirrels need cleaning."

"Later," Donald says.

I still struggle against him. "But —"

"I prayed hard for your recovery, lad. I'm not losing you now."

That is enough to stop me. "You prayed for me?"

"Aye. How else do you think you're alive? I know nothing about curing people." He points to the ashes of mullein and grunts. "Obviously." He grins. "I know what you're thinking. I'm a pagan."

"*I* don't think that. It's just —"

Donald holds his hand up. "I suppose if you asked my priest he'd say I skip mass enough to be a pagan." He coughs for a while before regaining his breath. "Och, I know I'm not perfect but somehow I don't think the good Lord would begrudge me drinking a wee bit more ale than I should . . . or even taking back what's rightfully mine."

"It's people back home, who don't know you, who think Scots are all pagans."

"Aye, that's what I heard about the English, how brutal you are. I find that hard to believe now. Depends on the man. I imagine it's much the same everywhere, even lands across the sea, including the Saracens."

"Even Saracens?" I say. "That can't be. They truly are pagans."

"They follow a different religion," Donald says.

I shake my head. "Haven't you heard the stories of the Crusades?"

"Aye, I have, just as I've heard stories about the English. And" — he looks at me pointedly, but not unkindly — "about people with overly pale hair, skin, and eyes. I may not be the best Catholic," Donald says, "but does that make me a pagan?"

I don't answer. I know what Father Fraud would say but he's wrong. I think about our church, and what the one in Donald's village might be like. I wonder if they sing the same songs? I wonder if the Psalter pictures are the same? I wonder if their priests use those Psalters to whack boys like me on the head when they're not listening? I suppose I'm no better than Donald when it comes right down to it. I ignore the priest and try to skip mass whenever I can. Does that make me a pagan?

Finally, Donald lets me start skinning the squirrels. He tries to help but I tell him to lie back or I'll yell at him just like Hugh.

"He's a good lad," Donald says, "with a noble calling."

"Physic?" I don't mean to sound so surprised.

Donald raises his eyebrows.

"I mean, there's nothing wrong with being a physic, it's just not what I'd call noble."

"Ah, the archer, the warrior — that is the noble one, eh?"

He coughs as I nod.

"Hugh is a healer, laddie. How much more powerful is it to save a life than to take one?"

I concentrate on skinning the squirrels, scraping their fur off with my knife. I could never be a physic or a healer. "I've had enough of illness, herbs, and remedies to last me a lifetime."

"Aye, but it's Hugh's calling. The battle is not for him. What is your calling, Adrian?"

"Bowyer, like my father," I say, out of habit. But Father won't allow it and even being an archer has lost its appeal. I always thought they were such noble callings. Now, as I gut the squirrels and remember Sir Geoffrey's death, I wonder what, exactly, *noble* means.

"My Mairi hopes Colyne will become a monk, perhaps even a prior."

I make a face and Donald asks me why, so I tell him about Prior Osmund and Nigel, and the reliquaries, jewels, and thievery. "The prior even stole the spectacles, something Nigel desperately needs!" I realize I'm shouting.

Donald stares at me.

"Stealing is wrong," I say, but that's not the only reason I'm upset. Every night, my eyes are so tired that my vision gets as bad as Nigel's. I know what it feels like. "The prior sold the spectacles so he could buy more jewels, something he definitely doesn't need."

"What are spectacles?" Donald asks.

"It's special glass held in a frame that rests on your nose so you can see clearly, if you have poor eyesight like Nigel." *Or me, by the end of the day*, I think to myself. "Nigel wants to be a scribe, so he needs the special glass in front of his eyes instead of holding a large piece of glass above his hand as he tries to write."

"You could be a scribe," Donald says.

I shake my head.

"You wrote a letter that looks like it's written by a prior!"

"Yes, but no one would hire me because of the way I look. If the lord of our manor needs a scribe, he'll hire Bryce, the reeve's son." I skewer the squirrels on sticks. "I'm not fit for farming. I can't be a bowyer, I can't be an archer, I can't do anything."

We're both silent as we watch the squirrels on the fire. Finally, Donald looks at me seriously. "Have you heard the story of Robert the Bruce and the spider?"

"I'm not interested in Scottish heroes."

"Ah, but he's not the wise one in this story. It's the wee spider that teaches him a thing or two."

"Spider?" I say, in spite of myself.

"Aye. The Bruce was hiding in a cave after six defeats by the English, wondering if it was worth all those battles, all the lives lost, and he noticed a spider, trying to spin a web from the roof of the cave to the wall." He has to stop to catch his breath. "She failed. He counted her trying — six times — and failing, just like he had. He decided that if she failed the seventh time, he was going to lose the next battle and should give up right then. But she didn't. On the seventh try, she succeeded. The Bruce went on to his seventh battle — and won."

Donald looks at me. "Don't give up, laddie. You'll succeed."

But I don't even know what my calling is anymore. I just wanted to be a hero.

That night I dream of slaying a knight on the battlefield, first knocking him from his horse with one arrow and then stabbing him with a saber. I'm feeling victorious until somehow, as often happens in dreams, things twist around so that it's now Sir Geoffrey who's lying dead, and maggots have started crawling into his open wounds and, as I try to hit them away, the dead body becomes mine and I wake up swatting at myself.

Still half asleep, I pull my tunic over my head to get at the horrible pests. I slowly realize it was a dream, but then I see my naked underarms and — St. Jerome's bones! — spiders have been spinning their webs in my armpits!

I scream, waking Donald, as I try to get rid of them. "They're stuck! Cobwebs! In my armpits!"

Donald is awake now, wide-eyed, and, St. Jerome's armpits, he starts laughing!

"You think this is funny?" I hold my arms up high for him to see the cobwebs that refuse to be removed.

He only laughs more, rolling back on the ground, wheezing, too weak to even sit up. "It's your own hair, Adrian!"

I stop. "Hair? In my armpits?"

"Aye, laddie, it's perfectly normal."

"But how did it happen so fast? Overnight?"

"You just hadn't noticed it before. When was the last time you bathed?"

"I — I was busy these last weeks."

"So were your armpits." Donald is still smiling. "You've seen men's armpits before."

"Yes, but the hair on Hugh's head is fair yet the hair in his armpits is dark."

"It starts out light but it turns dark," Donald says. "I imagine it may even do so for you, although you're so pale."

I stare at the hair under my arms.

"Not while you're looking!" Donald laughs again. "Just as you grow older."

His laughter stops and his face becomes serious as he stares at me, and I realize the importance of this moment. My feet are bigger, I'm taller, and now I have hair under my arms. I am growing into a man.

chapter the thirty-ninth

In Which We Are Both One-Handed Musicians

WE WALK FOR DAYS, BUT WHEN THE HEAVY RAIN STARTS
we don't even try trekking through the slippery mud. I make
a dome of branches like a cave so we have some shelter and
keep the fire going so we have warmth. It's actually good for
Donald because it gives him time to rest, and he seems to get
better. We have gone no more than ten miles, maybe less
since we left Hugh and Bess, and probably have fifty miles to
go to Donald's home. There is still a long journey ahead of us.

Donald is in good humor despite his pain. He keeps calling me the "tough wee spider." It's not exactly the name I'd
pick for myself — at least a badger is fierce — but I know he
means it as a compliment. We even have a hand gesture now,
instead of a wave. We curl our hands into a claw and wiggle
our fingers, like a spider. In fact, I feel like the spider as I go
off to find food and herbs for Donald because he's like the
failing Bruce and I'm small, but determined, and maybe
the only one who can save him.

The bad thing is that Donald's face paint is now gone. Between his sweat and the rain, it has all washed off. We'll just have to make sure he keeps his hood up to cover his face as much as possible for the rest of the journey.

I return with only old onions, but the sight of Donald cheers me up. He has taken his whistle out. It looks small in his grasp, not as long as his large hand and thinner than the width of his pinkie finger. His injured arm at his side, he blows into the whistle, which sounds like a bird. He looks around to see if it's all right to play, but he needn't worry because he's not able to blow it very loudly, so it simply sounds like a robin singing in the bushes. Besides, we'd hear anyone approach because they'd be slipping, sliding, and probably swearing.

As I watch Donald, I can't help but smile. He's a giant of a man yet he's like that gnome, the one my mother told me about when I was little, the good gnome who gives lifesaving drinks to thirsty knights and then disappears — unless you're a bad knight, then you're the one who disappears.

I like the music, but Donald takes the whistle from his lips and sighs.

"Why are you stopping?"

"I need two working hands."

I grin and raise my right hand.

Donald moves over next to me. He tries to teach me just the right-handed notes of a tune. It's not easy, especially since I'm not musically minded.

"Keep your first finger down on that hole," he wheezes, "until the chorus. Your second finger covers that hole on the third, sixth, and twelfth notes."

I try but it comes out awful, and we're both laughing, which sounds particularly funny since Donald is blowing into the whistle at the same time.

Donald shakes his head as he catches his breath. "I thought you went to school."

"They don't teach music at school!"

"Do they not teach you how to count at school in England?" He grins before I have a chance to get angry. Between coughs, Donald calls out numbers to the tune of the song, emphasizing where I'm supposed to put my finger down on the whistle's hole. "Let's practice once more, laddie. One-two-*down*, four-five-*down*, seven-eight-nine-ten-eleven-*down*."

This time, we play and I even recognize the tune. It's amazing how being a few notes off or not having the timing right can make it sound like a completely different song. He tells me the words that go with it, about a bird who flies away from the nest, and his mother is both sad that he's going and glad that he has his whole life ahead of him.

We're almost through the song a second time when we hear someone approach and we freeze, the tune dying into silence. Judas's bones! I should've been keeping watch!

The rain has stopped and the woods are a quiet mist. A fairly well-dressed man in a fine hat stands staring at us, not ten feet away. How did I not hear him?!

Quickly, Donald grabs his bowl and stick and starts clapping them together and moaning.

"Leper, sir!" I call out.

"You're a leper, my boy?"

"No, but the man I'm with is one so you'd best move on."

"You'll be a leper soon, too, if you don't move on."

"It's all right. I'm a postulant."

"I see." The man eyes us both.

Donald puts his head down. I stand up and gauge how quickly I can grab my bow, which I've left several steps away. When the man starts fishing in his bag, maybe for a knife, I leap over to my weapon.

"Calm down, boy," he says. "I'm just getting some food out for you and your" — he coughs, a very fake-sounding cough — "leper." The man gets two apples and a loaf of bread and puts them on the ground. "He plays very well for a leper. I suppose the illness hasn't reached his fingers yet." The man gives a sly smile. "One can gain much food, and even money, by posing as a leper. That's why King Edward sent them all out of London two years ago. There were probably more mock lepers than real lepers preying on people's good nature."

I start to speak, to tell him the whole story of Prior Osmund sending a leper to infect Scotland, but he interrupts me.

"Whist." He looks around furtively. "I'll make you a deal. If you haven't seen me, then I haven't seen you or the leper, all right?"

I nod. "I don't even know who you are, sir."

He smiles. "Nor I, you." And he disappears into the mist.

My heart is still beating fast and I finally take a deep breath and exhale. "Do you think he'll tell anyone about us?"

Donald shakes his head. "I think he has other things to worry about. He'd rather avoid people, and he's good at it. He managed to sneak up on us easily."

I clutch my bow. "I'm taking watch now."

"We'll take turns," Donald says, even though his face is haggard and I know he needs to sleep.

"No, we won't. You'll rest so we can walk far tomorrow."

He tries to argue but I make the crawling-spider sign with my hand every time he opens his mouth, and he finally closes his eyes, a smile still on his lips.

chapter the fortieth

In Which We Run Straight into the Enemy

THE SUN IS SHINING AND DONALD AND I WAKE UP
refreshed. I think we both feel as if we can face anything.
Which is good, because before long we round a corner, straight
into the standing horses of none other than Sir Reginald; his
squire, Gawain; and several other soldiers, who have stopped
to let their horses rest as the men stretch in their saddles.

I freeze. So does the squire, who, I'm afraid, recognizes
me. Sir Reginald stops drinking from his flask.

"Who are you?" He eyes me, and then Donald, who has
his head hung down and partially covered by his hood.

I hadn't even thought of a name for myself! Henry comes
to mind and I say it, quickly adding, "of Lanercost Priory."

"Indeed?" The knight begins to smirk, but when the
breeze blows Donald's hood and Donald clutches it, and
starts coughing, he backs his horse up, his face turning serious. "Who is that man?"

"A leper, sir!"

All of the men back their horses away now.

"Why did you not say so before?" Sir Reginald demands.

"It's all right," I say, "as long as you're five paces away. See? My rope is even marked."

"What are you doing with a leper, boy?" The knight's face is sour and pinched.

I pull out my letter quickly and head toward him.

"Leave the leper behind you!" he says sharply.

I drop the rope and Donald stands still, cowering.

I run over to the knight's courser with the letter I've scribed. As I hand it up to him eagerly, his eyes catch mine and his face looks thoughtful. Quickly, I step back, hanging my head to hide my face and show my tonsure. I thank Bess for coloring my hair and skin and hope the disguise works. I hope I look subservient, but really I'm afraid. Is it possible he could recognize me? With different hair, skin, voice, clothes, and no soot under my eyes this time? He has seen me only once. The squire has seen me twice, though.

I hear the parchment crinkle and the knight say, "This is a poor excuse for sealing wax. Why has the esteemed prior used mud?"

I swallow hard but, God be praised, my brain works. "Because the pagan Scots stole Prior Osmund's seal, and his parchment, too. Indeed, that's why the prior wrote the letter on the back of a poultice recipe. And that's also why he's so angry."

I can't help but look up at the knight, who now squints at the letter. I gasp at what he pulls out of his pouch. St. Jerome's eyes!

"The spectacles!" I hear myself say, and inside I curse myself.

The knight narrows his eyes at me. "What do you mean, boy, 'the spectacles'?"

"I — I've heard of them before but never seen them." That, at least, is true. I don't tell him that I know where they came from and whose nose they're supposed to be on.

"Why so interested?"

"My grandmother has failing eyes and she's an herbalist." That's also true. "I've wondered if having spectacles could help her."

He smirks. "An herbalist cannot afford such things. It would be a waste."

Now that I'm past the fear of being caught for my slipup, I find myself growing angry. And bold. Those are Nigel's spectacles!

I ball up my fists and step toward the knight, but Donald starts coughing, loudly.

A soldier gags, covering his mouth with his hood. He pulls his horse farther away. "Stay back, my lord," he says in a muffled voice. "The leper is already missing fingers."

I look back, surprised, and I see that it does appear Donald is missing two fingers. Then I realize he has folded them up out of view and remember how nimble his fingers are from whistle playing. I also see him wiggle his two remaining fingers just a bit, like our spider sign.

"Keep away, leper!" a soldier orders, and Donald retreats a couple of steps.

I look back at Sir Reginald, who takes the spectacles

from his nose. "Interesting." He licks his lips as he slowly folds the letter and holds it up in the air, flicking it back and forth as if taunting me to grab it. His eyes meet mine and lock them in so hard to his dark gaze that I feel as if they have skewered right through me, like I'm a pig on a spit.

He has me exactly where he wants me because his eyes don't leave mine, nor do they even blink. "You say this letter was written by the prior of Lanercost?"

I nod, but the murmuring among the men is not a good sign.

"Tell me, boy," the knight says with a smirk, "how could he write a letter when he's dead?"

I feel as the pig must feel held over the flame, only now I am being turned on the spit because I feel dizzy and burned.

"The Scots laid waste to Lanercost," Sir Reginald says coldly.

"Look how ashen the boy is," someone says.

All eyes are on me. I don't know what to do. *Think, Adrian, think! Ockham's razor! You're a boy who yearns to be a monk — yes!*

I drop to my knees, cross myself, and begin to pray. The words are for the prior's soul, but truly the prayers are for the souls of Donald and myself. And Nigel, because I worry now that he has been hurt, or worse. Also, it gives me time to think.

I hear some of the men praying for the prior, too, while Sir Reginald calls to his squire and mumbles something I can't hear.

I feel a hand on my shoulder and I jump. I look up and see Squire Gawain leaning down toward me, his back to the group of men. "Ten," he says, so softly and quickly that I barely hear it before he speaks out loud. "Rise, boy, my liege has a question for you."

The knight leans forward in his saddle, his eyes smiling and eager. "Tell us how many days you have been walking with this letter and the leper."

The men who were praying or grumbling have stopped and all look at me, expectant.

I look at Gawain, who has mounted his horse again, and can only hope the word he whispered in my ear is to save me and not a trick.

"T-ten, sir?" It comes out as a question, which I didn't mean.

Squire Gawain nods his head once.

"You sound doubtful," the knight says.

"I am distraught, sir, but, yes, now I remember it's ten because I've already finished counting all of my fingers and just this morning thanked God that I have ten toes to move on to, unlike my uncle, who lost three when he was drunk and plowed right over his foot."

While some of the men chuckle, Gawain says, as if he has just figured it out, "It was only eight days ago that the prior was so brutally slain."

The knight's face is sour as he glares at me. "Ten days, you say? That is slow progress from Lanercost. It's less than thirty miles from here."

"True, sir, but I can't walk fast because the leper is nearly blind and terribly afflicted. He can only take a few steps at a time before he must rest."

For the first time, the knight glares at Donald, and I fear his piercing, all-knowing eyes much more now than when they looked at me. "Perhaps we should put the poor fellow out of his misery."

I try not to gasp out loud. Even a few of the men are wide-eyed. The man who covered his face with his cloak backs up, as if worried that he will be called on to get close to a leper. I hate to think what Donald must be thinking.

Finally, my brain works, and then my tongue. Picking up Donald's rope, I say, "But, sir, it was one of the prior's last wishes for me to lead the leper to Scotland. Indeed, from what you have said, it was practically his dying wish. You wouldn't take that away from any man, would you, sir? Especially a man of God?"

It's bold of me to say, and challenging, but it puts the seed of worry in the heads of the others, and there's enough rumbling among the men and a half-coughed "Let's move on," for the knight to get the message although, clearly, he doesn't like it. He throws the letter on the ground and I grab it, giving him a relieved "Thank you, sir."

My relief is short-lived.

"I'm not finished with you, boy," Sir Reginald says, leaning forward in his saddle and peering at me. "You seem too . . . familiar."

I feel the rope tremble but I don't know if it's Donald or me.

Gawain finally breaks the horrible silence. "These children," he says with a strained laugh, "they all look the same, my liege. Begging, playing —"

"No," Sir Reginald says, examining me, "I think . . ."

Every second of silence worries me more that he'll find that place in his memory where I almost shot him with an arrow.

"I know!" Gawain cries. "He's the boy who was weighing fish in the market at Carlisle!"

"Yes!" I say.

"No." The knight shakes his head. "That is not he."

"My liege, he wore a large hood but I remember his face."

"The one whose father screamed at him so?" Sir Reginald says thoughtfully.

"Yes, my liege," Gawain says with relief.

The knight turns in his saddle toward him. "That boy could scribe."

Gawain turns pale and trips over his words. "I think — I thought — perhaps —"

"Boy!" Sir Reginald says, turning to face me. "Scribe something in the dirt there with a stick."

Gawain looks at me with alarm and, I think, pleading.

"Or can you not scribe?" the knight asks with a leer.

Gawain shifts nervously in his saddle and the other men look either amused or bored.

I pick up a stick. "What would you have me write, sir?"

Sir Reginald flings his arms out magnanimously so all I can see above me is purple and silver, glinting in the sunlight. "Whatever you like, boy."

I scratch away at the dirt, and when I'm done Gawain is shaking in his saddle with silent laughter, as are some of the other men.

The knight, too, reads what I have written, but his face

is as sour as Good Aunt's. He looks at me again, his eyes narrowing. "You and your leper had best be gone from my land by sundown or he will not live to see tomorrow." He turns his courser roughly, the other men following. "Come, Gawain, we must be off!"

"Yes, my liege," the squire answers, giving me a quick nod before leaving.

Donald exhales as if he has held his breath the entire time. "That was too close."

"I know," I say. "We must get moving."

After we're well under way, Donald stops for breath, leaning against a tree. "Tell me, laddie, what did you write on the ground for Sir Reginald to read?"

I grin. " 'Never fear: Spiderwort root will loosen even the tightest bowels.' "

Donald puts his head back and roars until his face is red with laughter.

chapter the forty-first

In Which We Cross Hadrian's Wall

THE NEXT DAY WE FORGE ON, AVOIDING SOLDIERS, PILGRIMS, beggars, and thieves. Donald is getting stronger but it's easier for him to walk on the road rather than through the woods. We are on the road when I hear footsteps behind us. Instinctively, I push Donald into the woods and peer out to see who's coming. To my surprise, it's neither soldiers nor thieves but children, mostly, with two women, one young and one old. I step out into the road because I'm curious.

A girl runs up to me. "Brother, do you have food or alms for us?"

"No," I say honestly, and she hangs her head. "I'm sorry."

"It's all right." She forces a smile. "We'll keep going."

"Where are you headed?"

The rest of the group has caught up to her.

She shrugs. "Nowhere. Anywhere. We can't stay in our village."

"Why not?"

"Our fathers never came back from the war. The reeve took our homes because we can't work the fields on our own."

"But the men may come back yet! The war isn't over."

The young woman steps forward. "Did you not hear, Brother? King David was captured some nights ago. If my husband were alive," she says, her voice shaking, "he would've returned by now. The war is indeed over."

"Aye," says the older woman, "and with it, our lives."

The young woman takes her hand. "We'll find a way to survive, Edith, don't worry."

"And feed all these orphans we've collected?" Edith asks.

The younger woman doesn't have an answer for that. "Come on, children," she says, and the group straggles down the road.

I go back into the woods and start to tell Donald what I learned, but he interrupts me.

"I heard."

"Sorry," I say, "that your side lost."

"Och, laddie," he says, shaking his head, "we've all lost."

We're silent for the rest of the day. I hadn't thought about after the war. Of women and children without homes and without a means to survive. I wonder how I could've missed that important detail when I planned to be an archer. If I'd been a successful archer, how many orphans would I have made?

That night, as we sit around our fire, Donald says, "I think you should go home, laddie. I can get myself the rest of the way."

We both know he'll never make it if he doesn't have me to lean on during the day, to feed him in the evening, and to protect him at night. I try to distract him with stories of my village, Father Fraud, the unholy trinity, and my journey, like I do every night. This evening, though, he's insistent because of the news that the war is over.

"It doesn't make any difference," I say, "it's still dangerous for you."

"You've saved my life enough times, laddie, and —"

"Exactly!" I say, cutting him off, and putting the squirrel I just cooked in front of him. "And I'm not letting all my efforts go to waste by leaving you now. You're still a Scot in English territory."

"We'll soon be at the border," he argues.

"And we'll see how you're doing then. If —"

I see movement out of the corner of my eye and stand up to look left. A small boy has my bag in his hand.

"Hey!" I cry. "Give that back!"

He takes off but I grab his arm, catching him quickly because the boy has a limp. And torn clothes. And big eyes like Otto.

"Sorry," he squeaks, "I'm hungry is all."

"Why didn't you ask for food?"

He looks at the ground. "Everyone says, 'No, go away!'"

I take my bag and let go of his arm. "Don't you have any family?"

He nods, pointing at his leg. "I ran away because I'm a burden. My father died in the war and nobody wants to marry my mother because of me. I wanted her and my baby sister to have a home. So I left. They're better off without me."

I feel sick to my stomach, and it must show on my face because the little boy pats my arm. "Don't worry, Brother,

301

I'll be fine." He gives me a wide smile that shows his missing front teeth. "My name's Lorcan. Mother says it means 'small but fierce.' See, I'll be all right!"

"Och, ye brave wee laddie —" Donald starts to say, but the boy backs away.

He's not smiling anymore and his eyes are wide. "That's a Scot!"

"It's all right," I say, grabbing his arm as he tries to run. "He's a friend."

The boy still pulls against me and it takes me a while to coax him by our fire. He stares at Donald.

"I'm going to see if I can catch you a squirrel before it gets too dark, all right? You look like you could use some meat."

He nods.

"Stay here and I'll be back soon."

I search for food, though my eyes are tired and it's hard to see. I aim at a scurrying — a rabbit or squirrel? — but miss because the creature runs under a log. I ready my arrow and step quietly to the other side of the log to catch the animal as soon as it emerges. When it pokes its head out I almost let my arrow fly until I see its eyes with black stripes underneath. It's a young badger. We stare at each other for several moments until I shudder, then step back, leaving him be.

I do manage to catch a squirrel, but when I return to camp the boy is gone.

"What happened?"

Donald shakes his head. "He was too nervous around me and bolted. I did get him to take my dirk, though."

"Your knife? Now you have no weapon at all."

"I'm going home, laddie. That wee bairn has nothing. And no one."

It's true. "Do you think . . ." Something catches in my throat and I stop.

"Do I think what?"

After a deep breath, I say, "Do you think he'll survive?"

"Aye," Donald says readily, "I do."

I look at him. "Really? How?"

"Spirit."

"The Holy Spirit?"

"Nay, his own spirit."

Maybe Donald is right but I can't help but feel angry, although I'm not sure with whom. It wasn't his mother who cast him out. And certainly his father didn't want to die and leave them. I know the boy is being noble by taking himself away from the village. Still, what kind of world is it that would put such a heavy burden on one small soul?

"What about you, Adrian?"

I startle. "What about me?"

"What will you do with your life, I wonder?" he says, lying down and closing his eyes.

There is not much I can do, considering who I am. I look down at my monk costume and wonder if I could ever be like Nigel. I suppose a priory might take me, even though I'm odd. At least I can scribe, although the idea of sitting and scribing all day makes my head hurt, not to mention my eyes. And praying and chanting at all hours would drive me to be an addlepate if I'm not one already. I could never make a good monk, like Nigel, but I understand now what he was saying about finding the truth.

And yet, who will accept me as a scribe? What will I do with my life? Donald must be asleep by now but I answer him anyway. "I'll be useless."

Donald sits bolt upright. "What!" He looks at me and holds my gaze. "You've saved my life! You're shepherding me, a grown man, through enemy territory all the way to Scotland! You're a scribe and an archer, and have a strong mind. If it weren't for you, I'd be long gone! Useless? I don't ever want to hear such foolishness again!"

His tirade seems to exhaust him and he closes his eyes and is soon asleep.

Maybe Donald is right that I'm not useless. I have done some things that are, well, surprising — I have even surprised myself. I suppose they are all useful things. But saving a Scottish soldier multiple times? How can I explain that to those in my village, or anyone, really? What am I going to tell them when I finally return?

I could say I got lost and that's why it took me so long to get home, which makes me an addlepate. Or perhaps I can say I got sick, but that just makes me weak. Or the truth — that I am a traitor. Hugh must've explained the truth to Father, but they can't share it with anyone. Who would understand? Truly, I think I'm doing the right thing, but if I didn't know Donald, and just heard about an English person aiding a Scottish soldier, I would think it dead wrong. That's what they'll think of me. And perhaps hang me for being a traitor.

It's a long while before I can sleep.

I'm awakened by Donald fixing us pine-needle tea. He's breathing heavily.

"What are you doing? You're supposed to be resting!"

He smiles. "I decided it was my turn to start breakfast. You needed the rest."

I feel the warmth of the sun and look up at the sky. St. Jerome's bones! It must be almost noon! How did I sleep so long?

"Do you feel better?" he asks. "Many a night it is you've been up late. Your body was catching up on sleep."

I shake myself fully awake as he hands me the warm tea. "Thanks."

I'm just getting up to find food when a pilgrim passes on the road close by. Looking through the trees, he waves and calls out a good-day. Donald, rather sheepishly, claps his wooden spoon against his bowl. The man nods and starts to take a loaf of bread from his bag, hesitates, and puts the whole bag on the ground, giving us a whistle.

"God bless you, sir!" I call out as I run to take the food. It's not only bread but four meat pies as well!

Many have given us food, believing Donald to be a leper, but never this much. We both feel guilty to be posing as a leper and his companion. I think, as I do every day, about the thieves and beggars in London who pretended to be lepers just to get free handouts, and I feel worse. Somehow, I resolve, I'll make up for this.

Still, the food gives us the sustenance we need to head north, and we're grateful. We're in high spirits, having gorged on the bread and each eaten a meat pie. The sun is warm. As we crest a hill, I see it. Hadrian's Wall. Again. This time I'm not scared of it, though. In fact, I'm almost happy to reach it because we'll be in Scotland, Donald's home, away from English soldiers, specifically Sir Reginald.

Donald is grinning as we climb over the wall. He points to a strip of blue water. "The River Tyne!"

We soon reach the cool, clear river, where we drink. The water looks so inviting as it reflects the sunshine that we put our tired feet in. Shivering and laughing with the tickling relief it brings, we turn to look at each other.

"Are you thinking what I'm thinking?" I ask.

Donald grins and steps into the water, and I splash in after him.

Soon we are scrubbing ourselves and our clothes clean. Donald is no longer a leper and, in truth, he looks healthier now. I'm no longer a tanned and dirtied monk. My skin and hair are bright white. Indeed, Donald has to squint at my brightness as much as I'm squinting from the sun.

He shades his eyes and jokes, "I feel like I'm looking at the sun itself!"

I laugh, feeling as powerful as the sun. "I'm nae a wee spider," I shout. "I'm Robert the Bruce!" I raise my arms and clench my fists, making my arm muscles bulge. In truth, they don't bulge much, which makes Donald start laughing, so I splash him.

"So, it's going to be like that, is it?" he says, still laughing. He paws the water, and even with just his good arm he makes a frothy whiteness like waves.

I splash him again and in no time the water is churning like a whirlpool because we're splashing each other so much and we don't stop until we've both fallen on our asses in the river, near breathless from laughing. When our laughter dies down, it's silent. Too silent. No birds singing, nothing. I look behind us on the riverbank and see an entire regiment of soldiers with swords and arrows pointed right at us!

chapter the forty-second

In Which I Decide My Future

"HE'S A DEVIL!" A MAN SHOUTS, POINTING HIS PICKAX AT ME.

"Aye," another one says. "I'll take care of the wee demon." The man rushes toward me, his sword extended.

"Stop! Right! There!" Donald yells, struggling to his feet. Even wounded and in just his short, wet breeches, he looks a menacing beast.

The man with the sword stops at the brink of the creek but doesn't take his eyes off me. I'm shivering in the water, wondering how long the standoff will last — and who will win — when one of the men on the bank struggles through the others to the front of the line.

"Donald?" he says.

Donald squints up at the man. "Malcolm?"

The man grins. "What are ye doing swimming with the devil?"

"He's no devil," Donald says, and I can feel him relax. "He saved my life!"

The man with the sword lets us out of the river and we put our clothes and weapons back on. I put on my cloak, too, because suddenly I feel chilled.

When Donald and Malcolm embrace I think, for a moment, that everything is going to be all right. But two men grab me and, when Donald yells at them, several more hold him back.

"You fools!" Donald shouts. "The lad has brought me through enemy territory all the way here. He risked his life to take me home. And he and his friend fed and sheltered me when I was so wounded I would have died! We should be celebrating him!"

The men stare at me but they don't look like they want to celebrate. A man with white hair and a black robe steps forward and speaks gently. "I'm afraid you're under the devil's spell."

"Och, for heaven's sake!" Donald shouts. "Malcolm! You know me. Tell them, I don't even listen to the priest! Why would I heed a devil child?"

"Aye, that's true enough," Malcolm says, but his words are met only with grumblings from the other men.

The men part and a tall man with a helmet and real armor emerges. His hair is dark and wild and his eyes look down on me over his beaklike nose.

Donald's face goes from rage to disgust. He spits on the ground. "MacGregor. You thief. I should've known. Who have you been stealing from lately?"

MacGregor sneers. "Don't go all holier-than-thou, Donald Stewart. You've done your share of stealing."

I feel my mouth drop open and I stop struggling. Donald? A thief? And I know this MacGregor must be right because Donald's shoulders slump.

"Only when I had to keep my family from starving — and the English had stolen my sheep!" Donald looks over at me and looks away quickly, with a pained face.

I realize my mouth is still open. But I don't blame Donald for stealing if his family was starving. It's what Henry's gang has to do. People don't just starve in cities. In the winter, you can starve in the country, too. And, anyway, the English stole from Donald.

"At least," says Donald, glaring at MacGregor, "I don't kill women and children."

MacGregor seems to have nothing to say to that, although his mouth is moving around as if he'd like to.

I know Donald would never kill women and children. He even saved an English boy. But this MacGregor will likely have no qualms about killing me. I start struggling again.

"Surely you can't believe the boy is a devil," Donald says. "Just let him go."

MacGregor smirks. "Aye, but what am I to do if my men think he is?"

"A fine leader you are, eh? You can't control your own men."

Now it's MacGregor who spits at Donald's feet. "Tie them both up!"

It takes four men to pull Donald away from me, although he keeps yelling at MacGregor. When I see MacGregor kick Donald in the back I want to yell, too.

"We'd be better off without this demon," a man says.

"Aye," the man with the sword says, pointing it at me again. "*What* are you?"

Suddenly, I'm not feeling the least bit scared. All I feel is rage. "I'm not a *what*! I'm a *who*! I'm a boy — a man — just like you!" My voice is so loud some of the men step back. "I'm not possessed just because I look different!"

"Poor wee lad," the white-haired man says, "it's not your fault that your body has been possessed. And yet —"

"And yet you want to get rid of me anyway? Well, you can't just throw me away!" I think about what Donald said last night. "I am *not* useless." I look around at the crowd. Some of the men meet my eye, others don't.

"All those who look like you," the old man says gently, "are the same. They —"

"What?" I cry. I nod my head at a man who stares at the ground. "He has black hair. Is everyone with black hair the same? And him," I say, looking at another man, "are all short, fat people the same? And what about you? You have white hair just like me. Are we the same, then?"

There's a murmuring and I hope the men are actually thinking, and maybe even agreeing with me.

"Silence!" MacGregor yells, barreling his way through the men. "Take the devil child away! He's poisoning your brains."

"You're the poison!" I say. "Why are you scared of me? A boy? Why do you kill children?"

There's a louder rumble from the men, and MacGregor hits me across the face so hard I fall down.

I hear a roar, as if from a wounded bear, and I realize it's Donald. They must be dragging him away because his screams are growing more distant. Someone lifts me up and makes me walk although I can't even see straight. The pain in my jaw is making my eyes water so I barely see my boots and the leaves as I'm dragged to a log, tied with my hands behind my back, and dropped on the ground.

I want to scream or cry, I can't decide which, but there are several men standing guard over me and I won't give them the satisfaction of seeing my pain. I have to think of a way out. My bow is on my back but it's useless to me with my hands tied.

There's a crashing through the branches and leaves and suddenly Donald, pushed by several men, is next to me. There's a rope around his waist, pinning his arms to his side. His face is bloody.

I stare at him as he drops onto the log next to me. "Are you all right?"

He nods, but before he speaks he spits out a tooth. "What about you, laddie?"

"I'm fine," I say. We're both lying, but sometimes friends do that for each other to keep their spirits up.

There are several more guards now, probably because of Donald, so we can't discuss any escape plans. Not that I have any. My head is ringing and it hurts to think.

Donald taps my arm and makes the spider sign with his hand. I have to smile, even though it hurts my face. We still don't talk but I feel more hopeful.

After a while, Malcolm comes. He stands over us with his feet apart, hands on his hips, and yells, which I wish he wouldn't do because my head still hurts. Besides, I thought he was a friend. I hang my head and see Donald's hand nearest me making the spider sign.

I give him a defeated look, as if to say even your friend is against us. Donald's head is down and he's trying not to smile. When I look in his eyes, they're twinkling. He glances toward Malcolm and makes the spider sign again.

Ockham's razor! Malcolm *is* Donald's friend. He's only pretending to be on MacGregor's side! He's really here to help us!

I decide to listen to Malcolm's ranting. There is probably some useful information he's giving us.

"So," he says, "the warden will be here by nightfall and we'll have the trial then. He will decide what to do with the boy."

"Warden?" says Donald, who has just lost his grin.

"Aye, of the Middle Marches."

Donald and I look at each other.

"Scottish or English?" I say, before I can stop myself, because if it's Sir Reginald, of the English Middle March, I am in serious trouble.

"Does it matter?" one of the guards says. "He rules them both."

"What?" Again, I can't stop myself from speaking.

"Sir Reginald," Malcolm says.

"But he's English!" I say.

"His wife is Scottish," one of the guards says.

"And," another adds, "he takes money from both sides, which makes him powerful in both the Scottish and English Middle Marches."

I groan. "He's a thief!"

The guards behind me laugh.

"We're all thieves," one of them says.

"Aye, but not like Sir Reginald," another adds, with no hint of laughter.

The others murmur in agreement.

"But he's supposed to be a man of law!" I say. "Instead, he's a worse thief than anyone!"

Malcolm inspects the fingernails on one hand as if he's completely bored and not even listening. But, I realize, he could've silenced me if he wanted to. Instead, he's letting me speak. He must want the other men to hear.

So I oblige. I tell them all about Sir Reginald and the prior and the stolen goods and Nigel. When I get to the starving townspeople who had to support the priory while the monks got fat, the guards are enraged.

As I'm talking, I'm reminded of Nigel and his search for the truth. I think of what I always believed to be truths — Scots are pagans, thieves are bad, knights are noble, girls are weak, war is glorious — and how all these "truths" aren't real at all. They're things I was taught or everyone believes, just as all people who look like me are supposedly angels or, more often, devils. I didn't believe Nigel when he said that scribing was power, that seeking the truth and sharing it is mightier than being a soldier.

Now I see what he means. And I resolve to seek the

truth myself. Instead of hiding and letting others decide my fate, I will follow my own truth. I will finish Sir Geoffrey's mission. I may not have saved his life but I can finish his life's work.

I will go see the bishop of Durham myself.

That is something the people of Ashcroft can be proud of. And so will Father. And so will I.

I'm so excited that I tell the soldiers my plan. "I'm going to tell the bishop of Durham exactly what has been happening in his realm!"

They stare at me. And then they laugh.

"You're just a wee boy!"

"Aye, and an odd one at that!"

"That's a man's job!"

Donald stands up and turns to face them. "He is a man! You just can't see it yet." He smiles at me. "I'm glad you finally have."

"But," one of the soldiers says, "why would the bishop talk to you?"

"He doesn't have to. He just has to listen. And I'll write it all down, everything I can remember, so he'll see I'm no fool. I even know who's wearing Nigel's spectacles."

Another man rolls his eyes. "And what if Sir Reginald and the bishop are friends?"

"That's why I'll write it all down, and scribe copies, and give them to other members of the clergy. And any merchant and scholar and lawyer in Durham who'll read it."

Donald's eyes are twinkling now. "Aye, you wield much power in that hand."

"Och, it's a waste of time, laddie. You said yourself the prior is already dead."

"I can still stop Brother Bernard and the others! Besides, the truth is never a waste of time."

"Sir Reginald's arriving!" someone shouts.

"Well," says the gruff-voiced guard, "we'll let the warden decide what happens to you and your fancy ideas of running all the way to Durham."

I watch the horses in the distance — there must be at least a dozen of them — approach the camp, and I slump, wishing I could disappear.

Malcolm clears his throat. "MacGregor's bringing out the ale tonight for the warden and his men."

"What?" the gruff-voiced man says. "What about us? His own men?"

"Why don't you go get some before it's all gone?" Malcolm says.

"I'll not leave my post!" the man replies.

Malcolm shrugs. "Suit yourself. Hamish and Gordon, if you two want to go have a wee dram I'll take over for you."

"What about me?" a young voice says.

Malcolm laughs. "All right, Ian, you too. Bring some back for old Jock here."

"More than a wee dram!" the gruff-voiced man orders.

I look behind me and see we still have three guards, and one of them is Jock, who wants Sir Reginald to seal my fate. How will we get away? And how far could we get on foot, anyway?

"MacGregor is angry with you," Malcolm says to Donald,

his voice indifferent. "He doesn't much like being made to look a fool. Still, he knows not to turn on one of his own." I'm relieved to hear that until Malcolm yawns, and adds, "The boy, though — who knows what's to become of him?"

Malcolm looks at Donald. "Because of our long friendship, I'll help you get home to your family, whether this boy is a devil or not. You're fatigued. I'll let you ride Fire. She's right over there." He points behind us to a lone chestnut pony tied to a birch. All of the other horses are where Sir Reginald is now dismounting, on the other side of camp. I wonder if Fire is so wild that she can't be kept with the others.

"Ah," says Donald slowly, looking at me, "right. I'm not such a good rider, of course."

"Och, I know that," Malcolm says. "You've no skill at all. It's a good thing she knows what to do even with someone who has absolutely no experience riding." Malcolm raises his eyebrows at me. "All you have to do is hold on. Aye, she's a special girl, she is. She can run far and fast, through woods, even through the night."

Wait. I look at Donald. Does Malcolm mean for me to ride Fire out of here? Donald nods his head once and I know the answer is yes. But I'm still tied up. I can't even get on a pony, never mind ride, with my arms useless like this.

The guards are back with ale, and when Jock sits down to drink, Malcolm urges them all to face west to look at the sunset. Meanwhile, he slips Donald his knife and I feel Donald sawing at the ropes that bind my hands, even though it's hard for him with his arms still pinned to his side. When I'm free I quickly cut his ropes.

"Fire," he whispers.

But the men are all looking in the direction of the pony so I can't go now.

"Go around," Donald murmurs, "and stay low." He smiles. "All the way to Durham."

Malcolm looks across camp to where the other horses are, then gives us a nod.

I don't know how to say good-bye. "I —"

"Whist! Go!" Donald says sternly, although there are tears in his eyes. "Godspeed, Adrian. We will meet again."

As the men talk and laugh and drink, I sneak around the trees heading for Fire, stopping when I hear Sir Reginald's voice. Although it strikes me with fear, it also reminds me . . . the spectacles! I have no scroll to bring to the bishop when I make my case against Sir Reginald, but I could bring the spectacles. I must. And then return them to Nigel, their rightful owner.

I double back to where the horses are. Donald is standing now, and he and Malcolm and even some of the guards are pointing toward Malcolm's pony and shooing me in that direction, but I have to get the spectacles. I make my thumbs and forefingers into circles and hold them in front of my eyes to explain to Donald what I'm doing. He shakes his head fast. I don't want to leave him distressed but I must go. I hold up my hand and make our spider sign. His shoulders slump and he still shakes his head, but he holds his hand up, too, wiggling his fingers, our sign of strength.

I creep over to Sir Reginald's mount and fumble to find his saddlebag. I feel the warmth of the horse as he steps back, pushing against me, and snorts. I remember the way Sir Geoffrey spoke softly to his horse, so I do the same, even calling him Lightning because I don't know his real name. I can't see in the dim light, so I'm still fumbling with the clasp of his saddlebag when a large hand clamps down on my arm, and I freeze.

chapter the forty-third

In Which My Journey Is Just Beginning

"WHAT ARE YOU DOING?" A VOICE HISSES.

It startles me but for some reason I'm not scared, maybe because the man isn't raising an alarm. I turn and see it's Gawain, Sir Reginald's squire. I don't know if he thinks I'm stealing, which I suppose I am, but I don't have time to explain. I manage to sputter, "Spectacles."

He stares at me for a moment, nods once, and lets go of my arm. Deftly, he fishes them out of the bag and hands them to me. Maybe he knows how Sir Reginald got them.

"Thank you," I whisper.

"Gawain!" It's Sir Reginald's voice.

"Coming, my liege!" Gawain calls out. "Godspeed," he whispers as he slips away.

I know I should go but I see some parchment sticking out a tiny bit from under the saddle. I grab it. Could it be the accounting from Prior Osmund?

I open it. It's not. My disappointment is replaced with curiosity, though, because it's a map . . . with *MacGregor's land* written on it and an *X*, followed by *20 head of cattle* and *take cattle through the Pennines.*

The Pennines are the mountains west of here. Sir Reginald must be planning to steal cattle from MacGregor! Much as I dislike MacGregor, Sir Reginald is worse. And I want to prove that Sir Reginald is the one everyone should be suspicious of, not me.

Quickly, I scroll the map around an arrow and secure it with the string that tied it under his saddle. As I leave on Fire, I'll shoot the arrow at MacGregor — not to hurt him, but for him to see the truth.

"Bring the boy!" I hear Sir Reginald yell.

St. Jerome's bones! I run as fast as I can toward Malcolm's pony. In my haste, I drop the spectacles' case and it opens. Fortunately, the spectacles don't fall out, but I see an inscription inside the lid. *Fra Nigel, Lanercost.* I know *Fra* means a brother or friar. Brother Nigel! His name! Evidence, clear as the spectacles themselves, for the bishop of Durham that Sir Reginald is a thief! This will seal Sir Reginald's fate.

"Ockham's razor!" I say out loud.

That's when I hear the footsteps, or rather the halting of footsteps, as Sir Reginald, MacGregor, and many men face me, just yards away. They close in, surrounding me.

God's heart! I am backed against a low rock. Scrambling on top of it, I'm panting with fear. This is it. I am dead. I face my enemy and realize I'm now eye to eye with these men, taller even than some of them.

"So, boy," Sir Reginald says, leering, "we meet again. This time, you will not get away."

"And neither will you!" I say, my voice loud in my ears.

Instantly, his face turns sour. "You are the one on trial here. Seize him!"

The arrow! I raise my bow, pointing the arrow with the map around it at Sir Reginald's right eye.

"Stop!" he yells.

At first, I think it's a command for me, though I don't move, my right eye fixed on his.

"Back away!" he orders. "The boy is a sure shot."

Ha! He's scared. As well he should be. "You'll want to see what's on this arrow, MacGregor!" I shout. "It was hidden under Sir Reginald's saddlebag."

The knight startles. "How dare you steal from —"

"No, sir! How dare *you* steal, is the question! From the poor, from the ailing, and even from your fellow men, like MacGregor!"

"What?" MacGregor says, facing Sir Reginald, and the other men look at the knight, too.

Behind MacGregor and Sir Reginald, I see Donald and Malcolm, readying the pony. I don't see how I can get to it. Escape seems impossible. But behind the helmets and heads of the crowd, I see Donald's arm rise and his hand makes the spider sign.

I can't return the sign because my hands hold my bow, but I give a nod.

A battle cry and shouting come from behind the men, and through the confused crowd Fire appears, rushing at me.

I let my arrow fly at the feet of MacGregor, but the men scatter as if I mean to harm them. It distracts them long enough for me to launch myself from the rock onto Fire's back. As soon as I land on the pony, she takes off, with me grabbing on to both her reins and her mane, tangling my bow in the process. I lie low on her back since I have no defense now.

I hear MacGregor shouting, and Sir Reginald yelling at his men to chase me!

"That's my mount!" Malcolm shouts. "I'll go after him!"

"The four of you go!" MacGregor orders.

I groan. If it were just Malcolm, I'd be all right. "Come on, Fire!" I plead, clutching on to the flying animal.

"He's a good man!" I hear Donald yell, and I want to look back but I'm too scared I'll fall off. Is he telling me that Malcolm's a good man or is he telling the others that I, Adrian, am a good man?

I'm far enough away now that I can't hear what Malcolm says in reply. It doesn't matter. I know he's on my side. But whoever is with him may not be.

I crouch low on the pony's back and want her to go faster to get away, but slower so I don't fall off. I keep whispering, "Faster — no, not so fast! Faster! No, slow down!" But she doesn't listen to me, anyway. Like Malcolm says, she follows her own road, and it's as if she knows that we're in a race and she must win.

I yelp and close my eyes when Fire rushes through trees, the branches scraping my head, as I pray to St. Jerome for my very survival. The air rushes past and I remember the feeling from Lightning, although I think Fire goes even faster. As she descends a hill I'm sure I'll be tossed off, and I clutch on to her even with my knees, which only seems to make her go faster.

She slows a little when we cross a river. The cold water splashes me and I'm grateful for Fire's warmth as the night air rushes past my wet legs. I cringe as I see that she's heading for a line of trees, an entire forest, and I prepare for the worst. Once inside the wooded area, however, she stops altogether.

"What are you doing?" I ask her, as if she'll answer. "Keep going!" I dare to look back and I see a pack of men on horseback up on the hill behind me, silhouetted against the dusky sky. I'm hoping they'll turn around, but instead they come barreling down the slope toward me.

"Move! Go! Please!" But Fire is frozen. It seems that she's even trying to make her breathing as quiet as possible, so I do the same.

"I saw him!" a man says. "He went into those trees!"

"Nay!" another answers, and I think it's Malcolm. "Fire went that way."

"He's in the woods, I tell you!"

"I know my own mount!" Malcolm says, sounding angry. "You saw a deer!"

"Are you calling me blind?" the other man shouts.

"Nay," says Malcolm, "I'm calling you stupid!"

The man curses at Malcolm. "I have good eyes!"

"Maybe," Malcolm says, looking straight at the woods where I am, "but you, my friend, do not have as many eyes as a wee spider." He turns his horse and trots away.

Fire whinnies softly at her owner. "Hush," I whisper.

"We can't give up!" a man calls after him. "We need the boy. And you, Malcolm, don't you want your pony?"

"Fire will come back on her own. I'm not worried."

I peek through the trees and see a man throw his arms in the air, shake his head, and trot off. The others soon follow and I breathe a sigh of relief. Fire lets out one more whinny, louder this time, but the men don't hear over the noise of their own horses.

That's when I notice the lone horseman at the top of the hill, hunched over in the saddle. He must never have come down because the others are still behind Malcolm, climbing back up the hill.

The man at the top of the hill raises his left arm and, in the moonlight, I see him make the sign of the spider.

Donald. I grin and make the sign back, although he probably can't see me. He knows I'm here. And I know that, someday, I'll see him again. We might play the whistle and recount our adventures like men do. Maybe I'll meet his family, even teach Colyne to read and write.

But for now, I have my calling. I'm going to finish what Sir Geoffrey set out to do. "Come on, Fire," I say, urging her onward under the rising moon, "we're going to see the bishop."

It must be many miles to Durham but I'll get there. I have no idea what I'll encounter but I know now that I will survive. I'm the Badger, tough and scrappy. I'm the Spider, small but determined. Mostly, I'm someone *useful* from the village of Ashcroft. My name is Adrian Black, and I am a man.

AUTHOR'S NOTE

I WROTE THIS BOOK FOR THE MANY READERS WHO WERE excited at the prospect of an adventure set in the Middle Ages, a period I've always loved. History, especially medieval history, is like fantasy — only it's based on how people really lived and what actually happened, which, I think, makes it particularly compelling. Although I took the liberty of updating the language to make the book more accessible to today's readers, the events in this story are centered around battles that actually took place between the English and the Scots from October 7 to October 17, 1346. I followed Adrian's trail myself, starting at the imaginary village of Ashcroft, south of the real village of Penrith, visiting Mayburgh Henge, Brougham Castle, Carlisle Castle, Carlisle Cathedral, Lanercost Priory, Hadrian's Wall, and the surrounding countryside. These places still exist and I hope readers are able to visit some of these fascinating sites and see where Adrian hurried past a Neolithic monument at dawn, stopped at a lord's castle, sought sanctuary in a massive cathedral, jumped from a scriptorium window, and hid in a Roman latrine. You can have the same adventure.

Many thanks to the museum curators, historic site managers, and professors who answered my questions, especially Professor Joshua Eyler at George Mason University, who did independent research on my behalf about the possible attitudes toward those with albinism in the mid-fourteenth century. Thanks also to fellow authors like Rebecca Barnhouse and Karen Cushman, who helped directly or indirectly. Thanks to my husband for driving me around England and Scotland for research, being my sounding board, and putting up with my lapses into old English. He is indeed a noble knight. And thanks, as always, to my agent, Linda Pratt, and editor, Andrea Davis Pinkney, for their help in making this book possible — what an exhilarating ride!

~ FOR MY FRIENDS ONLY ~

I have scribed some words and their meanings for you. Like you, some of them I knew already but some of them I didn't. I don't like being in the dark and I didn't want you to be, either.

As I have learned on this journey, there is power in words.

ADDLEPATE — a person who is confused *(which I am NOT even though Good Aunt claims I am)*

ALMSHOUSE — a shelter for elderly or poor people *(but the rules are strict and there is lots of praying)*

APPRENTICE — a person who is learning a craft from a professional; an apprentice works about seven years for free in exchange for the training *(which I would happily do if Father would only apprentice me)*

ARCHER — a person who uses a bow and arrow *(like me)*

BAILIFF — a person who works for the lord of the manor and is in charge of villagers or townspeople, much like a reeve, but gets paid and enjoys a higher status *(generally unfriendly to boys on the run; to be avoided)*

BOWYER — a person who makes bows for archers *(like Father)*

BUTT — an archery target, often a bale of hay with a target painted on it *(which I can hit better than any man in our village, except maybe the blacksmith)*

FISHMONGER — a person who sells fish and seafood *(raw, but if you're clever, like Henry, you might be able to get him to cook it for you)*

GARDYLOO — from the French for *look* and *water*, it's a warning that a chamber pot is being emptied out of the window onto the street *(the "water" being the water people have passed from their bodies; you DEFINITELY want to get out of the way)*

GROAT — a coin worth about four pence, or pennies; three groats equal one shilling *(especially nice if you have three of them)*

JOURNEYMAN — a person who is experienced in a craft and has already served an apprenticeship but is not yet a master craftsman *(like Peter)*

KIRTLE — a woman's dress or gown *(like Jane's, which I got mud on — I'm still not sorry)*

LAUDS — the early hour of the day, immediately after dawn *(too early)*

LEPER — a person who suffers from leprosy *(like Thomas)*

MATINS — the very early hours of the day, before dawn *(definitely too early)*

MARCHES (WEST, MIDDLE, AND EAST) — lands on the border between England and Scotland, far from the capital cities of London and Edinburgh, where wardens are appointed to keep law and order *(and it's very hard to tell whose side you should be on)*

MICHAELMAS — the feast day of St. Michael, occurring on 29 September *(also occurring five days before my birthday!)*

Physic — a person who makes you well again *(unless it's Roger at the manor, in which case you're far better off getting herbal remedies from Grandmother)*

Postulant — a person who wants to join a monastery and is in a trial period *(like me, only I was just pretending)*

Prime — morning hour, after *Matins* and *Lauds*, usually around seven o'clock *(early enough)*

Psalter — a book of psalms *(which Father Fraud uses mostly to whack me over the head)*

Reeve — a person who works for the lord of the manor to oversee his estate, sometimes including tax collection *(NOT as important as a bailiff even if Reeve Elliot thinks so)*

Reivers — thieves terrorizing the *marches*, or border, between England and Scotland *(careful: sometimes those who are supposed to be keeping order are themselves thieves)*

Reliquary — a container for holy objects, such as the bones of a saint *(as in "St. Jerome's bones!" only I haven't actually seen his bones, it's just an expression, and one that gets me hit over the head with the aforementioned Psalter)*

St. Aldegundis — a saint who protects children, among others *(she is on the pilgrim's badge Bess gives Hugh to keep him safe)*

St. Crispin's Day — the feast day of St. Crispin, occurring on 25 October *(and my prediction of when the war with the Scots would be over)*

Scribe — a person who writes *(like Nigel . . . and like me)*

SHILLING — a coin worth twelve pence, or pennies *(a very nice coin to have)*

SUMPTUARY LAWS — regulations that limit the type of food, drink, clothing, and other luxuries people may have, for moral purposes, but also to regulate social class *(yes, I'm talking about Reeve Elliot)*

SURCOAT — a tunic worn by a knight over his armor, often indicating for whom the knight is fighting *(like Sir Reginald's purple one)*

TONSURE — a shaved spot on top of the head indicating that a person is a monk or in the clergy *(which I would not recommend, especially if it's done by plucking out your hairs, unless you absolutely have to)*

WATTLE AND DAUB — a type of building construction where upright pieces of wood are connected by woven straw and the openings are filled in with clay or mud *(like my house)*

WHIST — an expression to stop someone from talking, similar to "Shh!" *(nicer than "Shut up!")*

YEOMAN — a farmer who owns land for himself rather than merely working the land for the lord of the manor *(which is what Uncle wants so he can buy his way out of battle)*

Godspeed, friend!

—the BADGER

ABOUT THE AUTHOR

Kathryn Erskine is the acclaimed author of many distinguished novels for young readers, including *Seeing Red*, which *Booklist* magazine hailed as "powerful" in a starred review; *Mockingbird*, winner of the National Book Award; *The Absolute Value of Mike*, an Amazon Best Book and ALA Notable Book; and *Quaking*, an ALA Top Ten Quick Pick for Reluctant Readers. Kathryn lives and writes in Charlottesville, Virginia, with her family.